WAS A

SUMMER

IN

SAN FRANCISCO

# coldest winter i ever spent

## ANN JACOBUS

Carolrhoda LAB
MINNEAPOLIS

Carolrhoda Lab®
An imprint of Lerner Publishing Group, Inc.
241 First Avenue North
Minneapolis, MN 55401 USA

For reading levels and more information, look up this title at
www.lernerbooks.com.

Image credits: Westend61/Getty Images; Naatali/Shutterstock; getgg/Shutterstock.

Main body text set in Janson Text LT Std.
Typeface provided by Adobe Systems.

**Library of Congress Cataloging-in-Publication Data**

Names: Jacobus, Ann, author.
Title: The coldest winter I ever spent / by Ann Jacobus.
Description: Minneapolis, MN : Carolrhoda Lab, [2023] I Audience: Ages 13–18.
    I Audience: Grades 10–12. I Summary: Eighteen-year-old Del is in a healthier
    place more than a year after a suicide attempt, but her aunt's terminal cancer
    diagnosis forces her to confront the demons she has been keeping at bay.
Identifiers: LCCN 2022008816 (print) I LCCN 2022008817 (ebook) I
    ISBN 9781728423951 I ISBN 9781728479156 (ebook)
Subjects: CYAC: Emotional problems—Fiction. I Terminally ill—Fiction. I
    Right to die—Fiction. I LCGFT: Fiction. I Novels.
Classification: LCC PZ7.1.J38 Co 2023  (print) I LCC PZ7.1.J38  (ebook) I
    DDC [Fic]—dc23

LC record available at https://lccn.loc.gov/2022008816
LC ebook record available at https://lccn.loc.gov/2022008817

Manufactured in the United States of America
1-49218-49345-8/8/2022

For my parents.

# A NOTE TO READERS

This book involves discussions of suicidal ideation and references to suicide. If you are experiencing thoughts of suicide, have any questions about suicide, are worried about a loved one and seeking guidance, or simply need a listening ear, you can call or text 988 or call 1-800-273-8255 (TALK). Both of these numbers connect to the confidential, anonymous Lifeline network of crisis lines in all fifty US states.

# 1

## Sunday, June 21, 2015

"Bay Area Crisis Line. This is Del, how can I help you?"

Silence. Breathing.

Not unusual.

The phone number on the caller ID is blocked. Also not unusual. We answer calls that feed in from the national suicide hotline. Three of us are in the stuffy call room tonight. Two more should be in any minute.

I doodle a lighthouse on my notepad. "If you'd like to talk to me, I'm here." My midnight-blue nail polish is already chipped.

"This is, uh, Jane," a girl murmurs.

"Hi, Jane. How are you this evening?" That's probably not her real name. It doesn't matter.

"Not good." She sounds my age—eighteen—or a little older, but her voice is alarmingly flat.

"Are you feeling suicidal?" We ask everyone as soon as possible. Hearing this question would've been a huge relief for me a couple of years ago.

"Yes."

"Do you have a plan? How you would attempt suicide?"

Standard assessment. I steal a sip of my decaf latte. Twilight from the barred bay window illuminates our eight computer-and-phone stations along opposite walls.

"Yeah."

"Will you share with me what it is?"

"I'm at the Golden Gate Bridge."

I bolt upright. "Now?"

"Yeah."

She not only has a plan that's lethal. It's *imminent*.

Ohmigod. I've never had a Level Five. Two months of intense training just bolted from my brain.

"I, um." What to do first?

Locate her.

I wave frantically at my shift partner, Isabel, who's engrossed in her own conversation.

"Are you on the San Francisco side?" I ask Jane, sort of calmly. *You might not be able to handle this.*

I hold up my fingers at Isabel: *A FIVE.* She jerks a nod and asks her caller to call back.

"Yeah."

"You're on the bridge now?" I fumble, click, close, and finally open the internal messaging function on my computer screen to communicate with Isabel and the volunteer coordinator, Quentin. Was supposed to do it first thing.

Jane responds in slo-mo. "In the parking lot. In my car."

"Okay thank you for letting me know that will you tell me what's going on Jane? Why you're there?" I'm in hyper-drive.

Deep breath. Slow down. Get in sync with her.

Isabel has alerted Quentin, and now she's listening in on her phone. She'll gather info in case we need to call 911. My job is to concentrate on Jane and to deescalate the situation.

"I've been thinking about it. A long time," Jane says.

"I'm really glad you called us. Has anything happened recently that made up your mind?"

"My mother died."

"When was this?"

"A month ago."

"I'm so sorry. That must be incredibly hard."

She doesn't answer, probably going, *Duh.*

I know exactly how hard it is. My mom died when I was thirteen. Dr. Vernon says I still need to come to "better terms" with her death.

A recent big loss for Jane. Not good.

An IM from Quentin pops on my screen: **Identifying info? physical description, make/model of car?**

"Are you still in your car?"

"Yeah."

"What kind is it?"

"A rental." So she must be at least twenty-five to be able to rent. She may have come to San Francisco just for the Golden Gate Bridge. They're putting up a safety net soon and we cannot wait.

Isabel's typing stuff to Quentin and filling out questions for the dispatcher.

"Is there anyone in the parking lot with you?" My hands shake like I just drank four real espressos instead of a double decaf.

"No."

"Any other cars?"

"Yeah. But nobody." Her voice is as hollow as a moon crater.

"Is your car on?"

"No."

She knows I'm trying to get info and is resisting. Best to drop it for now. Jane's got to trust me enough to keep talking and I have to help her find a reason to hang on a little longer. Come on, Del!

"Do you have other family?"

"Yes."

"Father?"

"He's with another woman. None of us really talk."

"That's rough. I'm sorry." Any physical description will help. I type: **Low flat voice, mid-twenties. Slight Midwestern twang?**

"I have a brother," she says. "We're not close."

A new volunteer, only two years older than me, is speaking to someone in Spanish, and another call blinks the lines. Isabel has to answer, quickly assess for suicidal intent, and then ask them to call us back since we're short-staffed. A Five needs full attention from at least two people. Where the hell is Jackson?

"Do you have friends you can confide in?"

"My friend Alex."

"Do they know where you are?"

"No."

"Would you be willing to talk to them?"

"Her. No. I just want to . . . jump."

Breathe out. Breathe in another one. "Jane, would you be willing to go to an emergency mental health clinic?"

"Going to hang up," she mumbles.

Crap. "No! Wait! Please keep talking to me."

She doesn't respond.

Quentin IMs: **Isabel is calling emergency.**

I scribble "Alex" on my note pad, to remind me to bring up her name again. She might be a reason for Jane to hold on. Now what?

"Jane, I'm so glad you called. Will you please keep talking to me?" I repeat.

She sighs but doesn't disconnect. The car door opens and *ding, ding, ding*s. Slams.

"You're getting out of your car?" My voice trills an octave higher.

"Yes." Obviously.

"Would you, uh, be willing to wait in your car a little longer?"

"No. I want . . . to walk." Out toward the bridge. She must know that the pedestrian walkway closes at 9 p.m.

It's 8:36.

"Please keep talking to me. Do you have any firearms or other weapons with you?" If police are on their way, they need to know what to expect.

"No."

"Any medications with you?"

"No."

At the other end of the room Isabel informs the 911 dispatcher of the situation and the info we have on Jane. They'll contact the bridge police, who should know exactly what to do since this happens regularly over there.

We inform our callers of any action we take. "Jane, we've contacted emergency services. They'll be there any moment."

She doesn't react.

I've got to keep her on the line until they arrive. I've got to find something that might keep her tied to life.

What made her call us in the first place? The same thing that made me leave a trail to that closet.

Ambivalence.

When you're this close to the edge, there's no point in talking about the overwhelming, screaming pain. You just want it to end. But there's still that small part of you that wants to live. I've got to grab onto that for Jane.

"How long have you been friends with Alex?"

"I don't want to talk about her."

"Okay." I blow out a puff of air in frustration, bouncing a hair strand over my forehead. "Do you have any pets?" A lot of people who call us like their pets a lot better than their family.

"No."

I don't say, *If you survive today, you really should get one.* I try another tack. "How long have you been feeling like this?"

"A long time. Since I was fourteen."

Been there. But we're not supposed to volunteer personal info and Quentin's listening.

"Are you seeing a therapist?"

"Yeah." Pause. "It's not helping."

"Are you taking medication?"

"Not now."

Also not good. "Coping with depression can be very tough. Sounds like you feel really tired of it."

"Yeah," she says. "I'm not going to do it anymore."

Shit.

Training! "How have you gotten through rough periods before?" I hope not like I did, with vodka.

"Daydream about how I would end my life."

That shuts me up. "Um, anything else?"

"Yeah. Talk to my mom. She was the only one who understood me. And stood by me."

Like Aunt Fran.

I'd probably be dead without Aunt Fran. Jane must have someone. "What about other family or friends?"

She sighs. "They're so sick of me and my problems."

"Do you believe they'd rather you be dead?" It just slips out. *Smooth move, Del.* But I totally get it. When I—or my mom for that matter—couldn't cope with life as well as other people, everyone wanted us somewhere out of the way.

"In the end, absolutely."

"Sounds like you feel really alone, Jane."

"Yes." She says this firmly. She's far enough out on the bridge that the wind crackling around her phone makes it hard to hear her. I turn up the volume on my headset.

"I'm so sorry for your grief. And pain. What you're going through is tremendously hard." Thank the Higher Power we know where she is. I repeat, "I'm really glad you called us."

The timer on the phone says we've been talking seven minutes. Feels like about one. Or one hundred.

"Can you tell me more about your brother?"

"He's younger. He's perfect."

So many dead ends. I've sweated through my sweatshirt.

"Do you live in the Bay Area?" I ask.

"No." She pauses, then to my surprise mumbles, "It's beautiful."

She's standing in the twilight on the brightly lit, massive Golden Gate Bridge as cold tendrils of fog sweep from the Pacific Ocean over and through the cables and stanchions. And maybe looking at the glowing city to the east.

"It is. Tell me what you see."

"Fog. The bay. Like a movie." Her tone is too flat to sound impressed, but this has definitely distracted her.

"What else do you see, Jane? Can you see the sunset?" Today is the longest day of the year. Tomorrow will be shorter. You wait all year for summer and before it even gets going, the days start turning darker again.

"The sky . . . silvery. And purple. Through clouds." She pauses, says almost with a sense of wonder, "A ship . . ."

"What kind of ship?"

"A cruise sh—"

A car door clunks.

The voice of a police officer calmly says, "Jane."

"They're here," she says, as if informing me about the location of a stack of books.

I exhale. "Jane, thank you for talking with me, for making this effort. It means a lot to me that you'll be safe tonight."

Someone takes her phone and says, "This is Officer Ho."

I identify myself and the Bay Area Crisis Line and quickly summarize pertinent info.

"We have the situation under control," he says. "Thanks for your good work."

"Hey, thank *you*," I say.

They're specially trained. They'll take her to the SF General psychiatric ward, where she'll most likely be admitted for seventy-two hours—then hopefully released to someone who can be with her until she's out of danger.

We have no way of knowing caller outcomes for sure, though, and have to let each caller "go" once we hang up.

I disconnect. Two cleansing breaths help slow the adrenaline pumping through my system. A sip from my watery latte wets my dry mouth as I lean back in the cushy ergonomic desk chair. Suicide Prevention Girl strikes again!

I fucking hate suicide.

# 2

This spring, when I saw that Bay Area Crisis was recruiting volunteers, I immediately, enthusiastically applied. I was just about to turn eighteen and was finishing up my senior year, courtesy of Cyber Academy. I needed something to occupy me this summer, more meaningful than answering the phones and vacuuming at Aunt Fran's art gallery. The adrenaline from tonight's call says I made a good choice.

Now, I pop a few jelly beans while I log in info about "Jane's" call for funding purposes. Everything's anonymous and confidential, though. Jane sounded like someone named . . . Sierra, maybe. But never knowing what happens to her and being at peace with that is part of the job.

"Good work, kid!" Isabel gives me a high five. She was born in Brazil and is studying at UCSF to be a psychiatrist. Her older brother completed suicide when she was twelve.

The others call me "kid" because I'm the youngest one here.

"You too." My voice warbles. "Thanks for having my back." Two other volunteers finally showed up and are on calls. So we're keeping our voices low.

But Quentin returns from the staff room and bellows, "Good job, people! Great work, Del!"

My cheeks warm as we fist-bump. Quentin's bushy black beard could shelter small critters and stinging insects.

He adds, "Whenever you're ready." He disappears to his office and I grab my phone and backpack.

The reason we debrief after high-risk calls is so we don't get burned out or take a caller's problems home with us. This will be my first time.

I'll remember this call for the rest of my life.

;

After my shift, it's like I'm walking on stilts made of plastic drinking straws. The cold night air and the blanket of darkness at the bus stop weigh me down. A neon-green Heineken sign pulses across the street. This must be how people feel after alligator wrestling.

By helping Jane, I hope I'm paying the universe back a little for my own bad choice. Fine, *choices*. Still, some strange brew of acid and tar is gurgling just below my esophagus.

It's San Francisco-summer-freezing and I forgot my sweatshirt. The LED display for the next bus says four minutes. Good. Aunt Fran turns in at the freakishly early time of 9:30 lately and I want to tell her about this call. Among other things.

In two months, I'll be moving into a dorm at SFSU to start my freshman year, like a normal student. Aunt Fran isn't thrilled with the prospect of me living on campus. Hearing about my call with "Jane" will help convince her of my maturity.

The Russian Hill bus pulls up with a squeal of brakes. I'm composing an upbeat text to Nick. He's an old family friend from Dallas who arrived three days ago for an undergraduate summer internship at a UC Berkeley lab. He's premed, just finished his freshman year at UT Austin.

Nick will like the "Janc" story. He's a "helping" kind of guy. In addition to being super smart and totally hot. He doesn't know yet that I'm in love with him.

**Just talked a lady on the GG bridge out of jumping!!! 'Sup with you? How's it feel to be at Cal? Berkeley's a trip, right? When are you coming to the city? [starry eyed emoji]**

I impulsively tap send as I climb on with three other passengers.

Oh, crap. People are packed in the bus like fast-food French fries. The thought of shoving my way into all those bodies makes me pant. I should wait for the next one.

No, I've got to get home.

I beep my pass and wedge my way in. My vision goes all overexposed.

Exhale. Exhale. Count breaths—in through my nose and into my belly. Release slowly. Inch back. My forehead's pressed on the cool, grimy pole I'm clutching as dozens of human bodies leech my life force and I try to imagine something other than suffocating. And I was having such a nice evening up to now.

*Nick's going to think that text, and you, are dorky. Too many questions. Why'd you put 'sup?*

A searing, musky reek tinged with fruity alcohol hits me.

An old guy with matted, grizzly hair, oily clothes, and dirt-haloed nails sits right below me. His bloodshot eyes, open too wide, dart around the bus. He mutters, "Smell it my brain has been shot out what's in your wallet?"

Everyone pretends he's not there.

Junior year when I was really depressed, I could barely get out of bed, let alone shower. Poor personal hygiene can *so* be the least of your problems.

"Not much in my wallet," I admit.

He mutters to the floor, "All y'all educated fools you wanna boyfriend? Welcome to San Fran-fucking clan and a whole lot of fucking nothing." He looks at me. "You're a child common sense lord have mercy all y'all gotta pay attention."

"Right?" I say.

I think everyone has a spark of instability inside. My mom's spark—or wildfire, really—was bipolar disorder. My cozy bonfire is garden-variety anxiety and depression.

So far.

Deep breaths. Out slowly. One, two, three. The man sits quietly now, hands folded in his lap.

My latest meds help slow my racing brain and loosen the asphyxiating tightness in my middle. They provide a force field that keeps the sharp fear and electric jitteriness about seven feet away from my face.

But I could end up like this man someday—in a public place, drunk, unwashed, talking trash, scaring people, lost in some sealed panic room in my brain.

The bus lurches. Three people slam into me. A scrawny girl with dark, unbrushed curly hair in an oversized gray hoodie grips the upper bar, her bony knuckles near mine. She's my height and about my age.

A pinkish, shiny, jagged scar winds down the tan velvet above the artery inside her wrist. She observes me with eyes that are dull as a dead bird's.

Cold sweat bursts from every square inch of my skin. *So many of us.*

Being alive is

Too much

*Can't hold it*

Up—
*Back*
*Anymore.*

I lunge, yank the cord, and cry, "STOP! I'm getting off here!"

The driver scowls at me in the mirror.

Can't breathe!

Shoulder forward.

The back door opens and I stumble down the steps. Momentum pulls me away from the bus.

I smooth my hair down with shaking hands. Lean against the glass bus shelter and deep-breathe cold, fresh air.

I check for my phone and wallet.

Another deep breath. Focus on the neighborhood market across the street.

A man buying milk at the counter, the white light from inside spilling onto the sidewalk.

The line of parked cars on the hill with their wheels all turned toward the curb.

A tiny blinking jet moseying across the black, starless sky above.

Maybe that was a slight overreaction. But that girl. She's me.

And here I thought I was finally swimming out from under the Great Pacific Garbage Patch of my own suicide attempt.

;

I walk the rest of the way home in the cold dark, hiking up the last part of Russian Hill.

When I finally let myself into our apartment—step onto the soft carpet and into the pool of warm gold from the brass lamp on the entry table, smell traces of the spruce-and-cedar candle she likes to burn—I hear Aunt Fran's soft snores through her door. I used to have a strict curfew along with an actual "in bed" time. Just in the last few months, she's relaxed her vigilance. She trusts me.

I wish she were waiting up.

# 3

## Monday, June 22

I'm rollerblading along the Embarcadero, dodging joggers and balancing a cold-press kale-cucumber juice in my SFSU stainless-steel water bottle. Exercise is critical and it's a cool, foggy morning. I'm mainly cleaning at the gallery today so no big deal if I arrive sweaty.

I'm all better this morning after a soothing evening of working on my latest collage. Good thing, because I have to convince Aunt Fran to sign the online license agreement for my freshman housing and submit the payment. Which may be a little sticky. She wants me to live with her in cushy seclusion until I'm more . . . independent. Stable.

At least I have a better chance of convincing her than I do of getting Dad's approval. He lives in London, managing a medical nonprofit. He's relieved that I'm here on the North American continent, and not on his. He definitely won't like the idea of me being on my own. Dr. Vernon urges me to work on improving our relationship, which is unlikely because it'd involve having to talk to Dad.

I love talking to Aunt Fran, but I didn't get a chance this morning; when I left, her bedroom door was closed and her guided meditation app was playing. Maybe I can catch her during a moment of downtime at the gallery today.

My phone buzzes. A text from Nick! I weave between automobiles and cross to Bay Street.

*CLANG!* Whoa! Where did that streetcar come from?

I accelerate across the tracks before I stop and read.

**Feels great! Cal is cool. Congrats, awesome work with the bridge lady. We should celebrate. Not sure about my schedule yet will get back to you on timing. Say hi to Fran.**

Yes! I roll in curly lines into North Beach singing a made-up song about true love.

I'm supposed to be at Aunt Fran's art gallery, the Lone Star, by 10 a.m. It's a tad past that. No sneaking in—the front door dings to announce my arrival. I plop on the floor to remove my skates and stow my water bottle in my backpack.

Louis, a former model and Aunt Fran's assistant, comes down from his office upstairs. He's in Nantucket red chinos and a blue-and-red plaid blazer, loafers, no socks. Fran would never hire anyone who didn't have a strong sense of style. Aside from me.

"You're late." He stands on the bottom stair illuminated by the skylight and demands, "What did you do with my receipts?"

"Good morning to you too. I don't know what you're talking about." We got along okay until I started working here.

"You know exactly what I'm talking about. The pile of important sales receipts that were in my office yesterday." His arms are crossed.

I indicate the size of a Big Mac. "Um. About yea tall?" I pad in my socks across the pale bamboo floor, past large and small paintings to the supply closet under the stairs. "Including a couple of pink and yellow ones?" I chuck my blades in with a solid *thunk*.

Before Louis can explode on me, Aunt Fran breezes in. It's already 10:40 but she can show up whenever she wants. She opened this gallery ten years ago after making bank in financial consulting, so she's got nothing to prove at this point.

"Morning, sugar," she hollers. Did I mention that she's six-feet-two barefooted? And a stealth ginger, whiter than—well, sugar. She waltzes across the room in a leopard-print tunic jacket, a chic mustard-gold dress, and cognac-brown heels. "Another blue-sky, bright, sunshiny day in the world's most stunning city!" She has a Texas accent you could cut with a bowie knife. She thinks she shook it.

"Which sugar were you greeting?" Louis asks with a straight face. He's tapping his loafer.

"Both of us," I say. "*Sugar* is plural. It's a noncount or mass noun. Like *water*." A final-exam test question at Cyber Academy.

Louis responds with a sweeping eye roll.

Aunt Fran bullet-trains for the coffee in the back. She grins at Louis before beaming at me from behind her thick-rimmed mother-of-pearl glasses frames. Her nose is a little big for her face and her chin's small in relation to the rest of her, so it tends to double. She's beautiful. "Naturally, I was greeting all my sugar," she drawls.

"Ha!" She loves me best.

To Louis, she says, "You look fabulous today, darlin'! Are you ready to go over those numbers with me?"

"I would be," he huffs. "But while I was in the process of scanning all the first-quarter receipts, they disappeared. Perhaps Delilah can account for them?" If looks could throw lassos of barbed wire . . .

"Check the big trash bag," I say. "I was vacuuming yesterday."

Fran startles. "You threw them away?"

"They were all over the floor!"

"They were being *sorted*," snaps Louis. "Please. Never. Throw away. Anything. In my office. I'll be responsible for that." He fake-smiles. He'd be nastier if Fran weren't here.

I fake-smile back. He knew I would be vacuuming. Why sort crap on the floor? Louis always thinks the worst of me. I can tell he's waiting for me to rip off some piece of art and sell it to buy meth. Or maybe to slit my wrists in the bathroom.

I pull a dust mop from the closet and push some floor grit around. Hmmm. Meth is one thing I never tried.

Kidding.

Aunt Fran says firmly, "Del?"

"Fine," I say. "Sorry. I won't throw anything away in his office." She hates it when we're "ugly" with each other.

She heads back to the kitchenette for coffee and Louis follows her. I need to talk to her about my housing. I'm dying to tell her about my success with "Jane" too. And maybe I'll even tell her about Nick. But not with Louis around.

A large painting is down and leaning against the wall. *Sea Trash Number Three*. Blue-and-green sea turtles with real plastic six-pack holders and shopping bags varnished on, and a solid five-figure price tag.

Aunt Fran points to the canvas and raises her penciled eyebrows at Louis.

He says coyly, "The exercise app magnate and his CFO wife. They just left."

She squeals and grabs him in a hug.

"I already sent Caroline champagne," he adds. Caroline Kong, the Lone Star's current featured artist.

"You are on fire!" She's beaming so hard she may burst a blood vessel. I roll my eyes as I lean into the century-old mustiness of the supply closet.

"Oh, also," he says, "I left a message on your desk about Friday's flight lesson." Yes, now we all know he had to answer the phone because I wasn't here yet. Too bad the gallery doesn't have a slingshot and some water balloons for his pointy head.

"Thank you, sugar." She fumbles her silver thermos closed.

"I didn't realize you were piloting small aircraft," Louis says.

"Learning, anyway. It's now or never. Next up, private jets!"

Louis snags his leather briefcase from the back desk. "I'm headed over to Pocket Wars. Ciao for now." A video game company that's buying art to fill their new headquarters.

"Oh, Louis?" calls Aunt Fran as he opens the front door. *Ding.* "I have a doctor's appointment at three this afternoon. NorCal Trust may be coming in."

"Perfect. I'll sell them Number Five," he calls over his shoulder.

"Atta boy! Go get 'em, tiger," says Aunt Fran. *Ding* goes the door again.

"But you just went to the doctor," I say.

She pauses by the stairs, readjusting her thermos, the newspaper, and her chocolate faux-leather handbag. "That was to the lab for tests. Dr. D'Silva called me in to discuss the, um, results."

# 4

Aunt Fran had breast cancer when I was nine. But she beat it. She goes in once a year for checkups. Or for lab tests and discussions, I guess.

She's still leaning against the banister, her arms loaded.

"Guess what?" she says. "Speaking of jets, I had a flying dream last night."

"Cool!" We're total dream nerds. "Where did you fly?" I lean on my dust mop.

"Over my—and your dad's—old neighborhood. Jerry was with me. I woke up so happy."

"Oh, yeah, from high school, right? Wait. Isn't he dead?"

"Yes." Her free hand flutters, flashing a ring with a fire-red garnet the size of a ping-pong ball. "Motorcycle accident."

"A long time ago, right? What was he like?" I ask quickly. "He must've been amazing if you loved him." She almost never talks about her past.

Her eyes get a little glassy. "He was. I used to call him Doll Boy, he was so cute. Isn't that silly?"

"Ha. Mom used to call Dad Baby Cakes."

She runs a free finger absently along the top of the thermos. "Jerry followed me out here. He wanted to get married. I was a fool. I never met anyone else like him."

This is news. "I'm sorry. He was from Dallas, right?" A black-and-white yearbook photo of the two of them is on her bedroom bookshelf. "Why didn't you marry him?" *Or anyone?*

She doesn't answer, is staring unfocused out the front window. If she had her own family she might not have taken me in, so I'm secretly, selfishly thankful she didn't.

"I've had flying dreams," I say, trying to win back her attention, "but I think it's when I'm feeling in control. So, um, not very often." I smile at my self-dig.

Aunt Fran says, "I think it's a yearning for . . . how we were . . . before we were born into our bodies."

"Hmm." We both contemplate that for a few beats.

Eventually, she asks, "How was the hotline last night?"

"Ohmigod! I had a Level Five! That I deescalated! A woman on the Golden Gate Bridge." My face warms with pride as I wait for her burst of enthusiasm.

"Good heavens."

I tell her the whole story, watching her face droop into deep seriousness. She sets the thermos, the paper, and her bag on the step.

"How did all that make you feel, though, Pumpkin?" she asks, arms crossed. She's never liked that I'm "around all that suicide."

"Great, of course! She's not fish food!"

Aunt Fran flinches.

I nudge the mop across imaginary grit on the floor between us. *So much for your clever plan to impress her.*

"Of course I was worried," I say. "Petrified that she would hang up. That they wouldn't get to her in time. But I kept her calm and on the line." I add, "I'm good at this."

"You are indeed, darlin'. But was it a trigger for you?" The

H-shaped wrinkle between her eyebrows deepens. She's staring down at me over her glasses, and her chin's bunched against her neck.

"No way." I ignore the image of the girl's scarred wrist and the memory of hurtling out of the packed bus like a cannonball. "Helping someone like that helps *me*, more than I can explain. It's like a lifeline."

Yes, the day was long and intense, and I had a slight meltdown, but this is The Truth.

She picks up her stuff and gives me a one-armed hug. "Well, I know Dr. Vernon agrees. I'm really proud of you." I breathe in her sweet waxy-flower-with-a-hint-of-orange perfume.

"Oh, what's the latest from handsome Nick?" she asks. Aunt Fran's childhood friend Nancy is Nick's mom.

"Still settling in at Cal. He says hi."

"Isn't that sweet!" She regards me over her pearly frames. "Plans to get together yet?"

"No, and if you bug me, I'm not going to tell you when there are." She adores Nick and would love to play matchmaker. On the one hand, I'm glad she approves. On the other hand, her meddling will almost for sure backfire.

"Yes, ma'am," she says. "Speaking of plans, don't forget the show tonight."

"How could I?" I've been dreading it for weeks. We have benefit tickets to a sold-out bawdy cabaret about Icelandic librarians for our birthdays. It's also an "exercise" for me in handling large public gatherings.

Fran's heading upstairs to her office now. The talk about my freshman housing has to wait. Just as well—it's almost time for my meeting.

# 5

"Hi, my name's Del. I'm an alcoholic."

It's noon in the Nob Hill church basement where it smells like charred, stale coffee and those cellophane-wrapped red-and-white-twirl peppermints. Blowing off the meeting crossed my mind, but after "Jane's" call and the incident on the bus last night, that's an even worse idea than it already was.

"Hi, Del!" chimes the group. I started coming to AA meetings a year and a half ago. I kept coming back. My friend Savannah mostly goes to teen Narcotics Anonymous, but this group, "Foundations," is my favorite and a social gathering I handle fine.

Fluorescent light makes everyone look ghoulish, and the metal folding chairs are their usual hard, cold selves. But the warmth and camaraderie generated in this room could power the city through a dark night.

My phone dings.

Cell phone use is majorly against the rules. Fortunately, a truck thundering by outside covers the noise. I unzip my backpack a half-inch at a time and glance inside.

Omigod! A text from Nick! Only, my phone goes dark before I can read it.

My foot jiggles. We continue the greetings around the room.

Some meetings are open to the public. This one is closed, only us alcoholics allowed.

"Hi, Bill." "Hi, Esmerelda."

Inside my pack, my fingers blindly scrabble over folded registration papers, pleather wallet, an open lip balm tube, empty med container, chewed bubblegum in a tissue, and loose coins, until they wrap around my phone, waiting for my chance.

Esmerelda M, my legendary sponsor in the faded navy-blue hoodie, crew cut, and awesome high-heeled boots, winks at me from near the podium. She's a software engineer at Google and she's speaking today. Everyone will definitely pay attention.

I already know her story. Eleven years ago, she ran away from home when her mother's boyfriend raped her and her mom was too fried to do anything about it. Ez lived on the streets, drinking, snorting, and eventually shooting up until a church group helped her into rehab, and eventually into college and computer science.

A bass musician, a residential real estate agent, a sales associate for a wine company, and Randy—who's basically unhoused—all introduce themselves as I wait for some kind of distraction.

For the record, in addition to having bipolar disorder, my mom was an alcoholic. Sometimes the two go together.

I'm dying here. So to speak. No way can I wait for an hour to see Nick's text! I could excuse myself to go to the bathroom . . . but wait—

Bill R, a cranky software sales associate, is reading off announcements and everyone's attention is wandering. He's been sober for three years and never seems too happy about it.

Now's my chance!

At just the right angle inside my pack, I open Nick's text.

**Are you free next Monday night?**

I almost squeal in glee but cough instead. Sadly, it's a whole week away. As a rule, Monday nights are packed with social obligations, so who knows if I can squeeze him in.

Just kidding.

**YES! In meeting. More later**, I text back.

White-helmet-haired Bill R is looking at me. I pretend to be searching in my backpack for . . . a pen. Ah, here's one! I hold up and examine this modern marvel.

Until last summer, Nick and I hadn't seen each other since Mom's funeral. Then, about a year ago, Nick and his parents were in town and Aunt Fran forced us all to have dinner together, a surefire attraction killer. Afterward, though, the two of us got coffee in North Beach. With the adults out of the way, it was easier to appreciate his transformation from soft-spoken nerd to soft-spoken *handsome* nerd.

I walked him to his hotel and we made out in the revolving door. Then again at the elevator bank as a bellhop and a late check-in pushed past us. His kiss was sweet and espresso-tinged and is seared permanently in my brain.

I should take him to the beach! Convince Aunt Fran to let me use the car again. Then get my hands under his shirt, over those muscles in his back—

"Del!"

The room's gone silent. All heads crane my way. Bill R glares at me like a giant bald eagle.

"What?" *Holy crap, did you say all that out loud?*

Oh. I've been tapping my pen against the chair. I stop.

"Did you have a question?" Bill demands.

Esmerelda says, "She's sending out an SOS in Morse code. 'Help. Trapped in a room full of old drunks.'"

Everybody laughs.

"Sorry," I mumble.

With an exasperated sigh, Bill R resumes reporting on the intergroup meeting from this past weekend, followed by details of the upcoming Fourth of July AA Beach Barbecue.

I can't wipe the Nick-centric grin off my face.

# 6

## Monday, June 29

I've got to get out there! Nick is sitting in the living room with Aunt Fran—god only knows what she's asking and telling him—while I'm obsessing over the height of my ponytail. Okay, I'll leave it mid-head, with this simple grayish-purple wool jacket over a white T-shirt and jeans. I switched my nail polish to "Silver Bells," took off three rings, and removed all earrings, except one pair of medium white-gold ones, and my favorite silver locket that was Aunt Fran's grandma's.

Plus these gray ankle boots—oh, and a swipe of lip gloss.

I shove the crap on my floor under my bed just in case, but it's unlikely he'll come back to this part of the apartment. One last trip to the toilet, mop my wet underarms, one last check in the mirror, clean teeth, and on that freshly sprouted zit a dab of cover-up—that just makes it stand out in an outlined, bull's-eye kind of way.

When I force myself to march into the living room, Aunt Fran booms, "Here she is! And don't you look snazzy!"

She's been teaching me how to make the most of my wardrobe. Supplementing it too, big time. I flash her a grateful smile. She's letting me take her Prius, which has been off limits since I sideswiped a support pillar in the garage, then backed into a Land Rover. No joke.

She probably feels guilty about the librarian musical. It was packed and I got claustrophobic. Plus, we ran into friends of hers who looked at me with unmistakable pity because of my long-ago attempt and hospitalization. Most of Fran's friends either feel sorry for me or outright distrust me.

Nick stands, burnished by the California golden-hour light streaming in.

His dark hair is shaggy but flattering. Those shoulders stretch for yards. He's filled out since last summer.

"Nick!" I practically tackle him and breathe in his woody lime smell. He hugs me back firmly, then pulls away. Maybe he's embarrassed to be physical in front of Aunt Fran. He's wearing cool glasses.

"I—you—you look really good!" I enthuse. My cheeks burn. When he was ten, he was an X-Men and Iron Man fan.

"You too!" he says. He takes my hand and shakes/squeezes it.

We're like blithering dorks, staring into each other's eyes.

"Cheese straw?" asks Aunt Fran, holding out a plate of buttery, freshly baked ones.

Nick laughs and takes one.

She asks, "Do y'all have time to sit for a minute?"

"Uh, sorry, Aunt Fran," I say quickly. "We can do that next time. Nick's here through August." If anyone could scare Nick off, it's her. I still remember the time in middle school when I went with Fran to visit Nick's family at Christmas. His dismayed face when she teased him about the thin hair on his upper lip is forever seared into my brain.

Nick nods. They've already been chatting for a while and he does look a little shell-shocked.

On the other side of the couch, a big black Lab stares me down like a glossy hellhound in a vest. "Whoa," I say.

"Meet Noor," says Aunt Fran.

"Omigod. A guide dog?"

"No," says Nick. "She's my new service dog. Helps me out."

"Oh, a service dog," I echo. He never mentioned this. He's got a degenerative sight thing to deal with. Maybe it's gotten worse.

The dog's sniffing the plate of cheese straws. "Noor," Nick commands. She adopts a pathetically sad expression and backs away from the coffee table. "She's still, um, in training."

I glance at Aunt Fran. She seems totally unfazed, but of course she's a huge dog person. She's still mourning the loss of her German shepherd, Rothko, who died three years ago.

"Um. We should probably get going," I say. "The movie's at eight-forty and we need to grab a bite first. Can, uh, Noor go to the movies?"

Nick says, "She can go pretty much anywhere."

Crap. I wasn't prepared for a third wheel. "Super." I give Aunt Fran a quick hug. "Don't wait up."

"You three have fun!"

Nick gives Fran a hug. "Really great to see you, Fran."

"Sugar, you know I love seeing you. Anytime." I bet if Nick and I get together, Aunt Fran will worry a lot less about me.

"Thank you," he replies. Something unspoken passes between them. Fingers crossed it doesn't concern an in-depth discussion of my psychiatric issues.

Noor snuffles the whole plate of cheese straws in one inhalation.

Nick's mouth opens but nothing comes out.

Aunt Fran gazes at the empty plate and says dryly, "Presto. A Labracadabrador."

# 7

I drive Aunt Fran's pea-soup-green Prius to Hayes Street. Nick grips the door during a yellow-light, left-hand turn. We are going a little fast, I guess. I park super carefully in an above-ground garage. My body feels stuffed with overfilled balloons that pop and jolt me from time to time. It's like Christmas morning when you're six and everyone's still asleep.

We chat about Nick's Cal schedule and rooming setup. "In late August I'm moving into a dorm at SFSU," I tell him. He says something generically supportive but otherwise doesn't really react.

After Nick unloads Noor from the backseat, I ask, "So what does she do to help you, exactly?"

"Warns me of stuff I might miss."

"Like . . . ?"

"Like a step, or a random skateboard. Especially at night. Or helps me find my glasses." He looks down at the concrete. "Stuff like that."

"Cool." That's a lot. We exit onto the street. "So, because of your retinitis—condition?"

He pauses to adjust Noor's harness in front of an Asian antique store full of old porcelain and wooden masks. "Retinitis pigmentosa. Yeah, I already don't drive at night. But I had to stop playing soccer this year because my peripheral vision is getting fucked up."

"Oh! That sucks." Soccer was one of our biggest common interests as kids. I sneak a look at him. His jaw is set.

"Noor, heel. I've been expecting it for a while. I just want to accomplish what I can before it . . . gets worse."

"You mean total blindness?" I blurt out. It's more serious than I thought.

"Worst-case scenario. Hopefully, that'll never happen, or if it does it'll be years from now." His face and voice have a no-big-deal set to them, but there's a forked furrow between his brows.

"How is it for your research at the lab?"

"Not an issue so far. We do so much on the computer, and technology is my friend." He smiles.

"Glad you got Noor." And I thought I had problems.

The three of us pass an art gallery exhibiting rubber-tire sculptures. He turns to me. "I'm honestly not worried about my *vision*—I can compensate. It's people's reactions to it that piss me off. Being treated as an invalid."

"For sure. Wait until you spend three days in a psychiatric ward and see how people skitter." We cross the street, dodging turning traffic.

"I bet." He grins. Not the deer-in-the-headlights response I typically get when I bring up this subject.

Ten years down the road, I could be off in my own internal world talking aloud to myself, and he could be tapping a white cane as we make our way into an Olive Garden. Who cares?

We're heading for the recently opened, trendy Beast Burger. That will probably be packed. Where I will seem normal and at ease.

"You're still planning on med school," I state.

"Absolutely," he says. "Family medicine, like, in under-served areas is what I'm thinking."

"That's so cool." I use the excuse that we're turning at the corner to hold his elbow. My fingers register the solid bone and layers of muscle, and I hang on maybe one Mississippi too long. He doesn't pull away.

"Getting this internship was a lottery win," he says. "It's super competitive, though, so I have to really focus." His melt-me eyes blink behind his glasses. "No pun intended."

"Ha!" I touch his navy flannel sleeve. He's making light, but his shoulders are a little hunched and his jaw's set. If there's one thing I recognize, it's anxiety. "I totally respect your ambi-tion." I pat him on the shoulder. "Maybe I'll come to Berkeley this weekend and we can grab lunch or something."

"That would be sweet." He pulls open the heavy teak door of Beast Burger for me, and the three of us make our way through fake hanging vines.

"Hey," he says, looking around at all the people, "cool! Crowded, though." He asks with concern, "Sure this is okay?"

I blush a new shade of blotchy and stop plucking at my hands. "It's fine!" Someplace quieter would've been a smarter pick, but I figured this would be fun, and also a good exercise. *You forgot you'd be all stressed about Nick too.*

I slip one of the green and orange tropical-themed takeout menus in my pocket for my collage file. We stand in line to order. "What about you? Still planning to study education?" he asks.

"Yep. I figure teaching is never a bad idea. Maybe little kids."

"You'd be awesome at that," he says.

My face warms yet again. "Thanks."

The jungle-themed restaurant is hot and humid, climate appropriate. I discreetly wipe my forehead with my sleeve. I'm sweating like a firefighter in the tropics, despite double clinical antiperspirant. My meds make it worse.

When our order's ready, Nick insists on carrying our wooden tray to a table, even though he can only use one hand—he holds Noor with the other.

"Gosh, she's surrounded by all this food and yet, so well-behaved," I deadpan.

"Must be my excellent training." His smile looks a little strained.

"Aunt Fran loves dogs. She could not care less about those cheese straws."

"Glad to hear it."

He doesn't notice the condiment holder and salt and pepper shakers as he puts the tray down. They all knock over. He jerks the tray and the burger basket slides off. I grab it midair before it hits the table upside down.

"Ha. Good catch," he says.

"Thanks!" Sight-related incident?

We sit. We take bites of our burgers and swallow. "Fran is really cool," he says. "How's it been, living with her?"

"Excellent. She's my anchor. I'll be moving into a dorm in late August, though," I repeat. Maybe he can visit me there.

He coughs and looks at something beyond the cash register. "How's she, um, been feeling?"

"Fine?" I put my burger down. "Why, does she look bad or something?"

"No! I mean in general. My mom's the same age, and she has a lot of aches and pains these days." He picks up his knife as if to cut his burger, but immediately sets it back down.

Fran and Nancy are both fifty-two. "Uh, that sucks. But Aunt Fran's strong as a horse."

"That's good. It's great you're around to help her out, though." He pops a saucy French fry into his mouth.

"Uh. I guess. I mean, I'd be around if she ever needed me, for sure."

We chat about Fran's gallery while I drive to the multiplex. Now that it's dark, Noor seems to stay closer to Nick's side and be more alert. In the dim theater, she herds him into the row after me. Once we're seated, she lies at Nick's feet.

He's chosen the latest superhero team mashup, with surround-sound collisions and explosions. Because it's a Monday night, it's not crowded, and even with the noise I unclench a little. Anxiety is exhausting. Actively worrying about seeing him, what to wear, what Aunt Fran will say, about driving, parking, and then the overstimulation of Beast Burger—would he notice if I took a little nap?

Just kidding. My attention flits to Nick's warm arm and leg, which pulse within inches of mine. Our hands brush twice in the popcorn bag and he offers me a sip of his blue Slushie.

Finally, I shift my leg against his.

*Hey, how's it going?* my knee asks his through the denim.

*Great! So nice to bump into you!*

When I sneak a look at him, he's smiling, and our knees sit in happy togetherness for the rest of the movie.

After it's over we stand outside on the sidewalk. Nick jams his hands in his pockets and looks up and down the street. I undo my ponytail and re-force all my hair into a messy bun. Noor stares ahead like a black-fur-hatted Queen's Guard.

"Want to see the ocean?" I ask.

"Um, okay!" he says.

# 8

I navigate to Baker Beach, to the west of the Golden Gate Bridge. On the way, Nick tells me about living in Austin and about his classes at UT. He does an imitation of his stoner roommate singing Miley Cyrus songs and I laugh too hard and run a stop sign. Whoops. Nick politely says nothing.

We're not really supposed to discuss callers, but I outline the basics of the situation with "Jane," and he's impressed. We park and pull a fleece blanket from the back. I slip off my boots. He leaves his sneakers on.

"Oh, wow!" he says once we're out of the car. "The view of the bridge from here is. Totally. Awesome." It's lit against the night sky, partially obscured by fog, like some elongated alien space transporter decked out with Christmas decorations.

Actually, the bridge kind of looms for me like the deadly weapon it is. We should've gone to Ocean Beach. Except it's farther away and colder, and the waves are too big.

Nick, Noor, and I amble over the beach. Creepy signs warn us that currents along here can be deadly as the tide rushes into and out of the bay and that people wading and swimming have drowned. I keep Nick between me and the water. "You cold?" he asks me.

The damp sand is frigid and abrasive beneath my bare feet.

I'm shivering. "Nah. A little." Nervous is more like it.

He throws the blanket around both of us. Now I grin.

I'm really *here*, on a dark deserted beach, with Nick, like I've played out in my mind a hundred times. Maybe we'll hook up! Is that okay? I'm so not sure what to do.

At Ridgefield—my boarding school since eighth grade—attitudes had the smell of double standard. Guys got points for having sex with anyone as fast as possible. Girls lost points if they slept with more than some arbitrary number of guys—like two—depending on how much time passed in between. And yet, virgins were losers.

Here in Cali, judging by my friends' stories, it seems like people hook up with fewer rules about who should do what. I think. Except giving consent. And people hook up first, then get "involved" after.

Please, can someone just give me some universally approved guidelines? Fair ones.

Nick interrupts my thoughts. "So, your depression and, um, anxiety are better." He states it like a fact.

"Yep. Definitely. Thanks to modern pharmaceutical advancements." We walk above the tide line toward the bridge, avoiding the frigid waves.

"Can I ask you something personal?"

"Sure." He kind of already did. Aunt Fran doesn't like it when people ask her if they can ask her something, but I don't mind because it lets me brace myself. Maybe it'll be about sex!

"What did it feel like to be suicidal?"

"Oh." Worth bracing for. But it's a legitimate question for someone who plans to be a doctor. "Well." I zip-line my silver locket along its chain.

My attempt sits in my head like a walnut-sized tumor.

Hopefully benign now, but not going anywhere without major brain surgery. I try not to think about it, but it's always there.

"I guess it's different for different people. Have you ever thought about killing yourself?" I know the answer, but I'm stalling.

"Abstractly, I guess a few times." The wind is at our backs. "I guess it's more like I've thought about death in general."

I suck in a deep breath of fresh salty air. "Junior year at Ridgefield. After I left Aunt Fran's at Thanksgiving to go back, I was already dealing with a kick-ass depression. Already in 'the void,' as I call it, where nothing matters, and classes, sports, and meals are way too much work. I'd gotten dropped from the soccer team for missing practice. We were supposedly getting ready for finals." I pause. "I was already thinking a *lot* about dying."

I stop walking. We're still leaning into one another, wrapped in the blanket. The tilt of his head and the expression on his face say that he's concentrating on my words.

"When my best friend got expelled, it snapped something in me. I kept picturing and planning all the ways I would end my life."

"Jesus. That's really tough."

We walk again. The warmth of his body steadies me.

"It was unbearable. Almost no one gets that. Living in my head was like being tortured. While also being strapped into a speeding, dilapidated car that's about to crash. Or explode."

"That could be challenging," he agrees dryly.

"I was willing to do *anything* to make it stop."

I'm proud to be doing well these days. Proud to be retraining my brain to be healthier. Still, inside me is always this writhing mass of one-inch-thick rubber noodles and live electrical cords that could burst out of an orifice at any time.

"Did you tell anyone?" he asks.

"My more balanced friends were not really hanging out with me by then. So, no. Matt knew, but he was gone."

Nick regards me sideways.

"My best bud sophomore and junior year. Platonic. He's gay." Awkward to have to specify that, but I don't want any confusion here. "He got kicked out for having alcohol in his room. That was mine."

"Oh. Man." He gazes down at Noor, trotting alongside him. "What happened to him?"

"I learned recently that he went to the art high school in his hometown, as well as to a good therapist."

"He forgave you?"

"Um, I wouldn't go quite that far. But he let me know how he was doing." Turns out we both do better apart.

"Then what happened? To you?"

"At that point I just shut down. There was absolutely no point to anything. The wellness counselor and my English teacher were, I guess, watching me, but I kept saying I was fine. Plus, the semester was, like, two days from over."

"Did you think about your family?" he asks softly.

Distant, blinking lights travel over the bridge. A tow truck maybe. "Of course. I knew it would destroy Aunt Fran and my dad. But I also knew that they would eventually get over it and then be *way* better off without me." I hesitate. "I thought about my mom too. That I might actually get to see her again." Her rare giggly laugh jingles in my head.

He stops. I do too. We're closer to the northeast end of the beach. Boulders hulk in the dark ahead, and the bridge threatens, extremely close and loud.

"We've never really talked about your mom," he says.

"About what happened, I mean. There wasn't a chance to say much at the funeral, and—"

"And Dad and I left Dallas pretty soon after that." He moved to London and I went to Ridgefield.

"Still. I could've made more of an effort to keep in touch right afterward. To check in. She was really awesome. Losing her like that—it must've been so hard."

"Thanks. It did suck."

He smooths down Noor's left ear, which the wind has flipped inside-out. "What did you think it would be like?"

"After I died?"

He nods.

An eddy of air lifts loose strands of my hair. The thousands of icy grains of sand beneath my feet prick. "A big nothingness. Which would be way better than what I was experiencing. But it didn't really matter. I just couldn't keep on any longer."

He laces his fingers through mine. "So what did you do?"

"I had some prescription meds, plus what I borrowed and bought. After finals I washed them all down with, um, peach schnapps."

"Ew." He laughs. "Wait. *After* finals?"

"I know, right?"

Now he grins. "Then what happened?"

He's listening, not in a rubbernecking kind of way, but in a trying-to-understand way. After my attempt, I've never really fit back in with the living in the same way again. It's hard to talk about it with anyone who hasn't occupied the same territory. Yet Nick's letting the subject be kind of *normal*. Shitty, unfortunate, sad, but not unspeakable. "There was this broom closet in the basement. I squeezed in behind a bunch of mops."

He shakes his head slightly. "Weren't you scared?"

"No. I wasn't feeling much of anything. Except relief that everything would soon be over. But I think a part of me hoped someone would find me before I died." *You didn't stay in your room where you knew they would find you, but when you dropped your hoodie on the steps to the basement, you left it.*

Sometimes a flash of ammonia and mildew from the closet, and that feeling of rocking in the cradle of the dusty, velour-y darkness, hits me even now, strangely empty of fear, regret, or relief.

"What happened next?" We're still leaning against each other under the blanket. Noor flops down on the sand, apparently concluding that we're not going to move anytime soon.

"My faculty dorm-parent did find me, like, less than ten minutes later, and called 911."

"Thank god." He jabs the toe of his sneaker at a strand of rubbery seaweed. "Did they pump your stomach?"

Maybe he's interested from a medical point of view. "I was still conscious, so they gave me a big container of activated carbon charcoal juice and made me chug it. Like licking the bottom of a barbeque grill."

He squeezes my hand. It says, *You're funny, I like you.* "Really glad you didn't die," he says.

My cheeks warm. "You and me both." It's true. I'm glad all the time that I didn't complete suicide. Except occasionally when I'm not.

Still holding my hand, he asks, "Remember the July Fourth parade in Dallas when you were, like, seven? Hanging in the park?"

I take a breath and gaze up at the stars. "Seven? I remember the summer after fourth grade. When I was about to turn ten."

"Yeah, then too. But the first time our families met up for

the parade." He pauses. "I thought you were really pretty."

"You did?" My heartbeat blips.

"Elf-like. Like Arwen." He chuckles at his kid self.

I in no way look like Liv Tyler, but it's flattering. Does this mean he likes me *now*? Is my breath okay?

He continues, "You were all quiet. Not much into the games the rest of us were playing. You were reading to some little cousin."

"Yeah. The crowds and noise. Anxiety was already an issue for me."

"I could tell," he says softly. "Even then."

I throw my arms around Nick's tall and solid body and press my hot cheek against his collar bone. His heart's beating near my face, nowhere near as fast as mine. He pats my back and I nuzzle his neck that smells like lime peel, fresh hay, and a touch of Thousand Island dressing.

I kiss him.

I'm making the first move. This is California. It's politically incorrect to always expect the guy to do it, right?

Wait. Does he have a girlfriend at UT? He certainly hasn't mentioned anyone.

Jose V and I mutually lost our virginity at Ridgefield earlier the fall I attempted. But the memory is hazy since I was so wasted. I also slept with Molly W—also while wasted—but it was Awk. Ward.

*You have no clue what you're doing.*

Nick's lips are distractingly soft and warm. The fog and salt and his bright spring soap swirl around us in the frosty air. My fingers tangle in his thick hair and knock his glasses.

He pulls them off. Slow. Or hesitant? It's a moonless night, and stars are smeared over the ocean and the headlands like spilled glitter glue. The bridge-glow is our only light.

A jet roars over us, headed for SFO. A cold jitteriness gels beneath my hot skin.

The dim, locked echo chamber of my mind is sucking me into it.

I kiss him again and focus on my fingers as they slide along his back, over his smooth skin and firm muscles. I sink into the sand, pulling him with me. In the distance, cars rumbling over the steel girders of the bridge thrum menacingly.

In my mind a tiny "Jane" figure stands on the edge of the bridge eyeing how many, many stories down the fall is.

I fumble for the fly of Nick's jeans. Should I give him a blow job? I know I'm going too fast but I want him so much. Have wanted him all year.

He moves my hand away but continues to kiss me. Only not enthusiastically.

*Del. What are you doing?* I guess I'm giving *my* consent nonverbally, but what about his? Should I ask? Does he have a condom? *You're getting sand everywhere. Maybe you shouldn't have told him that crap! You shouldn't have come to the beach! You need to slow down.* A night bird screeches. I can't breathe. *You'll probably faint.* Shit, racing thoughts. The waves pound. The deadly currents lurk. *We'll get washed out!*

An involuntary yelp escapes me and I jerk back. *Ohmigod, you're hopeless.*

Noor jumps on top of us and sticks her nose in Nick's face.

"Noor. Sit!" Nick commands.

She does, almost on top of him. She lays her big head on Nick's chest and breathes doggy breath at me.

"Crap," I say. "Where's a tennis ball when you need one?"

# 9

Nick gropes for his glasses, silhouetted against the foggy Golden Gate.

We both sit up, not looking at each other. "I should get back," he says.

I scramble to my feet, nonchalantly shaking sand from my clothes and the blanket. We slog silently into the stiff, chilled wind that cools my hot cheeks. Back up the beach, back over asphalt dotted with seagull droppings that glow in the dark.

Funny how neither of us has vocal cords anymore.

Kissing Nick again, at the very least, has been in the back of my mind all year, and at the forefront all week. The plan was to be sexy and irresistible, not needy and insane.

*But you are needy and insane.* I know. And maybe he's not interested in me.

Yet.

"Uh, I can drive you over to Berkeley," I finally say at the car, scraping my socks and shoes over my sandy feet. I'm not cleared to go to the East Bay, but Aunt Fran will cut me some slack. Talking in the car will be easier.

"Thanks. That'd be great." His voice has a waxy evenness to it, as if all emotionally revealing edges have been smoothed off.

We roll through quiet neighborhoods of Victorians, town-houses, and apartment buildings, onto the bright elevated free-way and toward the other big San Francisco over-water engi-neering wonder, the new Bay Bridge.

The silence between us weighs even heavier. We don't really know each other that well.

*No, he knows more about you than anyone else now.*

The old part of the Bay Bridge is so high. The upper deck could collapse and crush us like that one in the last earth-quake. I'm pulled to the distant plunge into the dark, cold water below.

I focus on the lane dividers. The sand in my pants. My grip on the wheel. And try not to breathe like a trapped animal.

Nick gazes out the window at the Oakland shipyards shim-mering across the black bay. Noor is curled up contentedly on the floor at his feet. My one shot, and I lost out to a real bitch.

I would've gone all the way with Nick. Would right now. He's hot. I trust him.

But my enthusiasm way outpaced his. Maybe by pushing it, I made him feel, like, unmanly for not taking advantage of the situation? Right, Dr. Vernon, I didn't *make him* feel any-thing. But he felt pushed. Does he even remember that kiss last summer?

Maybe he thinks of me like a sister.

But he's being all weird now. A jerk!

*Because you were a maniac.*

Nick finally gives me directions when we pull off I-80 into Berkeley. In the driveway of the small apartment building where he's staying, a blinding motion-activated light over the side door flashes on, interrogation style. *Do you seriously think you are worthy of this guy?*

"Thanks a lot for driving me back," he says. The fuzzy outline of his bedhead hair is in relief against the bright halo of light behind him, his face totally and unreadably in shadow. His seat belt un-clicks with a final sound.

"I—I had a nice time tonight," I stammer. Except for that last bit. Thank goodness the darkness hides my hot face.

"Me too." He adjusts his glasses.

I clutch my locket. "I know you're really busy."

"Yeah. It's basically 'round the clock." He opens his door before quickly leaning over and giving me an obligatory hug.

I say, "So, I hope we can hang out when you have time. But no pressure."

"Cool, thanks. See you." He climbs out, gets his dog, and closes the door with a *thunk*.

Turd on a stick.

# 10

## Saturday, July 4

A man with a two-foot-long braid down his back hands Aunt Fran and me our life vests and helps us slide a shiny silver aluminum canoe into the shallows of the Russian River.

We're an hour and a half north of the city. This is my birthday present to her—at her suggestion—and it's the Fourth of July. We've both been moody lately, and canoeing is quality time together as well as a desensitization exercise for me.

Speaking of time, it's run out on the whole dorm thing. I *have to* bring it up it in a quiet, relaxed moment and submit the form tonight.

The cool air is filled with the scent of the massive redwoods towering over us. The sun pokes lazily through the fog.

My phone dings in its plastic bag and I retrieve it. Savannah and problems with her mom. Sometimes I feel guilty for how great Fran and I get along. Except, Fran's tapping her foot.

"I'm telling her I'll talk to her later," I say, thumb-typing fast.

"This is our time. I'd like to have you here and now." She's all about the present moment, thanks to all the time she spends at the Buddhist center.

"Turning it off, Captain."

"Thank you. Are you ready?" she asks. She knows that deep, dark water and waves are tough for me, even though I'm a decent swimmer. Lots of sunlight, a mostly shallow, slow-moving river, and an oversized personal flotation device with Aunt Fran can go a long way toward conquering this anxiety. Baby steps.

"Yes, ma'am." I hold the canoe steady as she gets in, then push off and hop in back to steer. We're front-heavy but slide out into the gentle current and fall into an easy rhythm of silent paddling.

A mini-meadow of bright orange poppies and tiny yellow wild flowers slides by as the sun breaks through the billows of fog overhead. Aunt Fran turns and beams at me. "I haven't been in a canoe since Girl Scout camp at Lake Texoma, a million years ago. This is so far out!"

I deadpan, "Yeah, it's pretty groovy." Still, all the five-pound ice bags of stress and embarrassment I've built up over the past few days are melting away.

About halfway down the course, we pull up onto a shaded, gravelly beach where we make seat cushions of our tangerine life jackets. The sun burns hot now and the soaring eucalyptus tree above us fills the air with its minty scent. The first time I breathed it in was when I came to California at age eight and Aunt Fran took me for a ride through the Presidio in her shiny convertible. We talked about *beauty*. In nature and in people. I was probably waxing poetic on the virtues of my princess unicorn plastic watch, but she treated my opinions and questions like they were gemstones.

We unwrap our sandwiches. Occasional canoes and kayaks float and paddle by. Time to bring up how living close to school and with other students will help me—

"Heard from Nick?" she asks.

Deep breath. Nick would probably love it here. My face heats. "Yeah, we texted." Finally. His was brief. But we are still going to meet up in Berkeley. I don't know exactly when yet, or what it means, but I'm grateful.

"Hmm." She scoots up to lean against the tree and grimaces as she adjusts.

"Back hurt?" I ask, psyched to change the subject. I tuck two eucalyptus leaves into a napkin to take home for my collage file.

"A little sore. Just need something to lean against. Any plans to see him again?" She opens her bottled juice.

I sigh. She's like a bulldog. "Yeah, we might get together next weekend. If he has time."

"He's come all the way from Austin to be in the Bay Area for the summer. That's not a coincidence."

"He's wanted to go to Cal for ages. And even if you're right, all of a sudden it feels like a lot of pressure."

She studies me as she nibbles her eggplant and brie on whole grain.

"I think I scare him." I set my ham-and-Swiss baguette down.

"Why do you think that?" she asks.

"Because I was honest about almost killing myself. Plus, I might have, um, been a little anxious. And hyper."

"So what? Maybe he was a little awkward too. That doesn't mean things can't work out. You gotta want it, sugar!"

"I thought if you love something, you should let it go." Like me. Moving into a dorm.

"It depends. Sometimes if you love someone, you should go after them!" I wait for *You can do anything you set your mind to.*

But she says instead, "Speaking of letting people know how you feel, you do know that I love you more than life itself? And there's no one on Earth I'd rather spend my birthday with?"

I hide behind my bottled lemonade. "Yeah, I guess I do. And ditto."

"Thank you, cupcake, for bringing me up here. *This* is what the doctor ordered." She pauses. "But I have something important to talk to you about." Her bottle clanks against the gravel.

"What?" Uh-oh. She's going to *insist* I live at home for freshman year. Dammit! I should've brought it up first!

"At my checkup." She raises her pink-rimmed sunglasses and looks me in the eye. "The test results came back positive."

"Huh?" What test results?

"My cancer's returned."

"What do you mean? There's gotta be some mistake." Her breast cancer was eight or nine years ago. "You're in remission."

Aunt Fran says, "It's not what I had before. Though it's probably all related."

The peaceful river gurgles. A bird twitters. *Ha! You're being punked.*

The expression on her face is not a joke.

"I—do you—maybe something got into the blood or urine sample. Or onto the microscope slide!"

"I don't think so, sugar."

"How advanced is it?" A warped, giant-kneed me reflects in her sunglass lenses.

She focuses on the branch above us. "Not so advanced, but it's best to jump on it. I had my first chemo session last week."

*Chemo.* "You started chemo already without telling me?"

"Just wanted to get that first plunge out of the way. I go again on Monday, if you'd like to come along and join the fun."

Her voice is light, but there's a thread of hesitation in it. She's afraid I'll react badly. Afraid I'll fall apart. "Oh, Aunt Fran! I can't believe it! I'm—I'm so sorry." I scooch over the gravel and give her a hug. "Are you—do you feel it? Is there pain?"

"No, darlin'."

Bull-caca. Something's hurting her right now.

I'm always stressing over the next earthquake, climate change inundation, artificial intelligence takeover, or zombie apocalypse. I'm trying to learn not to.

Every once in a while, though, I'm right.

When I was fourteen, while I was visiting Dad in London for Christmas break, I chugged leftover cocktails sitting around from his office holiday party. The constant loud buzz in my head softened. The permanent clench and ache in all my muscles, especially my heart, warmed and soothed. I was the question. Day-old red wine in a lipstick-stained glass was the answer.

Aunt Fran's voice comes from far away. "Sugar, are you okay?"

The problem—or maybe the saving grace—was that I could never get enough. I'd kill for a Polar Bear shot right now. Or five.

# 11

As soon as we get home, I bolt into my room to call Savannah. I update her, then Esmerelda, and text a couple of my other friends. Nick's number is right there on my screen. Before I can talk myself out of it, I tap it.

It goes to voicemail. "Hi. Please call me when you get a chance," I say. "I have some sucky news."

Forty-five seconds later he calls me back.

"Del, what's up?"

"Hi! Are you out celebrating the Fourth?" I push shoes, clothes, and my oversized collage box aside and lie on the carpet. Aunt Fran's Andy Warhol print of Elvis in cowboy gear with a pistol is on the wall above me. Lichtenstein's *The Kiss* is behind me.

"No, at the lab. Snack room. Taking a short break." It's like he's working to sound normal.

"Sorry to bother you, but I got some bad news and really wanted to tell you." The rust-red throw pillow from my bed is clutched against my chest like a giant squishy heart shield.

"It's okay," he says to someone. "Hang on." He's moving somewhere.

"Aunt Fran was diagnosed with colon cancer."

"Oh, no. I'm so sorry."

I blurt out, "And I'm sorry about being weird Monday night. I know I . . . was moving kinda fast."

"No, *I'm* sorry. I really did have a good time and I didn't mean to be, like, a dick on the way back. Thanks again for driving me all the way. I guess I was just . . . um, uncomfortable. Things were moving fast—"

"I know. You can change the subject now."

He pauses. "When I came to the apartment that night, before you came out? Fran told me."

"What? About the cancer? You *knew*?"

"We were talking about . . . sickness. About when I was little and in the hospital . . ."

When he was eight he was racing his bike downhill and slammed into a tree, resulting in a serious chest injury.

"And it kind of just came up, that her cancer had come back. She didn't give me any details . . . and said she was working up to telling you."

I sit up. "She told you before she told me?" Outside my window, dusk is dimming the world.

"Probably she was worried. How you'd take it."

"The problem child."

He doesn't deny this. "How *are* you taking it?"

"Not. Well." *Everybody knows you're a whack-job and the slightest little thing will send you off the deep end. You should scream and chuck your phone at a window!*

"There's so much they can do," he says all calmly. "So many ways to fight it."

"Please don't minimize this." I scramble up and pace around my bed.

Long pause. "What do you want me to do?" he asks gently.

My chin drops to my chest. I want to say, *Be here now.*

"Sorry, I'm just . . . I don't know." I sit at my desk.

A sticky silence descends. *Good work, Del.*

He breaks it. "Something else I didn't tell you. The other night."

"What?"

"That if I do a good job in this internship, they'll help me transfer to Cal."

I sit up. "You-uh-really? A full-time student at Berkeley?"

"Really. The key is—with a scholarship. Otherwise, I'm staying in Austin."

"That's huge news!" So, to be near me?

*Probably not.*

"Are your folks okay with it?" I ask.

"Dad's all 'absolutely!' Mom thinks it's too far away. But I'm competing with tons of others so I really gotta go. I'm so sorry about Fran but it's awesome you're there with her. I'll see you soon, and don't worry, we'll get through this."

He could be a full-time student across the bay! He said "we," and that he'll see me soon. Yay! "Okay, go. Love you," I blurt out.

Horrified, I disconnect and bang my forehead on my desk.

;

I stay at my desk to work on my latest collage.

My best one, *California Dreamin'*, is framed and hanging in the kitchen, and *High Places* is on my wall in here. My art teacher at Ridgefield assigned my first one, then I did more as "therapy." I'm hooked.

I've always been sort of a hoarder, but saving cool stuff and then pasting it together pins events and feelings down. Prevents them from vaporizing out from under me.

Fran gave me books about collaging for Christmas, along with a big folder of her old maps from all over: California, Cape Cod and the Islands, Budapest, Bangkok, Paris, Nepal, Scotland, and of course Texas. I print out random antique ones from the internet.

On a long piece of butcher's paper, over an enlarged map of Northern California, so far there are fireworks, a comet, a streetcar, the SF Ferry Building's clock tower, a scale, a hand knocking on a door, brown autumn leaves, a mother kissing her child, and a billboard for life insurance. I'm enhancing it with pastels.

The title of this one is *Untitled*.

;

A little after nine, Aunt Fran and I turn off the lights in the living room. I sit next to her on the couch that faces the big windows. Savannah invited me and some other sober types to a fireworks-watching party at her parents' house, but due to recent developments I ditched it. She's been known to do the same to me, and not for a sick aunt, but she still thinks *I'm* being a brat.

Aunt Fran has a small glass of brown liquor, probably bourbon. She doesn't keep alcohol in the apartment on my account so she must've bought it in the last few days.

*Hmm. Wonder where she keeps it.*

"You told Nick before you told me," I say softly.

"Oh, sugar. I didn't mean to. It just slipped out."

"Why didn't you tell me right away?" She's known this for almost two weeks.

"Because I didn't want to upset you. Or influence your plans." She's rotating the gold bracelet on her wrist.

I jump up. "That's ridiculous! This affects me too! I deserve to know this as much as you do!"

"I was worried about telling you." She shields her chest with both hands. "I'm still worried." She exhales. "And I guess I needed a little time to process it myself."

Deep breath, Delilah. Sit down. Chill. This is not about you. *Oh, but it is!* I argue with myself. "Okay, then," I say.

We watch a huge red-and-blue ball explode in the night sky over Fisherman's Wharf, parts of it hazy in the patchy fog. The dark hunk of Alcatraz Island and its blinking lighthouse hulks behind it.

Muffled pops and rolling booms reach our ears a split-second later. I hated the noise as a kid. An even more gigantic white ball blows in a thousand graceful arcs and rains down over the bay.

Obliterated.

"Ohhh. Like a big dandelion!" exclaims Aunt Fran with enthusiasm lord only knows how she generated. "We should make a wish."

"Fine." I would wish for Nick's undivided love and attention and my own confident, seductive smoothness, but instead of course I wish that Aunt Fran's cancer gets zapped.

When I got sober, I had to admit that I was not in control. Aloud. That I was, in fact, powerless in the face of my addictive urges. Way harder than it sounds.

Then I agreed that I believed in a power greater than myself. In AA you don't have to believe in God. You just have to admit there is something bigger than you, outside of you, that is more powerful than you and your bad choices. Since it was crystal clear that my power was zip, I could sort of swing that. So, I agreed, in theory, to turn my life and will over to a higher power. To "let go and let [Higher Power]."

But that's so absurd now! Let go and let cancer take Aunt Fran?

Over my dead body!

Multicolored sprays follow a light waterfall that crackles. Golden chandeliers; puff balls; chrysanthemums, green planets with red rings; and red, white, and blue fountains brighten the empty black sky.

It's a relief not to have to talk.

Ghost clouds of smoke drift with the fog across the water toward Berkeley. Can Nick see these from over there? Muted flashes of light and color through the billows.

I steal a glance at Aunt Fran's profile. She gazes into the night with an expression of wonder like she's never seen fireworks before. And as if we have something to celebrate. When we're lit by the latest rockets' red glare, I find her hand and hold it tight.

# 12

## Monday, July 6

The deadline for SFSU housing has passed, but there are other ways to find a rooming/roommate situation near the school, so I figure I'll deal with that once Aunt Fran has her cancer back under control. Meanwhile, she's "invited" me to come with her to her next chemo appointment. Of course I accept, even though I'd rather have my fingers staple-gunned to the wall. I have to prove I'm not going to flip out.

We park deep in the bowels of a garage where an earthquake would instantly annihilate us. *Or trap you until you both die of dehydration.* I stop myself from pulling out my phone to see how many days it takes to do that.

In the med building elevator, I pretend to study the control panel so Fran won't notice my mild hyperventilating.

She signs in at the desk. Right away we're called into a big room with twelve sea-green, fake-leather recliners and IV poles planted at intervals like tiki torches. It smells like ammonia with a grapefruit juice chaser.

Aunt Fran chooses a recliner near the window. Onto the little table beside her, in her lap, and on the floor, I unload the contents of her oversized turquoise shoulder bag: her tablet and phone, a small pillow, the *San Francisco Chronicle*, the blue-gray yarn and the sweater she's knitting for me, *ARTnews*, *People*, a novel, a water bottle, vitamin-E hand lotion, sheepskin slippers with non-skid soles, ginger chews, and roasted salted pumpkin seeds. Apparently, when I was little, I liked to unpack her purse on the kitchen floor.

Two other people are already plugged up. As I organize, Aunt Fran greets each of them like she's on a debutante receiving line.

A nurse older than Aunt Fran, in a pine-green uniform, exclaims, "Fran from Texas!"

Aunt Fran glances at the nurse's name tag and says, "Hello, Janet! Delighted to see you! This is my niece, Delilah." She says to me, "Janet and I go waaay back."

"We're going to take good care of your aunt, Delilah."

I should certainly hope so. "Glad to hear it."

Aunt Fran already has a PICC line in her arm that they'll pipe the chemo into. The little tube-y plastic thing is crammed into the soft blue-white skin of her upper arm and secured with clear tape.

I told her I'm not squeamish.

False. It's true that blood doesn't bother me, but needles, long tubes snaked into veins, and small flaps of flesh edged with inflamed carnation pink push my squeam envelope.

Janet hooks up two bags of innocuous-looking clear liquids, enters information on the keypad on the IV stand, and then plugs the main line into Aunt Fran.

I turn away.

Whoa. The old man two chairs down looks like a leather-covered skeleton. With a freaking hole in his cheek. The jaw below is puffy-swollen and his eyes are bloodshot and drippy.

Next to him, his wife sits on a stool like mine and smiles at me. I smile back and try to hide how grossed-out I am.

Where to look?

The pretty woman farther down has thick, long black hair with a layered cut. She's maybe in her thirties? Here by herself, and the bright yellow straw bag next to her has a small disposable diaper sticking out.

I shake my head involuntarily and ask Aunt Fran, "Doesn't chemo make your hair fall out?"

"Possibly. Or at least makes it thinner. I think it depends on the kind used and how much. For me—before—it took a while. But I'm getting it cut short on Saturday."

"Oh." That might be hard. She's vain about her thick auburn hair.

She's studying me. "We all lose our hair, and nails, and skin cells. Every day."

"Usually not all at once."

"I'm a completely new sack of cells than I was seven years ago. You are too." She smiles wistfully. "That little Delilah with the two missing front teeth and the infectious giggle is gone forever."

"But I'm right here."

"Yes, you are, darlin', and I'm so grateful." She pauses. "What I'm trying to say is that the only 'you' is the one in this moment. Our bodies are secondary." She opens her water bottle. "I sure do wish you'd consider taking up meditation."

She's preached all this before. "I can't sit still that long."

She flips the footrest up and leans back. "You are what is behind, above, below, and beyond all that. As the Buddhists say, 'Those things of which I can perceive the beginnings and the end . . . are not myself.'"

"If you say so."

"Since today's your first day and it takes a little getting used to, we need to do at least two."

"Two what?"

She grins. "Silver linings."

A game of hers. "Seriously?"

"Yes," she says. "I look forward to dropping a few pounds with the chemo. I lost almost twenty last time, but put them all back on plus a few more since."

"Fine. I'm psyched to learn to cook better." Aunt Fran's taught me how to make omelets, pimento cheese, cornbread from scratch, and I already knew how to make blueberry pancakes. I also took a cake-decorating course at Ridgefield.

"Brrrr," she says. "I forgot how cold it gets in here. Sugar, would you kindly ask Janet for one of their mold-colored blankets?"

"You got it." I jump up, thrilled to escape for a minute. Aunt Fran trying to educate and reassure me today is mildly annoying. I don't want *her* to know that, though.

"Could y'all use a blanket?" Fran calls to the man and his wife. "Get two, please, sugar," she says to me without waiting for their reply.

"Yes, ma'am."

"Then I'm going to send you off to Whole Foods to get groceries and some hot soup for us for afterward."

"I can take the car?" Awesome! Plus, if she's organizing everyone as usual, she's obviously going to be just fine.

"Yes, you may. I might even nap a little and there's no need for you to sit here for the duration."

All I can think is, *Whew.* I give her a quick peck and bolt.

# 13

## Tuesday, July 7

Dad sent me a package. The size of a shoe box, it sits in the lobby mailroom, a little crunched with his return address and Queen Elizabeth stamps. He missed my birthday two months ago, so this is probably a late gift—and an attempt to make up for how little we've seen each other since I became a mentally ill teenager.

I bring the package up in the building's gaping, gleaming elevator.

When I unlock the front door the smell of something yum in the oven—jalapeño cheese grits, I bet—envelops me. Aunt Fran's in the kitchen in a bright pink-and-green paisley apron, looking like her usual energetic self. She bounded out of bed this morning to do her usual meditation exercises and then make French toast as if the chemo was just a bad dream.

"Oh, goodie!" She joins me at the black granite island. "A present from London!"

I rip the package open. Bubble wrap. An envelope.

Inside that is an Amazon UK "Happy Birthday" gift card for twenty-five pounds, about thirty-five dollars.

"Better late than never, I guess. It's nice. I'll use it. The poppable bubble wrap is a plus."

"Indeed, pumpkin," she says, but she's gloating. Probably thinking of the burgundy velvet top she recently bought me, and the cute navy fitted zip-up jacket she gave me on my birthday. Not to mention some killer black high heels.

Being competed over is excellent.

"You should call him and thank him." Aunt Fran presses her lips together. Dad and Aunt Fran went years without speaking.

"Uh, I can write him a note."

Aunt Fran grabs a sponge and wipes crumbs off the counter. "I've been meaning to call. I haven't told him the latest," she says to the cutting board. She sounds worn out from the thought.

"Well, *I* don't want to tell him!" I lean against the granite. He associates me with bad news as it is. "Does he even need to know? You're going to be fine."

"I would like him to know. How do you think he'll take it?" Her unsure expression unnerves me.

I grab the landline phone and dial Dad's London number. "Why don't we just see?"

Aunt Fran gasps. I hold my finger to my lips.

Dad answers groggily. I glance at the stove clock. Oh, crap—it's like 2 a.m. there.

"Um, hi, Dad. It's me. Sorry it's so late. But I just got your nice present."

"Well. Hope you like it," he says sleepily.

"I do, thanks. How are things?"

Aunt Fran's rinsing a mixing bowl in the sink but listening intently.

There's a slight delay. "Fine. I'm off to Vietnam and Cambodia next week. For a long stint. We're finally getting the health programs there going."

"Hmm," I say. "Dad, Aunt Fran wants to talk to you. She has some news."

Aunt Fran shakes her head and holds up her wet hands. As if that would prevent her if it were anyone else.

"What is it? You tell me."

I take a deep breath. "Her cancer has come back. Only it's not breast, it's in the colon. She's already started chemo."

There's a long pause. Fran's frozen.

"Dad?"

"I'm so sorry to hear it," says Dad slowly. "Very upsetting." To my surprise he adds, "I'm glad you're there with her. Would you put her on, please?"

"Sure." I hold the phone out to Aunt Fran, who makes no move to reach for it. "He asked for you," I mouth. I've always wished for siblings. If I had one, I'd be devastated if they got cancer. These two are so flipping wiggy with each other.

Aunt Fran dries her hands and takes the receiver. "Hello, Tom!" Her voice is faux-cheerful. "Well, it's not good news, but my prognosis is hopeful, and with a little luck the chemo will knock it out before it ever has a chance to get going."

I uncover the pecan pie on the counter and pick off a sweet, toasty pecan.

"Yes, I am too. Fine. Not sure. Mm-hmm. Oh, yes. Gosh. Mid-August would be great." Aunt Fran squinches her eyes shut. "No, it—it's important to me that you come. I'm sure. Okay, I will. Talk to you soon." She replaces the receiver in its holder, her face drooping. "He's coming in August," she says as if reporting a zombie invasion.

"When in August? He can stay here if I'm, um, living near campus." And I can avoid him.

She doesn't answer.

"Why do you—why is there tension between y'all?" I ask. I've always wanted to ask, but Dad's not the confiding type, and with Fran, so few subjects are off limits that I've always respected those that are.

The oven timer goes off, and she pulls the cheesy grits out with her mitt-covered hands. "I'm not sure there's tension exactly. You know how he is. Distant. It always felt that I was the only one reaching out. Guess I got tired of it."

"Hmm." I breathe in the scent of half a pound of baked cheese and butter tinged with green chilis.

She pauses, holding the steaming dish. "I got mad when he didn't visit Daddy while he was dying."

"Oh." Before I was born.

She places the casserole on the stove burners to cool. "I guess he did, a time or two, when Daddy first was diagnosed. But not at the end. He kept making excuses."

"How did Grandpa die?"

"Lung cancer. It took a long time, and he suffered miserably at the end." Her mouth is set in a grim line. "He was in pain and they wouldn't give him enough pain medication. For weeks he felt like he was suffocating."

"That's awful. And Dad stopped coming to see him because . . . ?" I wait for her to explain.

"He held a lot of resentment toward him for our parents' divorce. Daddy could also be a controlling SOB." She smiles sadly and pulls off the pink mitts. "But he sure did want to see Tommy."

"Dad never talks about him."

She folds the dish towel into a small square. "Tommy takes after our mom. Refined and reserved. I'm more like Daddy's side of the family. Big-boned, loud, and gawky."

"You're not gawky."

"Your dad was running his business then too, when Daddy was sick, and it was hard for him to get away. I do understand that better now that I'm running a business." Still holding the folded towel, she stares across the living room out the windows and says quietly, "Tommy and I had the same dream about him after he died, though. The same night."

"Really?"

"Yeah. We both dreamed he was all young and healthy and wanted to take us fishing." She gazes toward the bouquet of orange tulips on the dining table. "He loved it and rarely had time to. A couple of times, he took Tommy and me bass fishing on Lake LBJ and Texoma. Being around him when he was relaxed was a treat." She turns back to me. "So anyway, I knew he was okay. It gave me a real sense of peace." She sets the tightly folded towel on the granite counter and pats it.

I'm still wondering how to respond when she claps her hands and says, "All right, enough talk of cancer. Let's have some music!"

My speaker is on the counter from the last time I did dishes. On my phone, I pull up my "Dance Till You Drop" playlist and blare it on shuffle. Just what the doctor ordered.

# 14

The rest of the week feels mostly normal. On Wednesday I go to a Korean restaurant out in the avenues with Savannah and two other friends from AA. On Thursday after work, an AA friend named Cola finally has an opening for me at her studio. She tattoos a gorgeous semicolon on the inside of my left wrist. It hurts, but not as much as I feared. Aunt Fran's opposed, but she said that since I'm eighteen now I can do what I want. It's what I want.

By Sunday afternoon, the bandage wrap is off, but it's still red and swollen—like Fran's PICC line—not to mention oozing, so I put a big Band-Aid over it. But not before I text Nick a shot of it. He replies with a thumbs up. He's invited me to join him for lunch in Berkeley at a Mexican place.

This is a gift-wrapped second chance. *Relax and be your best self.* I visualize me smiling seductively and dropping witty one-liners. If Nick were in my life, I might even travel to Berkeley by BART train, at certain off-hours anyway. Despite the fact that it goes *under* the bay.

An Uber or a taxi ride to Berkeley costs over eighty dollars round trip. So with Aunt Fran's reluctant okay, I drive her car onto the lower section of the Bay Bridge. Out of the corner of my vision, the horizon jumps as the whole peninsula shakes, the bridge sways and buckles, and the upper deck cracks. A section will drop onto me and the blue Chevy Tahoe next to me, squashing us like slugs!

I blink furiously and shake that mess from my head.

A huge eighteen-wheeler thunders by, the sound waves and air pressure pushing me halfway into the next lane. I yelp and swerve to honks from the blue Tahoe. *There's no place to pull over!* Just get across. Focus on the black Jeep in front of me. Deep breath, in and out. The steering wheel is sticky from my sweaty palms and my heart is jack-hammering.

At least I don't have head space to worry about the meeting with Nick until after I manage to find a parking garage and navigate its dark, narrow levels.

At the restaurant on Shattuck Avenue, the smells of onions, garlic, cumin, and roasting meat swirl when I open the door. It's busy but not crowded. My stretchy, hot pink short skirt and scoop-neck T-shirt with no writing are sadly damp. I'm sporting lace-up sandals and I left in all my earrings and studs.

In walk Nick and Noor, fifteen minutes past the agreed-upon time. He told me once he's never late.

His face brightens when he sees me. "Sorry I'm late! Something came up and we weren't supposed to leave at all. But I did anyway." He kisses me on the cheek kind of near my lips.

He's flushed and a little sweaty too, maybe from running, and his plaid flannel shirt smells freshly acidic and chemical-y. But good.

"Hi, Noor," I say, smiling from that kiss.

"Let's order. I'm famished." He pulls me toward the counter and my arm tingles where his hand grips. His jeans hug his butt, not too tight, just right. He's wearing cool glasses frames, and soft stubble covers his strong chin and cheeks. He is so hot.

When we get our food and sit down, Noor lies between our feet under the table. Making sure no one plays footsie.

"Really sorry I don't have more time." He checks his watch. "Normally I get an hour."

"When do you have to be back?" I sip my lemonade.

Nick grimaces. "In fifteen minutes."

"Seriously?" WTF?

"Eat fast," he jokes. "I'm working for an absolute dictator. That I'm now in trouble with. How's Fran?"

"Seems to be doing fine. I went to chemo with her. That was a trip." I flake off a piece of fish from my taco.

"Good." He takes a big bite of his burrito. Chews. Swallows. "How's your dad?"

"Who knows?" He blinks. "Just kidding," I say. "He's fine. Sent me a gift card as his fatherhood membership renewal fee."

He grins, maybe a little uneasily. Long silence.

"So. How are all the frog cells?" I ask.

"Mostly thriving." A thread of melted cheese sticks to his chin until he wipes it off. "Until this morning. Everyone's salvaging presently."

Another pause while we both chew.

"Are you getting any time to see much of Berkeley?" I ask.

"Not really. It's such a cool place. Not to mention everything in San Francisco."

"Like me!" I blurt out.

"Uh, yeah!" His face says he meant the cable cars.

"I wish you had time right now. We could go to People's Park. Or the bookstore. It would be fun to browse with you." I bat my eyelashes.

He sighs. "Sorry, Del. I can't today."

"I was talking theoretically." Now I sigh. "Nick, this is hard."

"What?" He takes a chug of his juice.

"Knowing what to do." My finger traces the maze of my ear cartilage. "With you. Here. In fifteen minutes' time."

He puts his burrito down and tilts his head, as if to see me better from a different angle.

"I'm not good at this," I say.

He fumbles with his paper wrapper that crackles. "No, it's totally cool. But . . ."

"But what?"

"If I can focus, do a good job here—" He looks down at his lap. "Becoming a doctor takes so long. With my sight . . ."

"Oh. Right." I hadn't considered that. Try not to be so thoughtless, Del.

"I might not have that much time. Don't want to waste any of it."

"I see. Waste any with me." A real time-suck.

He blinks behind his glasses. Leans back stiffly. "No! It's— I don't want to ruin . . . we'll always be friends, right?" A red tide creeps back up his neck to his stubbly cheeks.

"Of course!"

"You know I'm here for you. Always. But work here is way more demanding than I expected." He pauses. "Are you going out with anyone?"

"What? No!"

"I'm glad," he admits. "But I don't think you should sit around, um, waiting for me. Now."

Heat boils into my face. I'm slow on the uptake. He's dumping me! *Except you weren't even together.*

He says, "I don't think it's going to work to be . . . more than friends this summer. I do want to see you and hang out. It's just that I have to bust ass. And you need to help out Fran."

"Fine, I'll leave you alone."

He shakes his head. "No, I don't mean it like that. Text. Call me. Anytime." He pats my hand, like a flipping physician.

I jump up and throw my stuff away. "Well, bye. Sorry I can't be what you want." I try to make it a joke. "A non-whack-job." *You told him too much!* "I told you too much." *Plus, you're jumpy and unpredictable. Needy. Sweaty. No one likes that.*

"That's not—" He shakes his head again, annoyed with me or maybe himself. Or both. "You mean a lot to me, Del. And I'd die if our friendship got fucked up."

I breathe out and stare at a crushed yellow tortilla chip on the floor. "I would too. Well, not *die*."

"But it feels like . . . timing's off."

"Whatever."

"Sorry." On cue, Noor steps in beside him. "I've got to go."

I watch them jog away.

*Now you've got the drive back over the bridge to look forward to.*

# 15

Driving Aunt Fran's car out of the Berkeley parking garage costs ten freaking dollars. I should've timed my meds for optimum balance and braved BART, but I thought maybe Nick and I might drive somewhere. *Silly you.*

It's the weight of my expectations again. All the time I've spent hoping, dreaming, and fantasizing is smushing me. Us.

I punch down on the accelerator and screech out into the street, speeding to the freeway.

Sophomore year at Ridgefield during the freezing, dark New Hampshire winter is when I started drinking in earnest. Illegal, of course, but there were numerous ways to obtain supplies and everyone was partying. By fall of junior year, with all the grades pressure, Matt and I were popping every pill we could get our hands on. I was cheating on my final papers and trying to for exams. When I got back from Thanksgiving break, I couldn't care anymore. Couldn't study or cheat. Then Matt got busted because of my vodka and, since he was already on probation, got expelled. That's when I couldn't even wash my hair. When I could barely move.

The evening after he left, I was slumped in the icy dark on a bench in front of the dining hall, in my gray wool school sweater, no hat or gloves, listening to a jet streak overhead.

It pulled the roar of the world behind it and I knew what I had to do.

Two days later, I took the overdose.

I'm through the tollbooth Fast Trak lane and onto the Bay Bridge. The air in the car thins like it's getting vacuumed out.

From the ER, I got checked into the psych ward, where an eighteen-year-old girl who kept beating her head against hard things was in the room next to me and a fifteen-year-old girl who was practically catatonic was in the other. I fit right in.

I hated it there, but at the time the whole world was a terrible place to be. In hindsight, it wasn't that bad. Mostly quiet, boring. Bare mint-green walls, spartan decor. I roomed one night with a pleasant, hysterically funny sixteen-year-old girl with OCD. In group therapy with other mentally ill teens, I learned about my illness and that I wasn't alone. Unlike in the movies, the doctors and nurses were laid back and patient. They gave me some strong meds and got me started on the path to finding long-term ones later with Dr. Vernon. After the raw screaming that had been going on in my head for weeks, it was all an improvement.

Maybe I need to check into a ward here.

I'm white-knuckling the steering wheel. The pores of my skin stretch to expel cold perspiration beads. Something from lunch is performing in my stomach.

Now the bridge buckles beneath my tires. The cars crowd me, will edge me off, and the hundreds of people driving them— all their malignant thoughts and nightmares are rising up into the fog, swirling around the swaying downtown buildings ahead, obscuring the jets above, full of fresh, flammable fuel, looking back down on the gasoline-filled and exhaust-spewing cars creeping like insects here and on every freeway fanning out from this point—immense interconnecting, polka-dotted, and overlapping lines and circles, everything rolling to extinction or infinity . . .

The bridge cables holding us up are fraying and about to snap. They cannot support all the weight of our expectations, our fear and greed, and the whole monstrous structure will smash at terminal velocity into the white-capped water twenty stories below that's laced with chemicals, rusting metal, rotting wood, and leaching organisms that haven't evolved for millions of years.

My heart pounds so hard, blood gushes are closing my airway.

Nowhere to pull over!

*Ohmigod, you're having a stroke! A heart attack! You're dying! STOP.*

No, just get across! This is a panic attack. Breathe out. Breathe out, breathe out!

Count breaths. Count cars.

Follow the white Tesla.

Exit downtown and get to Russian Hill.

*Or find some tequila.*

As soon as I get off the freeway ramp, I pull to the side of the busy street, turn on the flashers, unhook the suffocating seat belt, gulp air, fumble with my phone, and call my sponsor.

"Del!" Esmerelda says. "What's wrong?"

She's at work. But unlike Dr. Vernon, she answers her phone or gets back to me fast.

"Ez, I—I would honestly kill for three shots of chili pepper vodka right now. With an oxy chaser. I'm contemplating ways to obtain them."

"Where are you?"

"In Aunt Fran's car. Parked on the side of Fremont Street." I rest my head against the steering wheel. I used to have these more.

Ez says to someone else, "Hang on a sec. Nope, just gotta take this."

After three days in the psych ward I was released to Dad for a miserable time in London, mostly staring out a window at the cold rain or sitting through forced, silent meals with him. Then I came to SF to live with Aunt Fran. That was January of the year before last. There was talk of a residential treatment center in SoCal, but in the end I was subjected to outpatient treatment here with Dr. Vernon along with Fran's own version of a "program" that included AA meetings, curfews, chores, work, art therapy, and lots of time together.

"Del?" asks Ez, "Just hang on a sec, okay?"

I was so skilled at blaming everyone else for my problems, as a good reason to get drunk or high. With Esmerelda's firm guidance, plus Dr. Vernon's and Aunt Fran's, I accepted that my mental health issues are a permanent part of me that need to be respected, treated, and never ignored. They can also never be an excuse for seeking substance-fueled intoxication. Except if it's prescribed for me. I know I'm incredibly lucky.

My hazard lights click like a time bomb. Cars swerve around me. I pick at my tat scabs. *Someone's going to rear-end Aunt Fran's Prius.*

My self-pity had to be nuked—along with my anger at the universe for making me like my mom and then taking her from me. At Dad for being so missing-in-action. At myself for failing spectacularly and being a weak whack.

I'm *not* a weak whack. It actually takes exceptional strength to handle mental illness.

Ez told me scary stories about her past that I hadn't already heard in meetings. She said if it weren't for AA and God she would be dead. She has no question that God is responsible for her getting sober and strong, and for giving her the ability to help others.

She interrupts my thoughts. "Okay, tell me what's going on, baby."

"I had a panic attack on the Bay Bridge. Driving."

"That sucks. Where were you?"

"I met up with Nick in Berkeley, tried to be seductive with him but failed so bad he wants to be 'friends.'"

"'Friends,' right. Thanks for not popping a cap in his ass. Got any vodka on you?"

I lean my head back against the headrest. "Sadly, no."

"Del. This is good! That you called me. You're doing what you have to, to not drink. So, what're you going to do now?"

"I'm wiping that boy clean off of my . . . my hard-drive." I re-click my seat belt and take a deep breath. She wants action items. "I'll get home, somehow. Go plan my fall course schedule. Check with the club soccer team coach about tryouts. Then go to the gym to start getting in shape for fall season. I'll catch the six o'clock meeting."

"Are you going to be okay, baby?" she asks me.

"Yeah. I guess so." *He's so right to not get involved with you.*
"Sure?"

Someone behind me honks. I wave them around.

"Sure." They screech around, honking again. I kindly give them the finger.

"Atta girl. I'll meet you at six. Anything else you're going to do now?"

"Go buy a pack of cigarettes. Clean and moisturize my new tattoo."

"Sounds good. How's your aunt, by the way?"

"She's doing great. Thank heavens."

# 16

## Monday, July 20

A whole week later, my BAC shift with Isabel and Soo Jin goes fine—a couple of regular callers, referrals, HIV questions, etc.

During a lull, Isabel rolls her chair closer to me. "How's your guy from Texas?"

"Nick. Fine, I guess." He texted me once and I didn't reply. Every time he pops into my brain, I pinch myself and try to think of fried chicken or waterskiing. I was obsessing on him. No one likes that.

But in between crisis calls, I tell Isabel about our two meetings, including Noor, minus the most awkward sexual details.

"Sounds like he's trying to get himself to the Bay Area long-term," she says, raising her sculpted eyebrows. She told me it cost $50 to get them done.

The phone rings.

"Yeah. I guess. But so are lots of people."

"Maybe he feels a little overwhelmed right now."

The second line rings.

"Bay Area Crisis Line. This is Del."

Silence. The scent of fresh brownies on the volunteer table wafts my way. Mom used to make them from scratch, with a layer of caramel, for my soccer team. She was popular since we were supposed to bring oranges.

A girl says quietly, "Hi." There's a pause. "I don't know why I called." She sounds young, fifteen or sixteen at the oldest.

I say. "I'm here to listen. What's your name?"

"Uh . . . June."

"June," I repeat. More original than Jane. Even though it's July. "How are you feeling tonight?"

A sigh breathed into the phone is followed by another long pause. "Really, really shitty. I'm so tired of everything, I just want to end it all."

"Sounds like you're feeling suicidal?"

"Yes," says June. "It's not a good look for me."

We don't often get callers this young. Teens are more likely to use the 741-741 crisis text line or the Trevor Project line. Anonymous texting might've been a good option for me junior year, if I'd known about it. I couldn't bring myself to tell any-one—Matt, my teachers, Dad—*how much* I wanted to die.

"God. It's a relief to say it out loud," says June.

"Keeping that secret gives it power over you. Do you have a plan?"

"I've got some meds I saved plus a butt-load of my mom's mega-drugs. Mom thought my asshole stepdad took them."

"Will you tell me what they are?" I grab a notepad and a pen.

She tells me.

"How many do you have?"

She recites the exact number. My pulse picks up. Definitely lethal. "Do you have them with you now?"

"No."

Whew. "Are you planning on taking them today?"

She sighs. "No. It just gives me comfort knowing they're there."

Like the orange shoebox I once kept in my dorm room closet, filled with the same thing.

June's last two answers take some of the pressure off. She's a Three or a Four at worst.

She says, "Wait! Don't tell me you have an address-tracking thing! You're not going to send, like, a squad of anti-teen-suicide fighters over here, are you?"

I say quickly, "Everything's anonymous. And confidential." June hasn't blocked her number so we do actually have that, but I would only use it if she'd already taken those pills. "How old are you?" I ask.

"Sixteen."

"Tell me about your family."

"I live with my mom and sister." An emergency vehicle wails by outside through the phone.

"Do they know how you're feeling?"

"Pathetic," I hear Isabel say. She disconnects and rolls her eyes. A prank call.

June answers, "No. They know the Wolf-Man's not around anymore, but they have their own problems."

"The Wolf-Man?"

"It's a nickname. For a jack-hole I was hanging out with." June pauses. "My mom and little sister totally count on me. Too much."

"Sounds like you feel overwhelmed. Have you tried talking with your mom about what's going on with you?" I doodle a dandelion on my notepad.

She pauses. "No. She has enough to deal with. We moved out from my stepdad's place 'cause he was whaling on her."

"Don't you think your death would be hard on her?" I ask evenly. Illogical reasoning is totally typical when you're in crisis. We're meant to help callers figure things out for themselves, though.

"Yeah. I guess."

"You don't feel like you can keep going because your mom and sister depend on you so much," I reflect back to her, doodling a geometric maze.

"And the person *I* leaned on betrayed me," June says.

"Wolf-Man. Was he a friend or a boyfriend?"

"Fair question. I think I'm a lesbian but I was stuck on him. By the way, I, like, totally appreciate you didn't say, 'It's not that bad, petunia. Now, woman up.'"

"Ha." I'd like to reassure her that how things are and how she feels now will change. They did for me, although it took a while. But our concern is the next twenty-four hours and helping her to find her own coping skills. Besides, how can I promise her anything? "So you feel deserted and alone without the Wolf-Man. That's rough," I reflect and validate.

"Yeah."

I involuntarily relive Nick sitting across from me as he told me to take a hike.

"Are you eating okay? Sleeping? Getting some exercise?" A tiny bite of brownie nestles between my cheek and gum.

"No. None of the above."

"Self-care is one of your best mental health maintenance tools." Training manual verbatim. I haven't bladed or made it to the gym since the ridiculous lunch with Nick in Berkeley. The Ridgefield girls' soccer team was unimpressive, but at least it kept me moving.

June and I devise a plan. She promises to microwave some

soup, go out for a walk, and talk to a friend she trusts as well as to her mother. She also promises to call back if she feels desperate again.

I've walked a mile in those shoes, and I know what to say and do. All good. Great, even.

Suicide Prevention Girl to the rescue!

*How long will you get away with it?*

# 17

## Monday, July 27

Aunt Fran's been tired and a little cranky so I offer to drive her to her doctor's appointment. She's finished one session of chemo, three weeks on and one week off, and I think they want her to do up to six more. It might be too early to tell if the cancer is retreating, but probably it is.

I'm sitting in Dr. D'Silva's claustrophobic examination room exchanging texts with Savannah. Aunt Fran gets weighed out in the hall and gives me a thumbs-up when she comes in.

"Seven pounds." That she lost. Seems like kind of a lot for a month.

She peels off her stretchy pants and hand-knit sweater the color of cooked green beans and slips on a peach hospital gown. Aunt Fran doesn't care that her jiggly, bumpy old-lady thighs are on display and that I'm getting a flash of her pale breast through the opening in the gown. I focus on the stack of magazines to give her a little privacy.

"What's Nick up to?" she asks as we wait.

"Beats me." I wrestle my hair into an elastic.

She gives herself away with a sigh. Too bad for her. She's already over-meddled in this.

"I like your tattoo," Aunt Fran allows, staring at my inner wrist. "Remind me what it means, exactly?"

"That I'm the author of my life, and I chose to keep it going rather than to end it."

She nods with pursed lips.

Dr. D'Silva walks in, businesslike and smelling slightly antiseptic in a white lab coat. Aunt Fran introduces us and lights up when she notices the doc's chic high heels the color of raspberry jam.

Dr. D'Silva listens to Fran's heart and lungs and checks her abdomen. "How are you feeling?" she asks.

"Great! This chemo is a piece of pecan pie compared to what we used before."

"Glad to hear it. They've made advancements in these drugs since our last run with them." Dr. D'Silva pulls up something on the counter computer screen. "Fran, I'd like to show you the films, from *before* you started chemo."

She turns the computer screen toward us to reveal a misty-dark map, like a negative of a smeary night window someone splashed with mud.

"We'll do more scans after another session or two and measure our progress. Here is the cancer." Dr. D'Silva points at little and not-so-little blobs with her pen. "Here, here, and here. This is the large intestine, the liver, and the lungs."

*That's Aunt Fran's abdomen.*

Aunt Fran says, "Reminds me of a dress I had in the eighties. Navy-blue with white polka-dots, belted, small shoulder pads, cap sleeves. I wore it to a wedding with a wide-brimmed straw hat and felt like a grown-up."

My foot jiggles. I blurt out, "Those whitish things the size of eyeshadow holders are cancer?"

"Yes. Those are tumors." Dr. D'Silva points with her pen again at coin- and button-sized blobs. "These are nodules or smaller growths."

All those pale smudges suck the breath from me. "I—I thought it was just in the colon. What stage is this?"

"Stage Four," says the doctor.

The highest. The worst. "Meaning . . . ?"

Dr. D'Silva says gently, "Incurable, I'm afraid."

Aunt Fran pipes in, "But my breast cancer wasn't *cured*. It's remission we're after."

Dr. D'Silva nods. "This is an aggressive, rapidly growing form, as Fran and I have discussed. However, this last chemo round may have already slowed the growth of some of these masses. We'll know more after next month."

Aunt Fran reassures us, "I'm certain we'll diminish them."

I breathe in through my nose. Then out. "How exactly does cancer kill you? *This* cancer." I clutch my locket, sawing it back and forth along its thin chain.

"By affecting vital organ function, liver and/or lungs."

"So what is her prognosis?" Before last week, I had no idea what a "prognosis" was—the probable outcome of an illness. The word in my mouth is like three pieces of chewing gum and a glass sliver. Aunt Fran squirms on the examination table, tugging the skimpy gown over her bottom.

The doctor clicks the screen off. "The kind of turn-around—at this point—that you're describing has happened. I've seen it twice in my career. But in most cases, the disease progresses quickly, or more slowly thanks to treatment."

What is she saying? "So, her chance for remission, is . . . ?"

"Do you want me to be frank?" Dr. D'Silva says.

"Uh. Yes."

"Yes," Aunt Fran says with resignation. She likes the truth. But she doesn't think *I* can handle it. She's wrong.

"This is surprisingly advanced." Dr. D'Silva presses her lips together. "I believe this is what you will die from."

Aunt Fran blinks.

I stare at my tight fists to avoid their faces and all this information swirling around like I just stepped on a hive of killer bees.

The doctor adds, "But we can buy time."

"How much time?" I ask.

"Six months to a year, maybe longer if she can go four or more sessions of this chemo and everything else goes our way. It's impossible to say."

Dr. D'Silva clears her throat and swivels in her chair back to her computer screen. "There *is* something I'm worried about, Fran." She wasn't worried before? "Your platelet counts are low and your white cell counts are high. We'll have to watch that carefully."

Now I have to focus on the shiny beige floor and count brown flecks. Count breaths.

"How's your pain?" the doctor asks Aunt Fran.

Aunt Fran says in a low voice, like I won't hear, "There is some. In my side and back. Mostly later in the day, when I'm tired." Her slumped back and shoulders and loose, droopy expression suggest she is now.

"Let's up your dose of oxycodone." Dr. D'Silva scribbles out a prescription.

*Good idea! How about some for me too?*

"All right then," Aunt Fran says cheerfully. "Onward."

I can barely manage a "Goodbye" as Dr. D'Silva wishes us a good day and clicks out in her dynamite shoes.

# 18

I try hard not to let on, but Aunt Fran can tell I'm freaked out. She insists we go to our favorite restaurant in Japantown. I force down some house-made ramen and talk about the watermelon color of Fran's ahi tuna and flash-freezing raw fish to kill microbes, pretending her plan is working.

Afterward she drives us to Ghirardelli Square for hot fudge sundaes. We park in the garage and come up in the open courtyard.

It's a sunny day for once, but windy here and packed with tourists. I zip up my hoodie and hug myself as we walk through the outdoor shops to the ice cream parlor. "It's freezing," I complain.

"You know what Mark Twain said. 'Coldest winter I ever spent was summer in San Francisco.'" She's only quoted this 637 times.

"Yeah. Ha. But actually, Twain never said that. Nobody's sure who did."

"Is that so? I'm going to give him credit regardless." She marches ahead of me.

We sit at the small marble table in the warm restaurant and gorge. Aunt Fran has a dab of whipped cream on her nose and more on her smiling lips. She exclaims, "Let's not think about the future or the past but just enjoy the moment. This is certainly a moment worth staying in!"

The gooey hot fudge, the crunchy toasted almonds, and the smooth ice cream slide down my throat. Surfing on a sugar high, I realize there's so much we don't know yet. Cancer is beatable. The chemo is strong and effective, not to mention Dr. D'Silva. Plus, Fran's tough as a nickel steak.

I link arms with her as we stagger back to the garage, giggling. Her plan does work.

;

Nick calls me the next afternoon, while I'm at the bus stop. It's been two weeks and two days since we've had any communication. It's been about twenty minutes since I last thought about him.

When his name and number pop up on my phone, I let out a soft shriek. I drop and stub out my cigarette. I know, I shouldn't be smoking, but it's way better than vodka. Plus, it helped me kick my jelly bean habit.

I compose myself as best I can.

"Nick?" I say, like I almost can't recall who he is.

"Hey, Del! What's up? How's Fran?"

"She's great. We just finished the first round of chemo. Where are you?"

He chuckles. "They let me come home for a nap. Headed back in. What's her diagnosis again?"

"High-grade neuro-endocrine cancer of the colon that has metastasized to the liver and lungs. Stage Four."

There's a pause. "Whoa," he says. He reads medical journals for fun. "God. Didn't realize. That, uh, sucks."

"She's on high-tech chemo and doing great," I insist. "Tired, but otherwise fine."

Yes, the chemo slows her down some. She naps a lot, is staying close to home too. But it's nothing we can't handle.

"Excellent. How are you doing?" he asks.

"I'm great. Lots going on. Busy! You're lucky to catch me," I say brightly.

"Good! Glad to hear it! Okay, sorry but I gotta run too. I'll talk to you soon though."

"Thanks for call—" I start, but he's gone.

*You should've hung up first.*

I want to sink through the concrete under the bus stop shelter.

*A tall glass of Long Island Iced Tea would go down smooth about now.*

In eighth grade, one seemingly random Sunday afternoon, a neighbor took me to the hospital where my mom was on life support after her car accident. Contrary to what Emma H told the entire school, she was *not* drunk when she crashed.

That afternoon in Dallas, in the space of about twelve hours, the world turned into an artificially-colored-red Jell-O mold for me. It never firmed back up again, and it's wiggling wildly now.

The bus pulls up.

*You could get on it and keep going. Like, to Brazil.*

;

Aunt Fran's been coming in to work later than usual, so it's just Louis and me at the Lone Star this morning. He's manning the gallery floor and I'm tidying up Fran's office. The shelves in here are so loaded with heavy art books that they curve under the weight of them. There's a stack of real print newspapers on the desk because she refuses to read the news online.

A folded piece of notepaper juts from under the edge of the stack. It's crinkled and a little yellow.

I open it. There's no date or title, but it's in Fran's handwriting.

*Daddy*
*plugged with lines*
*that snake*
*to a plastic bag of*
*whisky-colored urine*
*clipped to the bed rail*
*or from*
*the bag of garnet juice*
*hanging from a stand*
*like a solitary, overripe,*
*rectangular fruit.*
*As the respirator hisses and thunks*
*air*
*into his cloudy plastic beak.*
*Tears are nestled*
*in white crepe-paper folds*
*beneath his sapphire-blue eyes.*
*What I gave up for him*
*sucked the beating heart,*
*pink lungs,*
*and soul*
*out of me.*

Crikey.

The stern grandpa I never knew. I fold the paper and stick it back under the newspaper pile, as if I can pretend I never saw it.

A motorcycle screams by and a jet roars overhead and suddenly I'm hyperventilating. My chest is impossibly tight, imitating Fran's words in the poem.

Part of me wants to scream for help.

My knees unhinge and I sink. Kneeling, I breathe deep breaths, concentrating on the smooth, cool, slightly springy bamboo floor under one palm and the Persian rug beneath the other. Dear God, please let Fran be okay.

Louis's voice sounds behind me. "Are you okay, Delilah?"

I whip my head around. How long has he been standing in the doorway?

"Yeah," I say, rocking back on my heels. My heart's still pounding and lines of sweat trail from my armpits down my ribs into the lace of my underwear. "Just . . . um . . . gathering my thoughts."

"Dropped them on the floor, huh?"

I smile. He smiles. Not fake. More like you'd smile at a chained rabid dog.

# 19

## Saturday, August 1

Aunt Fran is propped up in bed holding an album and fussing with stacks of old photos. Bad news blares from her television.

She looks up and answers my unasked question. "It's never a bad idea to clear out duplicates, and to add dates—and identify locations and people. I'll get them scanned too."

"Oh." I squash the thought of why she would suddenly want to organize her past.

She pats her bed and thrusts several pictures at me.

The one on top is of a pretty, middle-aged woman standing in a kitchen. On the counter is the ceramic rooster cookie jar we had in our house for years. Whatever happened to it? "Grandma, right?" I ask.

"I'm so sorry you didn't know her."

"Me too." She died in the eighties.

Fran pulls out another photo. "That's Daddy and me fishing on Lake LBJ."

"Ohmigosh. You were so cute."

"I'm about nine. I wasn't into the hunting-gathering aspect of it, but I loved being with him." The man reminds me a little of Colonel Sanders. And Fran was big for nine. She's posing in her tube top, holding up a fish the size of a sales receipt, grinning with oversized front teeth.

She hands me another. "This photo's from a couple of months before Daddy died. That's his favorite leather chair and he's reading the *Dallas Morning News.* Already so thin and gray . . ."

"Mm-hmm."

"It was right before he was admitted to the hospital. I kept taking leave from MacDougal here to go to Dallas and take care of him. His decline took a long time."

"How long?"

She points at the throw blanket at the end of her bed. "Hand me that, please, will you? Almost a year total. About two months in the hospital." She pauses. "He refused hospice care."

Can't blame him for that.

"I'd read to him, but sometimes I'd just sit quietly, holding his hand. Watching him grimace with pain." She stares off into the hallway.

I fidget. I don't want to interrupt her reverie, but this is . . . a lot. I need to get out of here.

She says, "He finally slipped away one night, while I was briefly out of the room. I've always regretted that. He was a social creature, but he was lonesome in many ways." She sighs through a smile. "You came in here to ask me something, though, didn't you, sugar?"

"Uh, yeah. I hope you don't mind—I have an invitation tonight to meet up with a couple of friends."

"Thank goodness." She flips the album closed. "You're eighteen years old. You're meant to be hanging out with friends. Staying up late. Dancing! Not sitting at home going through family photographs with your old aunt. Plus, you look fabulous, darlin'."

My thoughts exactly. My acting "normal" will be good for her peace of mind. "If you're sure." I give her a quick kiss.

"Couldn't be more so. Granny's necklace is so lovely on you." She nods at the silver locket. "And those are such cute sandals! They're terrific with that wine-colored top."

"If I can't drink it, at least I can wear it." Fashion made more sense to me when Aunt Fran explained it as *me as an artwork*. She also believes colors are good for our souls. "What are you going to do?" I ask. "After the photos?"

"Catch up on *Downton Abbey*. Charlotte may pop over." All the more reason to bolt. Big-hair Charlotte is one of her old sorority sisters. I've been to her fussy, matchy-matchy house in Pac Heights for Thanksgiving, back when I was in boarding school, and refuse to go back.

"You're feeling okay." I state, but it's a question.

"Feeling fine. Really, sugar."

;

A Lyft driver takes me to Bay City Bowl south of Market Street. It was a last-minute invite, which is good because I have less time to stress out.

The man behind the counter hands me a pair of sweaty-smelling bowling shoes.

The place is jam-packed and the noise assaults me. Maybe they didn't come! I invoke my handy breathing exercises. Oh, good. Isabel's tall boyfriend, Lars from Norway, stands beside her at Lane 5.

I trot over. Another guy with dark, chin-length dreads is

with them. Isabel says. "Hey, Del, this is Dalton. He's from Houston." She says to him, "Del's from Texas too."

"Cool," I say. "Yeah, Dallas originally." Is this why they thought of me? Like all Texans will get along? We shake hands. Mine is damp.

He sports a faded, yoked cowboy shirt and low-slung jeans. He's muscular and kind of cute.

They're all twenty-one and holding beers. Dalton hands me one. Isabel shakes her head almost imperceptibly. Maybe she told them I'm eighteen.

"Hi, uh, no thanks. I'll get something in a minute." I caress the bottle, then give it back reluctantly. His whole face falls.

*You do have that good fake EU student ID somewhere.* Ez would crucify me if she knew.

"So, you know Lars from UCSF?" I ask him.

"That's right." He reaches into his pocket and pulls out a toothpick. Pops it into his mouth. The pinky nail on his right hand is a little long. Ew.

"What are you studying?" I ask.

"Nano-engineering."

"Wow. Cool. Is another friend coming too?" I ask because this feels like a blind date and that's not what I signed up for.

"Yah, she couldn't make it," says Lars in his cute accent. The crash of pins and yelling nearby drown out whatever he says next.

Isabel says, "Let's bowl."

"Ladies first," Dalton says.

Isabel goes. She's compact, and graceful as a dancer. Lars's gaze doesn't leave her, and neither does Dalton's. She flashes a confident smile when she gets a spare.

Now, all eyes are on me and my heartbeat revs. My slippery

fingers almost slide out of the ball's grip holes. I discreetly wipe my hands on my jeans.

Other teams crowd the lanes. There are a lot of hip twenty-somethings in matching shirts, probably coworkers from tech startups. One group of old, leather-vested, long-bearded Hells Angels are bowling in orderly fashion in the far lane.

My left shoe pinches. Even with clinical-power antiperspirant, my armpits are soaked, so I keep my elbows close to my body. Mom was a good bowler. Maybe I can channel her. I time my stride but let go of the ball too early, with a *clonk*. It veers right, a little, then a lot, and plops into the gutter.

"It's been a while." I try to smile in that impervious, contained way that Isabel does.

Isabel does it properly at me. The guys are talking.

I clutch my orange ball again and aim for the middle. It wipes out the majority of the pins, leaving only two corner ones standing. Whew.

"Way to go," says Dalton, fist-bumping me as I sit down.

Am I having fun yet?

Lars gets a spare too and flow-dances his way back to his seat. We laugh. He and Dalton both drink.

"All right, ladies, watch out." Dalton sends his ball down the lane at rocket speed for a strike. "Obliteration ma*chine*."

"Wow," says Isabel. One arched eyebrow rises.

"Chug," he says to Lars.

Lars obliges. Afterward Lars splits "my" beer into his and Dalton's glasses.

*Sweet Jesus, you need one.*

Just one. To loosen my death-grip on myself and dull this extreme oversensitivity to everything. Even Cyber Academy's online prom was better than this.

Isabel's down to about a quarter beer too, and Lars offers to get another round. "Delilah?" he asks.

Speaking of sweat, a cold, dripping, clear glass bottle of lager topped with a lime, stuck in the sand and gently splashed by a small, nonthreatening incoming wave plays on slo-mo in my head. I clear my throat. "Lemonade, please?"

For now. Sometimes I have to dial down from one day at a time to five minutes at a time.

"Right on," he says, trying to make me feel better.

Dalton sits beside me. "Sure you don't want a beer?" he asks, right before he throws his head back and chugs what's left of his.

"No thanks. I don't drink. Used to, but it got a teensy bit out of control." It's not his business, but if I let people know I have a problem, i.e., am an alcoholic, usually they're understanding.

"So you work with Isabel?"

"Yeah. At Bay Area Crisis." We're volunteers, but if he thinks I'm employed he might think I'm a little older.

"Oh, right. A suicide crisis line?" He flinches.

I hold my tattooed wrist against my stomach. "We talk mostly to people who just want information, or who are depressed and need someone to listen. Any of us could end up there. In crisis. Under the wrong circumstances."

He snorts. "I don't think so."

"I'm glad you feel strong and mentally healthy and well balanced," I say evenly, crossing my arms. "You're lucky."

Sometimes, maybe even often, it's totally worthwhile to talk to someone about your own hard mental health experiences. But not him.

A laugh bursts from me that sounds, even to my ears, a little insane.

Dalton smiles like a stretched rubber band, then gets up and heads toward the bar. He says something to Lars, laughs and touches his head, and then looks over at me. And quickly looks away. Lars smiles too.

The intense heat in my face and neck mean I'm red as a pomegranate. Isabel works there too. Is he making fun of her?

No.

I *can* have a great time sober with people who are drinking. I was fine at Isabel's birthday party a month ago. Why should *I* feel loser-ish because this guy's disappointed that I refuse to drink, get drunk, and possibly hook up with him?

I'm homesick for Nick.

Isabel sits beside me. "So how's your aunt?" *She sees you as an interesting subject to study with clinical detachment.*

"She's doing chemo but feels pretty good," I say as the concrete in my stomach solidifies.

"Great. Glad to hear it."

Lars and Dalton come back, discussing some new hip-hop and hookah club in SOMA to move on to. Whew. I won't be able to get in.

"Okay," I sigh. "Anyone got a cigarette?"

Heavy silence.

"Morphine?" I've got everyone's attention now. "Just kidding. But I'm going to take off. Thanks, Isabel and Lars." I grab my backpack.

Isabel says, "Uh. Are you okay, Del?" Dalton focuses between his knees on the edge of his black plastic seat.

"Everything's fine. But it's time for my electroshock therapy."

# 20

It's after midnight. I could text Esmerelda but I try to save her for dire emergencies. I texted Savannah about my evening earlier but she's in the middle of another power struggle with her mom and has limited access to her phone. The occasional light swirls on the ceiling above my bed as a car whooshes past in the otherwise silent night street below. *Where are they going? Could you go with them?*

As soon as I got back from bowling I smoked two cigarettes, shivering outside in the alley, since Aunt Fran won't allow them in here and the building won't allow it in the lobby, per the state of California. It's, like, a felony.

Only now I can't sleep. Is Nick at the lab or home? Or out? By the light of a tiny lamp, I pull out my latest collage of growing things.

Aunt Fran's smeared, toxic x-rays are burned behind my eyelids. It's no longer working to just not think about it.

It's clear that the cancer's worse than she let on. How much time can we buy? Five years? Two?

I shuffle through my folders and boxes of photos, clippings, fabric, and found two- and three-dimensional stuff, settling on a small shot of a slanted-sunlit field of dandelions.

Aunt Fran's toilet flushes.

When something terrible happens to a friend, like they get mugged or have a car accident or their sister dies, I'm horrified and sad, but also secretly relieved that the lightning bolt of tragedy missed me. I hope that, like a lightning rod, they're pulling all the gathering bad luck away from the area for a while.

Her slow footsteps echo out to the kitchen.

So now *we've* got seven-story steel rods hoisted in the middle of the storm. We're getting hit by all the voltage out there. There's nowhere to run or hide.

Like when Mom died.

"Are you okay?" I ask, joining her. It's 1:46 a.m.

"Yes, ma'am." She's stirring baking soda in a glass. Her robe is misbuttoned. "I was trying to meditate but have a little indigestion and I'm out of Alka Setzer. How was your . . . going out?"

"Fine," I lie. I sit down at the kitchen island and prop my head on my hands. "No, it sucked. They were all older and . . . I should've stayed here and watched *Downton Abbey* with you."

"It was pretty darn good. Charlotte brought some wine," she adds. "She had to drink most of it. You know how that goes."

"Yep. Whenever she's ready for AA, I'll be glad to introduce her formally."

Aunt Fran snorts.

"Your buttons are crooked." I point to my chest.

"I like 'em like that."

"Isabel already suspected I was the biggest dweeb. Now there's no question."

"Get new friends," says Aunt Fran.

My face must give away my humiliation.

"Oh, sweetheart!" Alarm lights her face. She sits on the stool next to me and hugs me. "What happened?"

"Nothing, really, except one guy was sort of jerky, and maybe I was a half-ton wet blanket. But it's not just that."

"What else?" She strokes my hair.

"Nick said he just wants to be friends. Said I shouldn't sit around waiting for him."

Her face falls. "I'm sorry." She doesn't even ask me any more questions, a huge sacrifice for her.

"It was more than two weeks ago. But I just feel so sad."

She hugs me. "My poor, sweet pumpkin."

When she calls me that, I picture the cartoon one that morphed into Cinderella's carriage with all the mice footmen. "I don't even care about Nick or Isabel. It's sinking in," I mumble into the pink fleece robe I gave her for Christmas. "About you." She smells of winter-mint whitening toothpaste and her usual gardenia and oranges. And something faintly, sharply . . . rotten.

"No one said this is going to be easy."

"I know. But you have to promise not to . . . go anywhere. You've got a gallery to run, planes to fly, friends to entertain, and um, lots more art, fashion, business, and home maintenance to teach me. Plus, I'm not ready to be an orphan." Or even to move out in six weeks.

*To move out, ever.*

All my plans for my "normal," stable future hinge on Aunt Fran being right here to watch my back.

Her deep laugh fills the apartment. "Sugar, we'd have to off your dad to make you an orphan."

"Now there's a thought."

# 21

## Monday, August 3

The next day at Bay Area Crisis, my station phone is ringing before I can even get my sweatshirt off. Quentin's training a new volunteer in the corner, and Isabel's already here and on a call. I busy myself at my station, flashing her what I hope is a normal smile. I would slip her an origami-crane-folded Benjamin to not bring up bowling.

"Hi, this is Bay Area Crisis Line, how can I help you?" I log on as I talk and resolve to focus on and support our callers.

All I get is a grunt.

"My name's Del. Are you feeling suicidal today?" Somebody put up a calendar featuring dogs doing yoga poses.

"Nope. Got permission. Took a detour."

"Is this Matilda?" I recognize her mumbly voice.

"Yes. I don't even know where we are."

"I bet you're in your apartment, and you're talking to me, Del, at Bay Area Crisis Line."

"Oh yeah." She pauses. "Do I know you? There's a lot of scary people out there."

"Tell me about it. We've talked before, Matilda." Policy is that we don't confirm or deny that we've talked to someone

100

before, but Matilda's been calling for twenty years.

She has schizophrenia and lives with her son, who doesn't always take as good care of her as she needs. He's under a lot of pressure too. She checks in with us regularly.

"Matilda, is your son home with you?"

"No. Try talking to his father. He wouldn't touch household repair. Ridley says men are more lost when they're single."

"Have you taken your meds today?" I unscrew the top on my water bottle.

"I don't know." She hesitates. "Meds. I was trying to think of that."

"Can you get them?" I keep mine by my bed.

"I . . ." Fumbling noises come through the phone. "Here they are. Nope, didn't take 'em."

"Would you take them now? Get some water?" I take a sip of my own.

I wait until she's swallowed them.

"Great." We'll give it a little time. "Have you eaten breakfast or lunch yet?"

"I wanted pancakes. Frosted Mini Wheats."

"Awesome. Where are you standing or sitting right now?" Usually, it helps to ground her in her physical environment. Ask concrete questions.

"Back in his chair. Ridley was the one guy who could read my mind, usually when we were driving. But those long-term emission standards—no way I can play Ma Bell and I can't control my bills or get my care, so what am I supposed to do?"

I let her talk for a bit. Mom wasn't schizophrenic, but sometimes even as a kid I could feel the hypomania buzz off of her like radioactivity. Her racing thoughts and occasional paranoia sometimes mirrored in me—because I related so closely, according to Dr. Vernon. Or I went all opposite, calm and hyper-focused on her volatile moods, trying to soothe her as she bounced off the walls around me. Or when she was depressed, to engage her with gentle questions.

"—and they backed that truck right over it and then all she could do was call her sister and invite—"

"Matilda," I break in, "what are you planning to do this afternoon?" Getting a concrete next couple of steps usually helps her too. Living in her head must be confusing and so frustrating sometimes.

Another line rings.

"I've got to do a fresh coat of paint. Not the blinds."

"Sounds good."

Isabel is talking to someone more urgent, and the guy trainee is too. No one else is here yet. "Matilda, hang on a moment, a call's coming in and I'll be right back." I put her on hold and answer the other line—triage, as we call it. "Hi, this is the Bay Area Crisis Line, how can I help you?"

"Yeah. This is Arthur." His voice is so raspy and old, he's hard to understand. I hope he can call back in twenty minutes or so.

"Hi, Arthur. My name's Del. How are you today?"

"I'm feeling terrible."

"I'm so sorry to hear that. Are you feeling suicidal?"

"Yeah."

"Do you have a plan for how you would attempt suicide?"

"I'm going to take a bunch of pills."

Crap. That puts him at Level Three, if not more. "Thanks for letting me know that, Arthur. Hang on for a moment, sir. I'm so glad you called and I will be right back with you. Please hang on." I scribble down his number in case we get cut off.

We need someone else in the call room! When I explain that someone urgent is on the other line, Matilda graciously hangs up. I come back to Arthur as fast as I can.

"Arthur, thank you for holding. Tell me what's going on, sir."

"I've been thinking hard about it, and saving meds, but I only get a few at a time. It's going to take years. I'd give anything if there was a simple, non-messy way."

"So, how many do you have?" I should've asked him before.

He tells me. His plan is not yet lethal or imminent. He's depressed and thinking about dying, but he's not standing on a ledge.

"I'm on disability and partially paralyzed. Doc just told me I've got stomach cancer. Inoperable. Stage Four."

"Oh! I'm so sorry. That's some seriously bad news." He doesn't need a ledge.

"Yeah."

"How are you feeling?" Quentin and the new guy are chatting with Isabel and it's hard to hear over them. I shoot them a look.

Arthur wheezes. "That's my problem. I've got at least three other life-threatening conditions—emphysema, diabetes, and heart disease. I'm confined to this goddamned wheelchair. I pray the Lord my soul to take."

"It sounds like you feel really overwhelmed. Are you in pain?"

"Yes. To both."

"Do you have anyone there who helps you?"

"My wife died six months ago."

"Oh, that's rough, Arthur. I'm so sorry." So many people have it really hard, in ways I can't even imagine.

"Thank you. I miss her." His voice breaks. He's flipping

from anger to grief. "It won't be long now but the waiting is torture."

"You're all by yourself?" I'm not sure how to help him. "We can refer you to social services and medical help—"

"I'm in a goddamned nursing home."

"Oh. Okay. Do you have any other family?" I doodle pills and capsules.

"My son checks on me once every couple of months if I'm lucky. Yeah, I'm alone."

"Are you receiving pain control?"

"They're a bunch of idiots here. Yeah, I get some meds—" He pauses to wheeze. "But I just want to die. Can't someone help me commit suicide?"

"You—?" I blink and backtrack. "I—I can understand how you'd feel that way. Does your son know how you feel?"

"I tell him every time to put a pillow over my head. Put me out of my misery. But he won't." *Since he would end up in prison.*

He continues, "And these people won't help me. Can you guys help me?"

"Help *kill* you? Sir, we're a suicide *prevention* group!"

Silence. *Not exactly nonjudgmental and supportive, Del.*

He disconnects.

*Nice going.*

# 22

## Wednesday, August 5

Aunt Fran is spooning apricot jam on her sprouted-wheat English muffin when I join her at the table. Her new short haircut gives her a cute androgynous look, the auburn dusted with a lot more gray than I realized.

"What time is your chemo session tomorrow?" I ask, breaking a warm blueberry Pop-Tart in two. "I'll drive you."

"There's no need, sugar. I haven't forgotten how to drive."

"But *I* need the practice!"

Her eyebrows lift in quiet agreement.

"Louis can definitely spare me. From here on out I'm officially at your service. Shopping, cooking, nursing, laundry, driving, whatever. I'm your Happy Helper." Inside joke. I was anointed as one for a week in kindergarten and told her about it in rapture.

Maybe the way to get through this is to lean into it a little. Like Aunt Fran teaches me to do with everything that scares me.

Aunt Fran smiles. "I'm perfectly capable of doing all that myself. And you have school starting in a couple of weeks. When do you move into the dorms?"

"Oh! I decided not to sign up for on-campus housing."

Shoot. Maybe I never mentioned it. "I'll wait to move until next spring. Or whenever you get better."

"You know I love having you here." She shakes her head as she takes a sip of tea. "But, sugar, I don't want you to take any more time away from your pursuits to go through all this chemo and sickness mess. Charlotte will drive me, or thanks to you, I can get a ride on my phone app-thing."

"Don't be stubborn. If you turn me down it will hurt my feelings," I say through half-chewed Pop-Tart.

She clasps her hands and blinks twice. "Having you with me would give me great comfort. But what if it's not pretty? There could be upchuck and all."

"I'm not squeamish. If you throw up, so what?"

She regards me sideways in a sizing-up sort of way. She's half sold. "What about soupy-poopies?"

I scoff but dodge this. "I stop people from *killing* themselves. Helping you get through an illness? No sweat."

She beams me that *you're adorable* look that I would love to bottle and dab on my pulse points.

"When's your next appointment?" I ask.

"They switched me to Friday. Nine o'clock. I would really like having you with me. But . . ." Her eyes are glistening!

"No buts. It's a date."

I sip my smoky roasted decaf coffee, with the perfect amount of sweetener and half-and-half, as the morning sun illuminates the siding of the forest-green building on the hill's edge, along with the tops of the Cabernet-colored leaves on two plum trees. The city in the distance and a square of lapis lazuli blue of the sky rounds out the composition. It would make the coolest collage on top of a San Francisco city map. I would title it *Our Summer of Triumph.*

My phone dings with a text as I rollerblade to the gallery for my shift. The bottom falls out of my solar plexus when I see Nick's name. I'm on strike—not texting him—but he probably doesn't even notice.

**How's Fran?**

Am I ready to cross the picket line?

Of course.

I rollerblade and thumb-type at the same time. Calm, cool, rational stuff.

**Thanks for asking. Tired. But good**

**How's her pain?**

**Ok. She's got excellent pain meds**

**What have they prescribed?**

I dash across Columbus and sit on a bench in Washington Square Park in the middle of a group of senior ladies doing their morning Tai Chi in the fog.

**Oxycodone with ibuprofen, Ativan, Zofran for anti-nausea, and more I can't remember**

**Are you tempted?** Not a question I was expecting from him. I thumb in "no," then delete it.

**Yes. But being super vigilant. Have you been partying?** He'll say no, because he doesn't much.

**A little. New intern mixer**

My next question: **Mix with anyone interesting?**

**Everyone was interesting. Wished you were there**

Oh, really! The most recent Instagram photo of him and his lab group includes two girls beaming beauty-pageant smiles. That's why I almost never go on social media. Anxiety lighter fuel.

**How much longer are you here?** I ask.

**Fly out Aug 26**

Crap. Just under three weeks. What if I don't see him for decades?

I want to kiss him again.

How can I see Nick? At least so we're on better terms when he goes back to Austin. Maybe it would be easier with someone else along. Take some of the pressure off.

**Fran and I are going to Beach Blanket Babylon on 8-13. Want to come? May grab Italian first?**

Another crowd exercise planned months ago. Aunt Fran would be ecstatic if Nick came. I hit *send*, and then immediately regret it. He'll just blow me off.

**Definitely! Will put in for the time off now**

⁊

I take Aunt Fran to another chemo session on Friday morning. When we get home she lies down in her room, assuring me that "fatigue is normal." And she actually asks me to call her flight instructor to *confirm* her flying lesson for the day after tomorrow.

The next morning about seven, she croaks my name from her room.

I run in there. "What is it, Aunt Fran? Are you okay?"

"Okay," she says hoarsely. "Think I got hit by a moving van. Can you close the drapes, sugar?"

"Of course."

She looks awful. Gray and puffy. Glassy, bloodshot eyes. I feel her forehead. It's burning! I dig through her bathroom drawers to find a thermometer and slip it into her mouth.

"102.4!" I know from babysitting that for little kids that's not so terrible, but for an adult, I think it is. "I'm calling Dr. D'Silva."

"No, it's just the chemo. Caught up to me."

In the kitchen I get her a radioactive-green sports drink. Mom once sat with me all night when I had the flu, pressing cold washcloths on my forehead or neck, singing show tunes, and rubbing circles on my back. So I grab a wet washcloth too.

I fluff Fran's pillow and get her to chug the Gatorade. Afterward she lies back, only to bolt upright. "Oh, dear," she groans. "I'm going to be sick."

Her grandmother's antique porcelain wash bowl and pitcher are on her bookshelf. I grab the bowl and thrust it in front of her.

She heaves and throws up the green drink along with three partially dissolved pills. She closes her eyes and breathes heavily. Her expression rests somewhere between embarrassed and mortified.

I pat her back. "Aunt Fran, if you had any idea how many friends I've sat with while they barf, or how many times *I've* tossed my cookies, you wouldn't think twice about this."

She lets out what sounds like a bark, but is probably a laugh. When she falls back into her pillows, I cover her with her comforter.

;

For the rest of the weekend Fran can't eat, can barely get out of bed to pee, and sleeps all day. She does *not* go flying.

But this is "normal." A word I hang on to like a waterski-rope handle.

I force liquids into her and bring in her old CD player so she can listen to Tchaikovsky and Stevie Wonder. When she asks for disco, I'll know she's feeling better.

She's a little improved by Monday, though not enough to show up at the gallery. Louis is probably getting used to handling things without her at this point. After we go into the lab for her blood work and scans of some sort, Fran sleeps all afternoon and through the night too.

Now I get why people don't like chemo.

Dark silence has oozed throughout the apartment like slime.

# 23

## Tuesday, August 11

Dr. D'Silva's office called last night. Fran has to come in this morning to discuss her course of treatment, and we're squeezed between two other appointments. We think Dr. D'Silva wants to switch her chemo to the stuff they used before. I've spent the last few days doing online research about various approaches to cancer treatment, in case we need a backup plan.

Fran grips my arm and we walk at a turtle's pace through the garage. She's still weak. Climbing the three stairs from the garage level to the medical-building sidewalk, she grunts with the effort and I pretend not to notice.

The waiting room is packed, but they take us right back to an examination room. The nurse has Aunt Fran step on the scale in the hall, an old-fashioned one, and I hear the big metal weight grind and clonk as she slides it down a big notch. "Thirteen pounds!" says Fran when she comes in. That's not counting the five or so she lost before they started weighing her.

I force a smile and give her a thumbs-up.

Aunt Fran struggles with her gold cardigan, so I help her out of it, and then out of her stretchy black pants into the hospital gown. She leaves her large cotton-candy-pink lacy bikini briefs on. "Cute undies," I tease her.

"How are you feeling, Fran?" Dr. D'Silva comes in and washes her hands.

"Not too shabby," Fran says enthusiastically.

"Tired," I say. "She was sick as a dog after last week's chemo. But that's normal, right?"

"Yes. Any pain?"

Aunt Fran indicates her back, under the arm of her gown. "Here, at my ribs. Some in my mid- and lower back."

Dr. D'Silva examines where she's pointing, pressing gently a time or two, and Fran winces. "We'll call in a prescription for more oxycodone."

"What's causing her pain?" I ask.

Dr. D'Silva mashes her lips into a straight line. "Most likely it's the tumors, pushing against soft tissue or bone."

Aunt Fran flicks her wrist. "I feel like I've been tolerating the chemo pretty darn well."

"Um, until this week," I say.

Dr. D'Silva sits on her rolling stool. "That's what I want to discuss with you, Fran. I'm not surprised you feel tired. Your white cell and platelet counts are precipitously low."

"But those would only be affected if she had leukemia. Or lymphoma. Right?" I ask.

"It's from the chemo," Dr. D'Silva says. "It's too much of a strain on her system."

Silence.

Aunt Fran gives a little laugh. "So, does that mean I get to stop it?"

Dr. D'Silva spins the sparkly wedding set on her left hand. "Yes. I'm afraid so. I've conferred with three other colleagues, here and in Houston. We're in agreement."

"What does this mean?" I ask. "She's done with chemo?"

Dr. D'Silva's name embroidered in blue on her white lab coat rises and falls. She looks at us each in turn. "It means we have no defense against this quickly metastasizing carcinoma. She's not really a candidate for any other types of treatment."

"Won't her blood counts come back up?" I ask.

"Yes, they should if we stop the chemo. And we'll give her a transfusion."

"So could we try again later?"

"We could, but we'd have to see how long it takes"—she turns to Fran—"for your marrow to produce the blood cells you need, and meanwhile the cancer is spreading. Quickly." Again, she looks at each of us for a beat.

This sinks in. Like a bowling ball into the bay.

"Are you saying we should give up fighting this?" I burst out.

Dr. D'Silva presses her lips again. "What I'm saying is the chemo is not working and is not an option anymore."

"What about another kind of chemo?" I demand.

She shakes her head. "She cannot support any chemo at this point."

"What about alternative treatments?"

Fran pulls her chin back. "What do you mean, sugar?"

"You know—options that are . . . outside traditional medical approaches," I say. "There's a group in Mexico and one in Los Angeles that seem to be getting very good results. With, um, different drugs. And diet. And vitamins."

Dr. D'Silva and Aunt Fran turn to me in surprise.

I don't mention the coffee enemas because Aunt Fran will snort, and it does sound a little extreme.

"You should do whatever you feel will help," Dr. D'Silva says. "But . . ."

The edge of my seat is digging into my butt.

She says quietly, "I would like to refer you to hospice."

The light in the examination room vibrates at a much slower frequency. Waves of it play across my retinas. My limbs go leaden. "Hospice?" I cry. "For dying?"

"Hospice maximizes the quality of the time you have remaining. They make sure you can enjoy as much time with family and friends as possible. That you're comfortable."

Fran has slumped back in her chair. "Oh, my. Hospice. It's a shame that such a lovely organization inspires fear and loathing in people. But here I am, fearing and loathing."

*Because Dr. D'Silva has watched this monstrous disease devour thousands and she doesn't think Fran can come back from it.*

"Will I still come to see you?" Aunt Fran asks Dr. D'Silva.

My vocal cords aren't working again.

Dr. D'Silva is still smiling but looks like someone has poked her with a fork. She clears her throat. "I'd be glad to see you anytime, Fran. But if you elect to go with hospice now, I'll refer you, and their capable doctors and nurses will be responsible for you from here."

"That's settled, then," Aunt Fran says. "I'll talk to hospice." She glances at me. "And maybe we'll explore some other options."

She stands and wobbles. Puts out her hand. I jump up. Dr. D'Silva does too. "It's been a pleasure being your patient. Not for just one bout of this nonsense, but for two. A decade of care and saving. I thank you from the bottom of my heart."

"You have a Texas-sized heart, Fran." Small Dr. D'Silva gives Aunt Fran a big hug and squinches her face like it's painful. "I wish you all the best."

I help Fran dress, then we walk out of the office and pretend that she hasn't just given up on her life.

;

Back home, I get Fran in bed with water, meds, and a fresh cover on her duvet. I text Savannah, Maeve, and Kim, who are sympathetic but clearly don't know what to say. So I text Nick.

**They're going to stop Fran's chemo cuz her blood cell counts are too low. They've referred us to HOSPICE i.e. the doc just threw in the towel! Everything's up to me now.**

No reply.

# 24

At my BAC shift that afternoon, I try to concentrate, but anger burns on medium-low in my core. At Dr. D'Silva for being such a quitter. At Fran. She cannot just give up and give in! She's the one who says, *You gotta want it*. She has to fight!

I hate fucking horrible stupid death.

Aunt Fran is *not* going to do it!

A man who says his name is Osgood won't answer my question about feeling suicidal. At first I'm not sure he even realizes who he's called.

"This is Bay Area Crisis—suicide prevention," I repeat, tamping down my annoyance. "Are you feeling suicidal?"

"I'm feeling mighty down. Tired of it all. But it's okay."

So he did mean to call us. I write down the number on the caller ID. "Do you have a plan?" I ask.

"I'm at the park," he says.

Other than the risk of getting hit by a kid in a swing, sounds pretty safe to me.

He says that he lost his apartment six months ago and lives on the street. That he's lived on it before. That he hasn't been taking his meds for the last three months. He won't tell me what the meds are or what he takes them for.

He says, "Don't want any of them no more."

SF rents have been going through the roof and at BAC we talk to a lot of unhoused people: the old, poor, family-less. About 45 percent are mentally ill, 25 percent severely so.

As I doodle rain clouds, Osgood rambles about his daughter who is "a singer on TV," and his son who "plays football for the NFL" and signed a multimillion-dollar contract with the San Francisco Forty-Niners.

"Always been a fan," he adds.

"Wow, that's cool." He's most likely delusional. He believes what he's telling me, but it isn't the reality most of us know. "Osgood, it's been nice talking to you. I do have to open up the lines for other callers in the next couple of minutes."

He says quietly, "You go right ahead, miss. Thank you for your time. Reckon I've had about enough of this world. Been fightin' so long."

The way he says it makes me sit up. "Do you have a plan? For how you would attempt suicide?" I ask for the second time. I just had a Five a month ago. This can't be another!

"Can't say," he says. He seems to be breathing harder.

"Do you have any family in the Bay Area?" I ask, even though he just told me about his son and daughter.

"Family?" He seems to think. "Naw."

"Osgood, do you have anyone nearby, a friend you can stay with?"

"All died on me. Except Torrence here."

"A friend is with you now?"

"No."

"Can you call Torrence?"

"Don't need to."

"I mean, to stay with him."

"No."

"Where are you now?"

"Office building."

"You're not in the park?" I ask.

"Uh-uh."

"Is there someone you know in the building?"

"Found a whole pack of cigarettes on the sidewalk!"

"Really? That's cool."

"Headed up to the roof."

"Oh. The *roof*?" This is so not good. "Osgood, is there somewhere in the building you can sit down? I'll have someone come meet you." I message my shift partner, Jackson. **Might have a 5 here! Unhoused man, mentally ill? Heading up to a roof. Mobile crisis unit?**

"Going on up," he says. "Yep. Had to stop those dang pills."

"Osgood, please listen. I'm worried about your safety if you go to the roof. Would you maybe wait for a moment? Sit down somewhere? While we talk?"

Jackson gets off his call and alerts Quentin. They start listening in on my line.

"Don't you worry, miss," Osgood says. "No worries at all. I promised I'd call before I went. She kept her part of the bargain. Now I kept mine."

"Who did you promise?"

"A long time ago."

"What building are you in?" I fight to keep my voice steady. "What park were you in?"

"Don't rightly know."

"Are you calling us on your cell phone?" We'll have to locate him by contacting the cell phone company and triangulating his location.

"Borrowed it," he says.

"Who does it belong to?"

"Don't you worry, miss. It's just time. Gonna go see her."

Fuck! "Where are you now?"

"The stairs." He's breathing hard. "Sure are lots of 'em."

I hear a door clunk. "Here's the roof."

"Anyone else up there?"

"Nope. No one else here."

**See if he's willing to wait in the stairwell**, Quentin IMs me.

"Osgood, will you go back to the stairs for me? Please. And wait there? Just for a few minutes."

"Huh. Door locked."

"You can't go back to the stairs?" The room tilts.

"Naw."

"While you talk to me, will you please stay by the door?" My thick tongue wrestles the syllables.

"Wanna look over." He means the edge.

Jackson and Quentin are hunched over computers frantically trying to locate him.

"Can you please tell me the address of the building?"

"Naw."

"What street were you on when you came in?"

He doesn't answer.

Now what?

I need more oxygen. Quentin IMs me: **Get him to describe what he sees**—so we can possibly locate him by landmarks.

"Osgood," I say as calmly as possible, "tell me what you see up there." It worked with Jane.

"What I see? So many buildings." Distant honking and traffic sounds in the background.

"Anything else?" He doesn't answer. "How far up did you climb?"

"Reckon I'm up ten stories."

"Can you see any other buildings?"

"The pyramid. The water. Street cars below." He almost sounds excited, like a child. He's got to be downtown.

"Is the pyramid close by?" The Transamerica Pyramid. Quentin IMs me, **Keep trying for identifying info. We've got Verizon on the line.**

"The Walgreens," he says.

"You see a Walgreens?"

"Down below."

Oh, super. There must be five hundred of them in the city. "Osgood, I want to send someone to help you. Mobile Crisis is a great group and they help people who feel like you're feeling right now." They would be ideal for him. As long as he doesn't have a gun, since they're not supposed to walk into situations that involve weapons.

"I know them," he says amiably.

Has he tried this before? Also not a good sign.

"Do you have any weapons on you?" I ask.

"No, ma'am."

"But I need to know where you are. What's the street name you're on? Or even one near? Do you remember? Or the building number?"

Quentin IMs **Suggest a cigarette to buy time.**

"Don't you worry, miss. Thank you kindly for the talk. Goodbye."

Click.

"Oh no! Oh, shit."

Jackson stares back at me with wide eyes. "Fuck," he says.

I call back the number. It goes right to voicemail for someone named Melvin. I try again. Same result.

"What do we do?" I cry.

Quentin's staring at the turquoise industrial carpet. "Nothing we can do," he says, shaking his head. "I'm sorry. We couldn't get a location."

They didn't have enough time, because I didn't realize what was going on until too late.

Quentin leads me into his office for a debriefing. I fight to hold back tears.

"I screwed up," I say. A dozen photos of his baby daughter patchwork the wall behind him.

He reminds me that our job is hard, that I did help Osgood by being there for him, kept him talking for a long time, and may well have prevented him from attempting.

"One thing to note," he says, sitting behind his desk. "Besides dealing with someone with a weapon, Mobile Crisis can't go anywhere that's dangerous. That includes a roof. We would've called 911."

"Oh." More mistakes.

"Talk to me. Are you feeling okay?"

"I guess okay," I fib. I press my thumb into my wrist tat.

"You sure?"

All I can do is nod miserably. "Did I blow my probation?"

"No." He clasps his hands. "You're a good counselor, Del. But in the next couple of months, they need an intern over at the new trauma center—to help work with teens and youth. I think you would be even better at that."

"Really?" *He's trying to get rid of you.*

He rests his elbows on the desk and clasps his hands. "You're perceptive and connect well with people, especially young people."

His expression is open and honest. Maybe this is the silver

lining of being born with my skin on inside out and my organs stretched like tennis racquet strings.

"Is everything okay with you outside of here?" he asks.

I take a deep breath. "I guess not."

"Tell me what's up," he says gently.

"My aunt, the one I live with, has been diagnosed with cancer."

"Sorry to hear that."

Pretend everything's going to be fine and you're in control. "I mean, it's going well. The treatment and all." I open and close the locket around my neck. "Okay, no, it's not. It's awful. I guess I'm distracted. A little."

"Of course. That's a lot to be dealing with." He leans back in his chair. "All right. Give some thought to the trauma center. In the meantime, you might want to reduce your shifts here. Until your aunt's health improves. We have to take care of ourselves and our families before we can help others. Especially those in crisis."

Easier said than done.

;

On my way home through downtown twenty minutes later, my bus glides by the flashing lights of a police car and an ambulance. Medics are loading a body from the sidewalk onto a gurney. The area is taped off and I quickly turn away from the dark stain on the concrete and curb. Maybe it was an armed robbery or a homicide.

On impulse, despite a sickening, sinking feeling, I get off at the stop and approach one of the bystanders. A couple of police officers confer nearby.

"What happened?" I ask a young guy in a suit. He hugs his briefcase against his chest.

"A man jumped off the roof. From up there." He points. It's an old eight-, maybe nine-story stone building of doctor and dentist offices. "Old guy. Homeless, someone said."

Against the far wall of the building lies a Forty-Niners hat. I pick it up. The bill is frayed. It's black except for the round logo, where the white "SF" letters are stained with grunge.

The EMTs close the ambulance back doors. I hold out the hat. "Please. I think this was his."

The lady takes it from me. "Thanks."

The ambulance pulls away silently.

I blow out short breaths like I'm in labor or something and turn around. Across the street where cable cars run is a Walgreens.

*You cannot fuck up like this. Ever again.*

# 25

No way I can tell Aunt Fran about Osgood. My time at BAC is supposed to be affirming, encouraging—proving to myself and to her that I'm in a better place than I used to be.

I've never told her that I still sometimes have suicidal ideation—think about suicide—because she wouldn't understand and would freak out. I didn't come live with her until weeks after I attempted, and by then she was in hyper-psychiatric-nurse mode. But I know my attempt floored her.

Esmerelda says all the right things, but I still feel like a dried turd on a stick . . . that's being rotated and frozen over the void like a hot dog.

I work on a new Texas, London, and Bangkok map collage, featuring yin and yang, retro-fashion, dawn and dusk, dry ice, and the quote, "The coldest winter I ever spent was summer in San Francisco." *Dualities and Paradoxes*, it's called.

After an evening AA meeting, I bravely skate down part of Nob Hill on California Street. It's steep and I'm going too fast, leap a curb and then face-plant on the sidewalk. Miraculously, I only rip my jeans, jam a thumb and scrape my palms. My semicolon tattoo escapes intact. But some of the unbearable tension in my body leaks out onto the concrete via the skin left there. I don't cut, but I totally get how much physical pain can distract from and relieve mental pain.

Now I'm rollerblading along the level Embarcadero in the fading evening light, dodging humans, dogs, light posts, fire hydrants, and parking meters. I can smoke in peace and work off the electrical jolts that are erupting in my head and body.

The void shimmers like an icy heat mirage in the near distance. No one else can see it. Or has any idea what lies beyond it. *Nothing.*

Pretend you're in control.

Pretend harder.

I text Nick: **Can I call you? Please?**

I glide slowly on an open stretch of sidewalk near the water and keep glancing at the screen to see when he reads it. Finally, he does, and texts back:

**Five minutes**

I do a U-turn to head back since I'm getting closer to AT&T Park, which is packed with tens of thousands of rowdy Giants fans. Salt air mixed with traffic exhaust stings my eyes.

Five and a half minutes later: "Hey, Del! What's up? I was going to call you. About Fran—"

"Huge fail at the crisis line today."

"What happened?"

I tell him everything, the whole story, while I skate under the thumps and clamor of the Bay Bridge and around strolling tourist couples and evening runners.

"Oh my god," he says softly.

"Yeah." I'm back to the lit-up ferry building and it's dark now. A DON'T WALK sign glares.

"Sounds like he'd been planning it for a long time."

"But he called us. He talked to *me* for a long time. There's almost always that ambivalence. If I weren't such a dumbass,

I could've talked him out of it." I skate across tracks against the light, hear a loud clang, *then* look both ways. Fortunately, the oncoming streetcar is half a block away.

"What about Jane? You're really good at what you do."

"Thanks, Nick." I grip my locket chain with my free hand. "Um, did you see my text? The one before?"

"Yeah. I'm so sorry. Hospice! I meant to get back to you . . ." He trails off.

"It's only temporary. We'll get off it as soon as possible. Fran's doing great."

A pause. "I should probably call her, huh?"

I'm skating down Market Street, which has emptied of executives and techies, but not of unhoused people. "She'd love that. What's been going on with you?" I ask quickly, dodging a weathered young guy and his overloaded shopping cart.

He hesitates. "The same old."

"I wish you'd tell me more. I tell you everything. And then some."

He laughs. "A few of us are coming into the city tomorrow afternoon for a few hours. Wanna meet somewhere?"

"For sure!" I can't believe it! "Like for ice-skating? Maybe whale-watching?"

He laughs again. "I was thinking coffee, or ice cream."

"Great idea! North Beach. Where good gelato stores are on every corner. Or Fisherman's Wharf even."

"We stayed at Fisherman's Wharf last summer, remember?"

Yeah, I remember the revolving door and the elevator bank. Maybe this is our chance to create some new memories.

# 26

## Wednesday, August 12

The next afternoon, after my AA meeting and a shift at the gallery—where Louis and I have forged a working truce since he's kind of swamped, and surprise, surprise, I can actually help—I wait for Nick at Washington Square Park. It's a full city block, a big grassy plain studded with tall trees, playing dogs, winding paths, and clumps of dark earth overturned from rough ball games. The cathedral on the far side facing me has two spires, one for Saint Peter and one for Saint Paul. The bells ring three times for the hour, and startled birds take flight, dotting the blue sky like the musical notes of a song.

I'm sitting on a wooden bench, fidgeting with my rings, wearing a clingy white and navy-striped tee and a pale blue linen shirt over it, with jeans. And dressy low-heeled sandals that are a pain to hike in. But so cute.

*No expectations*, I tell myself. He's a good friend that I happen to really appreciate about now.

I check my phone. His text says that he'll be twenty minutes late.

**No worries**, I text back. But I know he has to be back at the lab by 5 p.m., so it means we won't have that much time.

This is getting to be a theme.

After pacing the perimeter of the park, I follow along with a group of elderly Asian women dancercising with big red paper fans, until a likely bus pulls up at the stop. Nick is unmistakable, getting off with Noor.

I rush him. He gives me a quick hug but pulls back. *You're pungent from power-walking and dancing.*

"Nick! Hey! Hi, Noor. Where's everyone else?"

"We split up."

Yay.

He adds, "Sorry I'm late. Took me longer to get here on MUNI than I thought."

"Ready for some gelato?"

"Definitely."

"Follow me." I grab his hand and pull him to the crosswalk. We head up the block. People glance at Noor first, then us. I bet they assume we're a couple, until he lets go.

"It's really good to see you," he says. "How's Fran?" He cranes his neck to look at me. I forget about his bad peripheral vision.

Part of me wants to go on and on about her. Part of me wants to talk about anything but. "Pretty good, all things considered." I tell him a little about chemo. "I've got a question for you though. Sort of a medical one."

"Sure."

"What do you think about special diets and cancer? Since we're off traditional Western treatments."

"What does Fran think?"

"She rolls her eyes and makes excuses when I bring it up, so I'm taking matters into my own hands." We reach the shop. "In here."

"What do you mean?"

I open the door for him. "I'm thinking of putting her on a special cancer diet. From a book."

Our arms touch as we scan the flavors through the glass of the refrigerator case. "Well," he says after a moment, "if it makes Fran feel better, then great." It might be my imagination, but it looks like new respect in his eyes.

"Yeah! That's what I figure too."

The guy asks Nick for our order.

"Go ahead," I say. I'm still deciding.

"Chocolate and, um, coffee, please," he says. A couple of his nails and fingertips are stained with some purple dye.

"Okay, mango and . . . coconut almond for me," I say. "Sometimes I feel like a nut."

Nick grins. While we wait, he stands close behind me and rests his chin on my head for three seconds. I don't move a muscle, aware of his whole body lightly touching mine.

We pay for our order. He stares at my skinned-up hands. "Get in a fight?"

"Rollerblading face-plant," I inform him.

"Yikes." He takes my right hand and gently examines both sides, then my wrist. Sparks skitter and bounce off the cash register from his touch. "You're keeping them clean, right?" He means the wounds.

"Except when I dumpster-dive."

We stroll back to the park eating our goopy, delicious gelato. The air temperature is unusually perfect, not too cold or hot. We sit on the sweet-smelling grass in the afternoon sun. Noor lies down on the other side of Nick. Back-to-back, we prop each other up. Our physical contact is burning a hole through my shoulder blades but I try not to obsess about it. Be cool, fool. Stay in the moment.

Mom used to run her fingers deliciously over my back in a rhyme called "Going on a Treasure Hunt." The last bit was "cool breeze, tight squeeze" and ended with her blowing on the back of my neck and gently pinching the flesh there: "Now you've got the shiveries!"

That's what I have. I'd like to sit here forever.

"How is it?" I finally ask.

"Awesome," he says, and I hope he means more than just the gelato.

He sets his ice cream cup down. "Not the ideal time to spring this, I know, but I can't make it for the Beach Blanket show after all. Professor Lin asked me to come with him to do a presentation at UCLA. I'm really sorry." He shifts and sits cross-legged next to me, close but no longer touching me. He does look disappointed though.

"Oh, shoot." I wish he hadn't ruined this stellar moment. My gelato's already gone, so there's none left for consolation. *You knew this was too good to be true.*

"No way I can say no. If I want his support for a scholarship."

"What do you have to do?" A Frisbee sails within inches over our heads and a guy yells, "Sorry!"

"Help with his presentation, video it, run errands. That kind of thing."

His dog is curled up all comfy against his long legs. "Is Noor going?"

"Yes. And I'm a little worried about that."

"You'll both do great. Sounds like you and Noor are the teacher's pets."

"Working on it."

So, did he want to get together today out of guilt, just to let me down gently? *You were letting yourself be too eager.*

He opens his buzzing phone. "Hang on a sec." He sends a quick text to someone. "Just confirming meetup time at BART."

He gets up and gives me a hand, careful of my wounds. We both hold on for at least three seconds once I'm standing, neither of us looking at the other. When he lets go, we brush off, throw our empty paper cups in the trash bin, and head for the bus stop.

I blurt out, "Maybe I can come over to Berkeley again when you get back? Before you leave?" Maybe going there by seaplane is an option.

"For sure. That would be sweet." He does like me. But like a sister, or an old friend. I get it. It's okay. *No, it's not.*

The bus pulls up.

"See you." He gives me a hug, and—to my amazement—a quick, chocolaty, full-on-lip kiss, before he bounds onto the bus with Noor. He waves from the window. I'm rooted to the spot, watching until the bus is out of sight.

# 27

## Thursday, August 13

"I'm making you a special breakfast treat," I announce to Fran, switching off the high-decibel blender as she shuffles to the breakfast table. "Sorry about the noise." She plops into her chair outfitted with cushions. Her face is doughy and droopy.

"I was already up. Trying to meditate. I'll start with some tea," she says. "Don't we have a . . . show tonight?"

"Yes. And turns out Nick can't make it after all." I flip on the electric kettle.

"That's a shame. I'm sorry, sugar." She's pulling at her fleece bathrobe. "I'm beginning to wish he'd stayed in Texas this summer."

Even go-after-what-you-want Fran sees that it's hopeless.

Maybe she's just tired. This will cheer her up. "A present for you came in. From me. Right there."

"Goodness! What happened to your hands?"

"Skating wipeout."

"Hmmm." Aunt Fran pulls back the cardboard around the package and holds up the book I ordered. *The Cancer Cure Diet*," she reads.

"Dr. Smith advocates sort of an extreme diet, but it's proven to reverse even the most advanced and virulent forms of cancer."

"Really? What are you supposed to eat? Uranium?"

"This." I scrape the contents of the blender into a hand-painted bowl. "Cottage cheese and the magic ingredient, cold-pressed flaxseed oil. A little basil and lemon juice. Pureed."

"What else?" She gazes at me over her red-framed reading glasses.

"In all honesty, not much else. Raw veggies. Some fruit. Water."

"That sounds like torture, not breakfast." She's not smiling.

"I thought we could at least try it." I garnish the gloop with fresh parsley and set it in front of her.

"We?"

"I'll eat it with you!"

She examines the book. "It's kind of . . . homemade-looking," she notes. "Oh my, it does say here that it cures cancer. Someone should call Channel Five."

"Okay. Maybe not in all cases," I allow, sitting beside her, "but in a bunch. Check out the testimonials in the back." I open the book to the right page.

Aunt Fran reads one and starts thumbing through the pages. "Root canal tooth removal?" she asks. "Hair analysis?"

"Those are suggestions. The diet is the important part."

She observes me for a beat. Sighs.

"Can't we just try it for a little bit?" I plead.

She huffs. "Of course. What can it hurt?"

"Yay!"

Fran dips a bright orange baby carrot in the mixture and pops it in her mouth. "Shoot. It's pretty good."

I dip a celery stalk. "Not bad! The lemon juice is key."

"How much was the book? If you don't mind my asking?"

"I bought the book for sixty-nine dollars." I clear my throat. "I used our credit card and will pay you back. The service would be three hundred dollars." I'm hoping she'll offer to pay for that since it will annihilate my budget.

"Thank you, sugar. A very thoughtful gift. May I ask what 'service'?"

"Where you can communicate with him—Dr. Smith—by email and he follows your progress. I haven't signed up yet but was going to run it by you."

"Doesn't that seem like kind of a lot?" Her jaw has a steely set to it that puts me a little on the defensive.

"Not at all when you compare it to the cost of chemo, or any other health services. Or even a doctor's appointment." That's a quote off his website, actually, but she pulls her chin back and looks at me like I've sprouted a mustache. "Okay," I say, "we don't have to sign up for that. But will you try the diet? For my sake? *You gotta want it!* To live! To fight this!"

"Yes, ma'am," she says, with enthusiasm.

I think it's enthusiasm.

# 28

"Oh, good!" Louis says to Fran with the phone to his ear when we finally stagger into the gallery. She still insists on walking down most days, though she gets a ride back up. Today, I accompanied her, holding her arm. She's wobbly, and I don't trust her alone on the steep hills. She hasn't told Louis yet—or anyone—about being on hospice care, and that's just as well.

Louis says to her, "I've got Jorge on the line and we seem to have a misunderstanding. Here's Fran." He holds the phone out to her and mouths, "Flaking out."

Before she can react, he jerks the phone back, staring at her. "Are you okay?"

She's ash-gray and swaying.

"Just a little tired," I inform him. "She was running a fever a couple of days ago."

We guide her to one of the chairs. Louis says into the phone, "We'll call you right back."

"Just need to catch my breath," she says, plopping into the seat. We were walking downhill.

I run to the small sink by the coffee maker, get a glass of water, and bring it to her. Louis watches us both.

He says to Fran, "Don't be mad, but you look ghastly."

"I had a reaction to the chemo this past weekend. Guess I'm still a little weak. I'm fine now, though." She puts her hand out for the phone. "Background?" I busy myself at the jewelry cabinet so I can listen.

Louis tells her, "Jorge says he's nowhere near ready and wasn't planning to be ready until *November*. He's slated to go up in four weeks! NorCal Trust and Pocket War Games are both interested in him."

Jorge Ortega is from West Texas and is one my favorite artists. His Lone Star bio describes him as "hyper-realistic, with Latin themes and colors, and magical dreamlike compositions." He works painstakingly slowly, which makes sense when you see the detail in his paintings.

Fran takes a deep breath and calls. "Hi, Jorge, this is Fran. How are you, sweetie?" She's using her best motherly tones.

She listens. "Thank you, I'm feeling fine." She glances at Louis. "Just a little fever and tummy upset. How is everything coming along?" Usually when she talks to an artist, she asks all kinds of questions about their families and the weather first.

Another pause as she listens with closed eyes. "Wonderful! I'm delighted to hear that. We are too, then."

I walk back to the coffee area. Louis is filling a water bottle.

"What's going on?" I whisper.

"She encourages letters of agreement with our artists, but she doesn't insist. This may be a case where we should have."

Fran says, "We discussed this almost two months ago."

Jorge's voice carries all the way over here. Can't tell what he's saying, but he's definitely worked up.

Fran soothes, "No, no, it's okay. I—we—I didn't call you in mid-June? I seem to remember . . ." Her face is contorted in

136

confusion and/or pain. "Oh. Well, maybe . . . Okay, November first, then. We'll . . . check you later."

Louis observes Fran with a half-frown. "You never talked to him then."

She shakes her head. "Apparently not. I'm so sorry to have let this slip."

"You've got a good excuse." He smiles. "Okay, damage-control time." He heads for the stairs.

"Louis?"

"Yes?" He's still walking away, clearly slightly annoyed with her. He's been covering most things by himself for weeks now.

Fran says, "Day before yesterday, my doctor referred me to hospice care."

He turns around in slo-mo, with a horrified expression.

"The need for damage control may be extensive, sugar."

I pipe up, "But only temporarily."

They don't seem to hear me.

;

That night I study Dr. Smith's site carefully—all the cancer survivor testimonials and his Q&A. Next, I google some burning questions and search for other options. There are literally hundreds of alternatives to Western medicine that have saved countless cancer patients. *Who refuse to give up.*

# 29

## Friday, August 14

Late in the morning the next day, I'm working at my desk on my 3D pop-up collage of each of Fran's chemo treatments—tiki torches to represent the IV poles, tubes, apricot-almond bars—superimposed over her favorite San Francisco postcards and pics. Including a dead end. No subtlety there.

I paste in a Walgreens coupon for Gold Bond healing lotion.

Vincent, the doorman, buzzes on the intercom to announce Harold someone.

Fran is resting in her room and I've got to go down to the Lone Star in less than an hour.

The doorbell rings.

I check the peephole.

Shirt buttons. A giant stands there. Can't see his face.

Fran calls from her room, "Del, can you get that? Forgot about our appointment."

"Yes, ma'am. Appointment?" I open the door partway.

"Good morning," says an unusually deep voice. "I'm Harold Lachance from Golden Gate Hospice."

"Hi," I say, still blocking the door. As if I could.

He's tall and ripped. Wide cheekbones and nose. A kind face. He clutches a navy-blue medical bag in one hand. He extends a hand the size of a catcher's mitt, but his handshake is gentle.

I have no choice. "I'm Delilah, Fran's niece. We're running a little late here. She never mentioned someone was coming today."

Fran walks out of her room, moving stiffly but with conviction, dressed in form-fitting jeans and a pea-green sweater.

They shake hands. "Come on in, Harold, and let me get you something to drink. We've got coffee, all kinds of tea, juice . . ." He's a couple of inches taller than Fran, but she's looking him in the eye. His shoulders are almost as wide as the doorway, and hers are sloped with fatigue.

"Green tea would be great."

Fran leads us all into the living room. The island of Alcatraz floats before us and a huge, loaded container ship cruises in from the Golden Gate.

"I'll get it," I say. If Mr. Hospice feels too comfortable here, he'll keep coming back, but if I don't do it, Fran will tire herself out running around.

When I return with a tray, Fran's on the couch and he's in the chair next to it, his back straight. They're chuckling and comparing notes on the south. I overhear that Harold's from northern Louisiana, near the Arkansas and Mississippi borders. They're laughing about something to do with the Sugar Bowl. He's probably only five or ten years younger than Fran.

Fran says, "Harold played football for LSU." Louisiana State. "Delilah lived in Dallas until she was fourteen," she adds.

"Are you an Aggie fan?" he asks me. He's talking about Texas A&M. He has only a tinge of an accent.

"No. Longhorns. Hook 'em Horns!" My index and pinky fingers make "horns," then do the appropriate "hooking" motion. Even having grown up in Texas, I know surprisingly little about football, but I don't think UT plays LSU. Different leagues. Whatever. I'm not here to make friends.

"May I take your blood pressure?" He turns to Fran. "Then I'll fill you in on what to expect, and you can ask any questions. Delilah, would you mind putting this box in the refrigerator?" He holds out one the size of half of a shoebox.

"Is that your lunch?"

"It's Fran's comfort kit." He continues to hold it out.

"What's a comfort kit?" I ask, making no move to take it.

"It's a collection of medications for urgent situations. It needs to be refrigerated. We'll review the contents in a moment, as you may need to know how to use them for Fran."

"Oh, all right." I take it and stash it in the fridge.

When I return from the kitchen, Harold is unwrapping the blood-pressure cuff from Fran's arm and saying, "I need to get a list of your current medications. We'll be responsible for all refills and prescriptions now."

Fran recites the names and dosages, then asks me to get all her containers from her bathroom in case she's forgetting anything. I do, though I regret helping them get their claws in Fran's care in any way.

"How have you been sleeping?" Harold asks as I park myself in the big chair across from them.

"Sometimes fine, sometimes not." She shifts in her chair and winces. "Dr. D'Silva gave me something to help, but I feel too darn groggy the next day."

"We can change your dosage or try another med if you'd like. How's your pain?"

She glances at me, probably hoping I'm not listening. She thinks saying out loud that she hurts will break some spell.

"I had a little flare-up yesterday—same area that's been bothering me lately, my ribs. But nothing serious. I was overtired."

"Dr. Berg may want to prescribe a higher dosage."

Fran leans at an awkward angle against the arm of the chair and then sinks back.

Harold says, "I'm here today to answer any questions."

"I've got one," I say. "Do we have to do this?"

Fran frowns, but he seems unfazed. "You are not under contract and can stop it anytime."

"Glad to hear it," I say to Fran.

He says to Fran, "If you fell tomorrow, heaven forbid, and broke a hip, we'd send you to the hospital. Then you could rejoin hospice afterwards. But for the most part, we don't call 911."

I stiffen. "What do you mean you don't call 911? I love 911!"

He takes a deep breath in through his nose. I'm getting on his nerves. Good. "We treat your symptoms here at home, and we have a lot of different things to do that with. We'll keep you comfortable throughout."

That's not really an answer, but I force my lips together as Fran smiles at him in agreement.

He asks if there are any particular areas of her body giving her trouble, and Fran mentions her eye.

"That's most likely the cancer," Harold says.

"In her eye?" I blurt out.

"Possibly behind it." Meeting Fran's gaze, he adds, "If you have tumors in your lungs and vital organs, they may have reached the brain as well."

TMI makes my stomach turn, but Fran nods resignedly,

like this is what she expected. It's nonsense. How could he know? He just met her.

She and Harold discuss ordering some oxygen and hospital equipment. Hospice will also help arrange for nurse's aides if it gets hard for Fran to bathe herself, for example.

That's a relief. I was wondering if I would need to do stuff like that.

"What about travel?" I ask.

He glances up from his notes.

I clarify, "Does she have to stay here, in town?"

"Nope, you're free to do whatever you like. We can refer you to hospice in another state for a week or longer if you want."

"What about another country? Like England or France?" Fran blinks at me. I haven't shared my research with her yet.

"I'll check. Maybe something could be arranged."

He pulls a form from his bag and hands it to Fran. A Do Not Resuscitate advance medical directive for any emergency responders. He begins to explain it but Fran assures him she's familiar with it.

She says, "I do *not* want extraordinary measures taken to keep me alive, should I, well, whatever." She throws both hands up. "Become unconscious or hit my head or something."

"Wait. What?" I gape at her. "You don't want medical care if you fall? Or split your head open?"

"No, that's not what we're saying," says Fran. "Not *no* medical care. Just no efforts to . . . revive me when I start to go."

I scowl at her with my arms crossed. Her sweater is sort of twisted on her, and her glasses are smudged.

Fran goes on. "They sawed open Charlotte's ninety-year-old mother's chest for emergency heart surgery, while she was unconscious. Boy, was she mad when she woke up."

"You're not ninety!" I cry.

Harold gives Fran a look that says, *Your ball.*

"Sugar, if the cancer continues to . . . grow, and I'm near death, I don't want CPR and other measures taken to revive me if I, say, have a heart attack or go into a coma." She looks at me. "I'll need to be allowed to die."

"But—"

"She can always change her mind," says Harold helpfully.

Fran winks at me, which pisses me off even more.

Harold says, "Delilah. The medical establishment has to do everything in their power to keep you alive, regardless of your age. Unless you indicate otherwise. Legally, in writing, with witnesses. And we *can* keep someone technically alive almost indefinitely."

I get up and pace to the far end of the room. "What about checking if her white cell counts increased? We were going to maybe do more chemo."

"When you elect to go with hospice, we discontinue all forms of treatment against the cancer. No more diagnostic tests are necessary. We'll treat all symptoms or complications—to keep you comfortable." He looks at Fran.

She nods.

I demand, "So the cancer will be progressing *unchecked*?"

"Yes." More softly, he adds, "We are moving toward acceptance that Fran is in her final stage of life."

I let my breath out.

Harold continues, "This is a difficult time. A lot of things to get used to. I promise you we'll be there for both you and Fran. Both of you can call me anytime, day or night. I'll be coming to check on you once or twice a week, Fran, until you need me more, then as often as necessary. If you start feeling uncomfortable, we'll up your pain medication or whatever else it takes."

He pauses before saying slowly and clearly, "It's real important to keep track of and stay on top of the pain. We can control it, but sometimes, if it gets ahead of you, it's harder to get you back to that baseline. Does that make sense?"

"Yes," says Fran.

It reminds me what's important here. "I guess so."

"Take your pain meds without fail, Fran, and if you have a pain spike, you're authorized to give her drops, Delilah. And call me."

"What drops?"

"In the comfort kit. I'll show you. We also have referrals for grief and spiritual counseling. Many patients find that this is an unexpectedly rewarding time for the whole family."

"*Rewarding? Seriously?*" I blurt out. I'm one absurd statement away from flipping the coffee table.

Harold clears his throat.

Three seconds of silence as they wait for me to get a grip.

"What happens when she gets to six months?" I demand. Calmly.

"We can extend her care. Or 'graduate' her—but that happens in very few cases. We're here to help patients and their families through the final phase of the patient's life, and to end life with dignity and peace."

"We're looking forward to a graduation ceremony." I get up. "Excuse me. I have to leave for work."

Harold has more to go over with Fran. "Delilah, how about we review the comfort kit next time?" he says. "I'll be here next Tuesday, and probably Friday."

"Fine."

I close the door kind of hard when I leave.

# 30

That evening, Fran and I are in the old Club Fugazi in North Beach along with lots of tourists. It's way smaller than the last show, more like a nightclub-saloon, and my crowd anxiety is at a low rumble.

*Beach Blanket Babylon* is the campy musical that's been running here for decades and that Fran promised to take me to. She wasn't sure about coming out tonight, but I talked her into it as I suppressed my disappointment that Nick's in Los Angeles and not here. He texted me again to tell Aunt Fran that he was sorry to miss seeing her. Fine. It's an overdue girls' night out and he will not ruin our fun.

I lead her right to our little stage-side table and sit her down. "Your lipstick's trying to escape." I point to the side of my mouth.

"Ah, hell." She swipes at it with two fingers. Her gold charm bracelet tinkles. "I haven't seen this in decades," she says. Her navy-blue chiffon skirt is sliding sideways and her white cashmere sweater hangs loose.

"I've never seen it," I remind her.

"Grandmama took Tommy and me to the theater in New York City," Fran muses. "Your dad and I were . . . twelve and eleven. Saw *Grease*, had lemonades at the . . . Plaza, and shopped . . . at that toy store . . ." She flicks her hand in dismissal of the actual name. "I thought we'd died and gone to heaven."

I try not to wince at her choice of metaphor.

The waiter approaches. "Ladies?"

"A glass of pinot grigio, please," says Fran. She glances at me, knowing it's not on her diet or a good idea with her meds. And that she's breaking her no-drinking-around-Del rule.

Two sips won't hurt her. "Ginger ale for me, please."

I want to hear more stories about her and Dad's childhood, but now's a good time to run something by her. "So they've been doing a bunch of studies on cannabis oil. It's having some amazing effects on tumor growth and cancer cells in general."

"Cannabis oil?"

"Yeah. Scientific studies, medical ones, have shown that the oil breaks down something, only in the cancer cells and they die. You start out with a little bit, like a gram a day in a capsule, then you gradually increase the dosage. That way you don't feel high or goofy."

"Never much liked pot, darlin'. Had to breathe too much of it secondhand. Besides, it is still illegal."

"Not for medical purposes, it's not. I've found a website where we can order if we have—"

She takes my hand. "You know I'm . . . so proud of all that you're doing." She wedges herself against the table and the back of her seat. "I'm taking enough substances as it is, sugar. I really don't want cannabis oil. But I appreciate that you did all this research . . . for me."

"Will you just think about it?" If there's even a slim chance that it can reverse what's going on in her body, why won't she try it?

The guy brings our drinks, and I pay. Fran's lips are pinched beneath her botched hothouse-tomato lipstick, and she flinches.

"Are you okay?"

She takes a glug of wine. "Your mother had such a struggle with her mental illness."

"Yeah," I say, rolling with this jump in conversational topics. "Remember when she bought that old Tilt-a-Whirl ride from the State Fair to set up in the backyard?"

Aunt Fran shakes her head.

"During one of her hypomanic cycles." Maybe Dad never told her.

Fran's still got a hand on her wineglass.

I continue, "I'm sure it stressed Dad out, but it was that same time she dragged us both to Disneyland with her, with about three hours' notice."

"Did you . . . have fun?"

"Totally. Mom and I screamed our brains out on Big Thunder Mountain Railroad."

"She was a charming woman. But her illness was . . . so difficult . . . when you had to sell your house," she says, frowning and releasing her glass that's between us.

"Yeah. We moved into that old apartment halfway to McKinney." It had something to do with Mom losing and/ or spending money. They never told me the details. I stayed in my school at least, although everyone knew we had moved to a rougher neighborhood. And that my mom was not like other moms.

Fran's eyes are closed.

I say quietly, "Her depressions were epic. When I was eight she spent months in bed. I remember that Grammy—her mom—visited and was mad that she wouldn't just get up."

"Her death. Such a tragedy."

I say quickly, "Did I ever tell you? After she died, like when I was having a hard time, I sometimes dreamed of her giving me a rose."

"Lovely." She reaches over and palms my jaw. "No child should go through that. But, darlin'," she says, "I may not be able to make it . . . through the whole show."

"Oh. Is there an intermission?" All she has to do is sit. Her breath is a little fast, though. I say, "Here, give me your purse." Inside her blue beaded clutch is a little tin with four of her pain pills. I give her one. That says, *Quick! Eat me.* And her wine says, *Come on, Del, just one gulp. You need it. She won't notice.*

She swallows the pill, leans forward, and puts her elbows on her knees to support her head. Her wine is *right there.* And she's not looking. I may have to go outside and call Ez.

People are coming to their seats now, staring at us and blocking our way. "Give it a few minutes to work," I whisper.

"Ohhh, dear," she groans. Her face gleams with a film of perspiration.

"Here, take another one," I say. Her pain medication tolerance has gone up a lot and these are some of the old lower dosage, so I'm not worried about her getting too much.

She pops a second pill without liquid and takes two deep breaths. But she's white and waxy as a magnolia. "We better go," she whispers.

"Really?" My stomach flips like I've stepped off the last stair, expecting the floor, and there's nothing there.

I jump up and help her from her seat. Everyone watches us as we weave through tables toward the front doors. She leans on me and lets out a sharp moan.

People clear the way fast. Out front, we slide into a taxi that two startled guys in matching blue tuxes have vacated. Now she leans heavily against me, panting, her forehead creased in pain, all the way up Russian Hill. When we pull in front of our building, the driver honks and I wave frantically. Joel, the night doorman, rushes out to help.

She can barely walk. Another moan escapes her, sounding like it came from a wounded animal, not a human.

We get her up the elevator and into the apartment and her bed. She's keening an unearthly muted wail. It's so clear to everyone, and finally to me, that she's deathly ill and shouldn't be in a chiffon skirt out on the town.

I ask in my crisis-line calm voice, "Are the meds helping? What's your level now?" Zero is no pain and ten is unbearable.

"Seven . . . eight," she pants, eyes squinched shut. She has a high pain threshold. Plus, I see her ratcheting it down a notch or two when I ask. She underreports.

"Omigod I'm so sorry!" I cry. "What was I thinking making you do this I'm calling Harold!"

The sheet in the kitchen has his direct number. My voice is all high and fast as I speak into my phone. "This is Delilah, Fran's niece, we tried to go out, but Fran's pain—she's in bad pain!"

"Where are you now?"

"Home!"

"Get the comfort kit from the fridge, Delilah. We'll get some drops into her and she'll improve quickly."

Harold helps me identify the morphine bottle in the kit and open the seal. I run back to Fran's room, fill the dropper to the right mark, and stick it in Fran's mouth.

Within five or six rough minutes, while I continue to

quietly reassure her and stroke her hand, the taut muscles in her face soften. Within a few more, she's asleep.

I hope asleep.

Yeah, she's breathing. Still in her dressy clothes.

I tell Harold that she's okay for now and disconnect.

What a fuckup I am, dragging her out and making her beg to go home. I stay at her bedside, still sweaty from all the running and from getting her big self up to the apartment and into her old four-poster bed. I slide off her skirt and nudge her under her sheets. Little by little, the familiar smells of the room—her shampoo and perfume—along with her bright coral geometric bedspread, prints and paintings on the wall, silver-framed photos, teak jewelry box, and random stacks of books everywhere soothe me with their familiarity.

We just dodged a hand grenade. So, thanks, Whoever. But I also just used up a ton of luck we will probably really need later.

I'm the adult and she's the kid. That's how I've got to think. But a soft moan escapes my throat. I want Aunt Fran to stop changing. It's crushing me.

And I can't let her see that!

*Why* am I doing all this by myself? Because Dad's in Southeast Asia. If he'll just get his ass here and do his part, we'll help Fran get better.

# 31

In my room, lying on the floor, I Skype Dad on my cell. I can't put this off anymore.

Dad answers, his short graying hair and long face radiating seriousness. "Hello, Del. Are you all right?" He's sitting at a desk with a framed print of some ancient stone temple behind him.

"Yes, I'm fine. I'm calling about Aunt Fran." There's a delay, and my own high, weird voice echoes back at me. "Where are you?"

"I'm in Phnom Penh. Cambodia."

"What's that sound?" Like someone is crackling cellophane around him.

"It's raining. Monsoon season. What's going on with Fran?"

"Funny you should ask. She started hospice care this week." My feet are propped up on my bed.

"I see. I've heard wonderful things about hospice."

Blood blooms through all my capillaries. This is like talking to a shiny automobile. Why would this be any different than discussing Mom's death, my mental health, menstruation, or a million other "unpleasant" topics?

"Really? That's all you've got? Don't you think it's time you came to help?"

"Sweetheart," he says in his firm, *don't be hysterical* voice,

"I will be there as soon as I can. Ideally in two or three weeks."

My vision narrows. "Two or three weeks? Her pain is getting much worse! You need to come now!"

"The project I've been working on for the last three years is coming to fruition this week. I can't leave now, or I would. Millions of dollars are at stake, not to mention dozens of jobs. Once things are rolling and I have personnel in place, I can take leave. But not yet."

"Dad, listen to yourself! She's your sister! You're her only family, besides me."

"If Fran is about to depart this world, then I'll drop everything and come. Is she?" he demands.

"Jesus, Dad, I don't know. She's definitely very sick. We all need to fight this together." The whine in my own voice makes me yank at the shag rug.

"What do the doctors say?"

"They don't really say much."

"Do they think she's within hours or days of dying?"

I study the jumbled pile of my shoes and boots on my closet floor. Three seconds go by. "No."

"Do you need help caring for her?"

"Yes! Hello! I don't know what the hell I'm doing! It's freaking me out!" At least he's not *under*estimating me.

"Hire a health aide or a nurse. If insurance doesn't cover it, I'll figure out a way to pay for it."

Like it's as simple as that. It's not even about the cost—Fran's got plenty of money. This would be even harder if she didn't. And Harold said hospice could help with hiring an aide, but still. "You're not hearing me. *You* need to be here." I've never stood up to him like this because I was afraid he'd . . . dump me. Now I don't care.

He responds by shifting gears. "Is she conscious?"

He knows the answer. "Yes. Of course."

"Confined to bed?"

"Not completely. But she's weak and having huge pain spikes." I'm focusing on the photo taken from the very top of the Golden Gate Bridge that's in my collage on the far wall, *High Places.*

"It may be a longer process than you realize."

"You're willing to wait until she's *unconscious* before seeing her?" I ask incredulously.

"I will get out there as soon as I can. Give her my love."

And with that, he's gone.

I slam the phone down so hard the protective cover cracks.

# 32

## Saturday, August 15

The next morning, I obediently follow Harold to the kitchen for the comfort kit lesson. Fran is resting in her room.

He opens the refrigerator and pulls out the box. "It was a mistake not to go through this drill with you yesterday," he says. "I underestimated how soon she'd need this."

"Yep. Me too." His number is now permanently in my phone and brain.

So is the fact that a bunch of drugs sit on the refrigerator shelf. And now on the kitchen counter.

Inside the box are several dark glass dropper bottles and some papers. He picks up the vial I already opened. "You know this one. Liquid morphine."

Esmerelda will have something to say about this.

He turns the bottle in his palm. "When she has pain flare-ups and her present pain med dosage is becoming ineffective, you'll give her drops from this again. It may happen without going out to the theater."

"Right. Drops for pain spikes." I pick up a purple-and-red linen dishtowel.

"Also, closer to the end, she may not be able to take her meds by mouth. We'll give her drops then too." He pauses. "Are you a drug user, Delilah?" He repacks the morphine into the box.

*Closer to the end.*

"No," I answer.

He doesn't say anything.

"Um, I used to be a sometimes drug user and, uh, a drinker, but I've been totally clean and sober for eighteen months now." I'm folding and unfolding the towel.

"Wow. Congratulations." His raised eyebrows say he wasn't expecting that for an answer. "Can you be around these medications without being tempted to use them?"

"Yes."

Harold gazes down at me, his face hard. "These are controlled substances, and even though we can get them relatively quickly, it can take hours to restock. Which is not at all 'quick' when you're suffering a pain spike."

I nod. Even a few minutes seemed too long to wait last night.

"It's extremely important that these medications are here for your aunt if the going gets rough. Do you understand?"

"I understand. I have no desire to take any of this stuff." I back against the dishwasher and drop the towel by the sink. Wait a beat. Cross my arms. "Okay, not *no* desire, but I want to stay sober way more. Me and not-sober are a bad match. And I want plenty on hand in case Fran needs it again."

"Glad to hear it. I appreciate you being honest with me."

He explains the next bottle, Ativan, for relaxation and sleep. I'm already personally familiar with this one. Fortunately, prescription drug supplies at school were not steady or reliable.

"How will I know how much of what to use and when?" What would a couple of drops do for me right now? *Mellow you right out.* I concentrate on Harold's cool, clunky sports wristwatch on his thick wrist.

"I, or one of my colleagues, will guide you."

"Okay. I can call anytime, right?" I grab the towel again and wipe my damp hands on it. Hold it.

"Anytime. As the days wear on, she'll build up a tolerance to all her meds. And her pain may intensify." Harold speaks slowly, as if he wants these words to sink in.

"It could also get better," I say. "Don't you guys have anything to help her *improve*?"

"I understand that you're worried about Fran's illness and prognosis. But hospice is about comfort. Not cure." He gestures with the liquid Ativan bottle for emphasis.

Yeah, Dr. D'Silva was the cure department and she gave up on us.

He continues, "When Fran's pain or agitation levels seem to be rising, or if she's uncomfortable in any way, call us and the doctor will prescribe a higher dose of her regular meds. While you're waiting for the new prescriptions, you can supplement with drops."

"Okay."

Harold explains another medication for agitation. He pulls one more bottle out of the box. "This one's for secretions."

"Um. Out of which orifices?"

He smiles. "In the last hours, the esophageal muscles relax, and saliva and phlegm build up in the back of the throat—producing what's commonly referred to as a 'death rattle.' This dries it up."

"Sheesh." A little TMI. "I don't think we need to cover this now. Maybe ever."

Harold says gently, "Don't be afraid, Delilah. The dying process is natural. While everyone does it in ways as individual as they are, we know what to expect and how to keep the patient and their families comfortable, physically and emotionally."

"But not. Everyone. Dies. Right? In six months?" I demand. It's so annoying how everyone is ready to jump to conclusions here. To the literal conclusion of Fran's life.

"Not everyone, no," he finally allows.

"That's all I need to hear. An exception. Give me a crumb here, okay?"

"Our society has gotten so far away from death that we don't know how to act in its presence."

"Run screaming the other way."

He chuckles, kind of a frog sound. "I've been doing this for over ten years. The vast majority of our in-home patients die at peace."

"Really?" I open and close my locket. "Doesn't the end of existence have people freaking out?"

"Sometimes, yes. Dying is a process. It's important, a luxury even, to have the time to adjust, prepare, and accept." He puts the box back in the fridge. "I can think of a couple of patients who didn't find peace until the last hour or two, but many go joyfully to whatever and whoever's waiting."

For some reason, my entire chest expands and my breath comes quicker. "How do you know?"

"They tell me." He sits on one of the kitchen island stools, which seems comically tiny supporting his big self. It's kind of endearing. He points to one for me.

I sit. "They do?"

"I've heard some wonderful stories. I've seen and . . . felt some amazing things." His eyes shine.

"Huh." Cinematically, the sun burns through the last of the morning fog, and the living room and kitchen brighten.

Even if it's just the brain easing our way into nothingness, I'm glad the dying are convinced they're going to . . . something. Not that Fran will need it, but still.

"You're worried about Fran," he states, "and what happens to people after death."

"Uh, yeah. For someday."

"Are you religious?" he asks.

"Not really. Sort of Christian, but we didn't go to church much." I shrug. "I think it's silly to believe in something for which there's no proof." Not sure why I say this since it's not really true.

"I could argue that we have 'proof' for very little. That there are an infinite number of things we haven't grasped. It's kind of arrogant to assume that if there isn't scientific evidence for something, it doesn't exist. That we have everything figured out, or soon will, when we are surrounded by infinities." He gestures with his large palms. "Don't you think?"

"What do you mean by 'infinities'?"

"Time stretching out in any direction." He sweeps his arm. "A moment broken down into smaller and smaller fractions. Circles—cycles everywhere. Seasons, day and night, life and death."

"Right." I actually think of those a lot.

"And what about love?" he asks. "How do we measure and prove that?"

I do believe there's some force bigger than me; it's just not easy to chat about.

He clasps his hands. "Stay open, Delilah. With Fran. Listen and observe. You've been given a sacred responsibility here and you may be surprised at what you take away from it."

"Okay. I'll try. Thanks." He just gave me another idea.

He picks up his bag and heads to the front door. "See you next week."

# 33

## Monday, August 17

Aunt Fran calls me into her dim room around midmorning, usually her best time. James Taylor, singing about love, plays at low volume from her old boom box.

She says, "I have something important to talk to you about, sugar."

Her face is all tight. Uh-oh.

I'm bleary-eyed from staying up late researching. "That's fine because I have something to ask you too." As good a time as any to announce my new plan.

She shifts beneath her blankets in discomfort.

"What's your pain number?" I ask. "You took your pills, right?" The clock says two more hours before her next meds.

"Yes."

I slide open her window a little to let some fresh air in and some stale, BenGay-rub-scented air out.

Aunt Fran points at the overstuffed chair beside her bed. "What were you going to ask me?"

I sit. Touch her hand. "I was thinking that both of us . . . could meet Dad in France. Like soon."

Her eyebrows pop up.

I forge ahead. "In the south. I want us to go to the sanctuary of Our Lady of Lourdes."

"Lourdes?" The H crease at the top of her nose deepens.

"It's this town in southern France where there's a shrine to the Virgin Mary. And a spring, or fountain or something."

"Yes, I know it."

"Where many verified miracles have occurred. Inoperable cancer cured! You won't have to do anything. They're all set up for sick people. They have a million hotels—I already found a really cute bed-and-breakfast. We can rent a car, and a wheelchair—"

"Del." She shakes her head. "No. No miracles."

"Why not?" She has the money for this kind of trip and loves to travel. She's won't do cannabis oil, proton therapy, hyperthermia treatments, or any of the other cures I've suggested. And we need more than just the diet.

"I don't want to prolong this. The diagnosis and my prognosis are not . . . arguable." She grips the blueberry wool throw in her fists. "I'd—I'd like to take things into my own hands."

"What are you talking about?" She won't look at me. Her short hair sticks out like downy feathers.

Her alarm clock tick-tocks. A wailing siren passes right beneath us on the street below.

We stare at each other.

"Do—do you mean *suicide*?"

"The proper term is 'advancing the time of my death.'"

I clench my fists. "You're fucking kidding me!"

"I'm very serious," she says quietly.

"There's no way I would do that!"

"I'm the one who would . . . do it." She clasps her hands. "It's legal . . . in Oregon. I just need help—to get it set up.

I've lost the—" She pauses. "The . . . way to . . . set it up. The papers. The planes." She gestures weakly with her hand.

"What about the special diet? You're not even giving it a fair chance!"

She smooths the sheet in her lap, then says quietly, "Dr. Smith is listed . . . prominently on QuackWatch."

"What?" It's probably another Dr. Smith. "I've seen the studies that prove that flaxseed oil works on cancer cells!"

"Darlin', a lot of people out there are happy to . . . take advantage of the ill and the dying. Help me set *this* up."

"*This* is a terrible, stupid idea! Like, 'when you have a moment, could you come in here and murder me, please?'"

"No," she says patiently, "it's 'will you help me . . . end my suffering?'"

*Mom curled up like a roly-poly in her own bed, and then stretched flat and on a respirator in the hospital bed.*

Fran takes a ragged breath. "It's getting worse. Fast. I can't . . . wait much longer."

"How can you know for sure—?"

"I know. When was the last time you were around a dying cancer patient?" Her voice is sharp.

I cross my arms. "When were *you*? Yourself doesn't count."

"Your grandmother died of breast cancer and your grandfather of lung cancer. I told you. I spent months with him. It was awful near the end. Dragged on and on."

That poem she wrote. I never asked about it. "But you're at home!"

She closes her eyes tight.

*For fuck's sake*, I think as I search the ceiling for help, *try not to be so self-centered.* "I don't understand why you want to do this," I say, as evenly as possible.

She grabs my wrist, which is still a little scabby. "Oh, sugar, there're lots of reasons. I'm afraid of the *pain* of dying."

"Me too. For you, I mean." When she's hurting, it makes me want to throw up. "But Harold says we can control it."

She shakes her head. "I'm afraid of putting you through all this."

"What? Oh no you don't! You can't use me as an excuse!" I shout. "Helping you die would suck way more!"

"What your grandpa went through, how hard it was for me—I don't want that for you. Plus, losing control of a body . . . is *inelegant*." She emphasizes the word, proud to have thought of it. "Sores, dementia, in . . . continence. We make it easier on all of us by—to . . . stream . . . the process. That's what I want to do. Stream*line* the . . . final stage."

I can't meet her desperate hazel eyes. I thought I knew her. I thought she loved me. I thought she was sane.

I blurt out, "You can't just leave me!"

She flinches. Stares at me.

"I—It's just—this is what I fight so hard against, trying to *stop* people from offing themselves!"

I don't say *including me*.

I hug myself and shake my head. "I can't. I won't! I won't help—bring about the end of your life."

Silence.

This is bullshit! She's out of her mind!

I back out and slam the door.

# 34

## Tuesday, August 18

I've called Savannah, who listened patiently but didn't offer much in the way of solutions. I've texted Esmerelda, who suggested informing Dad.

Yeah, right. I Skyped him but couldn't get through. Which, come to think of it, is actually a silver lining.

Nick would have something wise to say about this if I could ever talk to him.

Now it's morning. Harold arrives and checks Fran's vitals and puts in requests for a list of health aides, plus a bedside toilet. I corner him on his way out. "Have time for a quick green tea?"

"A glass of water would be great."

I get us each one from the kitchen and lead him to the two chairs and small game table in the far corner of the living room, since I'd rather Fran didn't hear us. Things are a teensy bit strained between us.

Out the big windows, a thick white fog blankets the bay and covers Alcatraz. The city's trapped under heavy cloud cover too. The gray light flattens everything and dulls all Fran's colors in here.

"Harold, what do you think about assisted suicide?" I ask in a low voice.

He doesn't miss a beat. "I'd want to know why a patient was considering it." He swallows about half of his water in two gulps and sets his glass down.

"To end their suffering." I use Aunt Fran's words.

"But we can keep almost anyone comfortable." He gestures with both palms up. "That's our whole reason for being. No one should have to suffer." A thick gold wedding ring gleams on his left hand.

"Okay. What about to keep loved ones from having to watch you die?"

Harold manspreads in the armchair. "Delilah, dying is an important part of life." He says this with no trace of irony. "Watching a loved one die is part of the grieving process, and the living process. It's not helping or right to 'protect' someone from it."

"What about kids?" Technically I'm an adult, but I don't feel like one right now.

"Kids may need help with loss and grief. But they'll accept death, when it's not hidden and pathologized—treated as abnormal, or unhealthy."

I set my glass on the table. My words catch in my throat. "I didn't accept my mom's death that well."

Harold tilts his head and scrunches his forehead in concern. "How old were you?"

"Thirteen."

"Did she die at home?"

"No. It was . . . a car accident."

Harold sits up straight. He says softly, "I'm sorry, Delilah."

"Thanks. Yeah, everyone freaked out when it happened

and then kind of shut down." Or at least my dad did. All my mom's friends faded away afterward. I didn't see as much of Fran back then. Maybe things would've been different if I had.

"That's a shame," says Harold. "Kids take their cues from the adults. They can be spared some details, but being honest with them makes loss *easier*." He inhales, his barrel chest expanding to twice its size. "I was fourteen when my grandma died of stomach cancer, after almost two years of suffering. Six months later, Pawpaw followed her. I helped nurse them both." He gazes out the tall window to the east. "Sat with them as they drew their last breaths. It was hard, but it shaped and enriched the rest of my life."

"Wow. You lived with them?"

"Yes, ma'am. Lincoln Parish, northern Louisiana." He holds up his glass. "We were so poor, Sunday dinner was fried water." He flashes white teeth that he doesn't often show.

"Who did you live with after they died?"

"My oldest sister and her husband."

MIA parents like mine. I sip my water then put it on the table. "Harold, what if someone wants to 'take control' of their death?"

"Are we talking about Fran?" he asks gently.

I nod.

He clears his throat. "I believe that control is an illusion, and that death teaches us that."

His words jab me in a way I wasn't expecting. "Okay then. Good to know." I throw up my hands in mock surrender. "All I *do* is try to control my emotions, my anxiety, my fear, my instability. If it's all an illusion then I'm in deep shit."

Harold chuckles. "Controlling ourselves is one thing. Controlling the world outside of us is another."

"You haven't even mentioned that there's always the chance to get better."

He opens his mouth to say something, closes it, waits another beat. "We have free will during the dying process like at any other time. But we all gotta die."

"I know that." It would be impolite to say *duh*. "But what if someone can't bear—is like, too fragile to go through it all emotionally?"

He blinks slowly. "They can and do."

The vacuum marks in the pale carpet hold my attention. *Harold doesn't understand who he's talking to.* "I might be the exception."

He smiles. "I think you should give yourself more credit, Delilah. The dying process, the final stage, is a rewarding and deeply important part of living. Most of us can go all the way through life and not deal with certain things. Choices we made. Lies we've told ourselves. Lies we've told others. If we have the luxury of the time to make peace with our lives, I believe we're meant to do it."

I want to grab his arm but refrain. "Do you think a person can still do that if they choose the time to die?"

"Maybe. But I fear that a person misses out—that the same full process doesn't take place when you make an appointment to die."

I blurt out, "I don't know what will happen to *me* if she dies."

He pauses. "Do you have other family?"

"Yeah, my dad. But we seem to do better apart."

He reaches over and awkwardly pats my arm. "We're watching out for you too. You'll get through this."

Harold picks up his bag and holds it in his lap. "Attending to people who are working to accept death on its own terms is my whole reason for being. So, you see why I can't support advancing the time of Fran's death." His firmness is reassuring.

"Is this the official hospice position?"

"No. Any number of people associated with hospice disagree with me." He glances at his watch. He stands.

"People do ask us about it regularly. As a rule, we allay their fears, the desire goes away, and they die on their own natural schedule. Peacefully." We walk to the front door.

"That's totally what I want for Fran."

He nods and turns to go.

"Harold?"

He turns. "Yes?"

"Isn't it hard being around dying people all the time?"

"Sometimes. There's suffering. And fear and loneliness. But we do our best to help with all that. It's an honor and a privilege for me," he says. "I can't imagine doing anything else."

# 35

That afternoon, Louis stands at the front door of the apartment with a bakery box. His lime-green T-shirt beneath his blazer pops against the beige foyer.

"Nice shirt. Thanks for coming by!" I take the box. Spinach quiche. "Yum. Thanks," I say. I might be thanking him too much.

"Been meaning to visit for the last two weeks," he says. "It's just been so busy."

"You're running everything by yourself." He needs more of my help, but I can't be away from Fran that much. "It's been a long week here too."

He politely refuses anything to drink and heads for the living room while I stash the quiche in the kitchen.

Fran shuffles out in her plum silk robe. "Louis, angel! Sight for sore eyes." She's breathing a little hard.

Louis leaps up. "Fran!" His face falls. He's barely seen her in person lately. They talk on the phone. But she's changing, and today she hasn't made any effort to prettify herself.

They embrace. She used to be wider than he is. Not so much now.

"How are you? How's Hassan?" She will not look at me. We've been exchanging only the most necessary information about meds, meals, and laundry.

"I'm fine. We're great. He sends his love. How are you?" He steps back and looks her over.

"Getting . . . as you can see. The cat dragged in. Feeling okay."

His mouth is open but nothing comes out.

Fran plops into the overstuffed armchair and slowly lifts her silk-slippered feet onto the ottoman. We sit too. "Tell me about . . . things."

He pushes his shoulders down and takes a breath. "I almost sold Caroline's Number Six, but they balked."

"Who?"

"The couple from Atherton. They're still thinking about it. Without you there to double-team them with me, I'm striking out more than I'd like."

"Nonsense," she says.

He runs his hand over his dark hair. "Meanwhile we've sold all her small ones."

"Price . . . is right."

"I have some more news. Or really, it's dirt." He smiles. "I ran into Johnny James at a party last night."

"Who's that?" I ask him.

"He owns a stodgy gallery and snubbed us last year." He turns to Fran. "I casually let it drop that Caroline's paintings are selling fast as overpriced yoga attire. He looked so disappointed."

"Ha!" I laugh.

Fran nods noncommittally. A couple of months ago she would have hooted. Hopped up and down.

There's a pause. Louis says, "Christie called and said she's ready to ship us the seesaw series. And Jorge's on track for November."

Fran's got a thousand-yard stare. "Okay."

Louis and I exchange looks. Her old enthusiasm is completely missing.

She says, "Have you ever told Del?"

"Told her what?"

"Told me what?" I ask.

"About your friend?"

"I, uh—" He grips the chair arms. He pauses. Breathes in and stares at his lap. "I had a close friend who commi—completed suicide a couple of years ago."

Ah. That might explain some of his hostility toward me, since I'm the suicide poster child. "I'm really sorry."

"Thanks." He crosses his arms tightly, as if to physically block us from getting more information out of him. "When do your classes start?"

"Next week. But I'll be adjusting my schedule. So I can be here."

"Good." He nods longer than necessary.

Silence settles over us all. Louis shifts as he studies Fran. She's staring out at the distant bay.

"Fran," Louis says quietly, "can I ask what you are thinking as far as the future of the Lone Star?"

"It has a bright one," she says with a ghost of a smile.

"Are you planning on selling it?" he asks.

I hold my breath. What *is* she thinking? For six months from now? For a year from now? A muscle in Louis's temple flexes.

She finally shakes her head. "No." She reaches for his hand. Holds it. "I want you to run it. Best you can."

He breathes out. Swallows. "Good to know. I promise you I will." He looks at me. "I hope I can count on your help too, Del."

"Of course." It's weird that he's talking like this, about what will happen after Fran dies. Even weirder that he wants my help with anything when he won't have to accept it.

He shifts again in his seat. "I'm glad that you're here with her."

"Me too." An idea pops into my brain. "Speaking of which, we need to hire someone to help. Fran doesn't like the thought that she can't be left alone for any length of time. But she can't." I add, "Dad's footing the bill, if insurance doesn't cover it." I don't say, *I've got to get out of here more.*

"No, I'm . . . a babysitter's okay," says Fran. She's concentrating hard and seems clearheaded this morning, but she still won't meet my gaze. "Maybe *they'll* help me," she adds.

I ignore that comment and stand. "Uh, could you help me with something in the kitchen?" I ask Louis, jutting my chin in that direction.

He gets the hint. "Sure." And follows me.

I get three glasses out of the cabinet. "She wants to off herself."

"What?" His hand covers his heart as if for the Pledge of Allegiance.

"Assisted suicide."

"Mother of God!" He lowers his voice. "That's so . . . difficult. What an idea." He blows out a breath. "Is she—why?"

"You should ask her. I guess she's scared. Dealing with more pain . . ." I trail off.

I fill the glasses with tap water and he glances at my tattoo. "Don't worry," I say. "It won't happen on my watch. Ice?"

"No, thanks. And . . . that's good to hear. Anything I can do?"

I ask, "Could you help with interviewing health aides?

I have no clue how to do that. But I've got a list of candidates from Harold."

"I'd be happy to. I could narrow it down to two or three and then you can see who's a good fit."

"Awesome! Thank you." I lower my voice again. "We need someone, like, *really* strong, in case they need to help move her around."

"Heard that," says Fran from the living room.

# 36

## Wednesday, August 19

It's almost 3 a.m. and I can't sleep. Nick's only here a few more days, and I'm dying to talk to him about Fran.

I toss and turn all night but finally sleep a little.

As soon as I open my eyes Wednesday morning, I text him. **Are you at the lab? Can I call?**

No response.

;

Louis, on the other hand, has texted me a list of health aides. I call them first thing in the morning. Two of them agree to come to the Lone Star at 9:30 and 10:00 today, and Louis and I interview them. We both like Libby best, only she can't start until Sunday, four long days away. We hire her anyway. Louis helps me set up direct payment from Fran's account. Thank goodness Fran's made big bucks. What would I do if she were sick like this and lost her job and insurance and *didn't* have money socked away?

On the way home from the gallery, I pick up some mild channa masala takeout for lunch. At home I coax Fran into eating some of hers and double-check she's taken all her meds. Her friend Lacey comes over to watch a movie with her.

Still no reply from Nick. And when's Dad planning to show up?

After my AA meeting, I've got plenty of time before the extra BAC shift I've agreed to cover tonight. So I take Fran's car, without permission, to Berkeley. She'll understand.

Even though I've driven this route recently and have the GPS, I'm beyond out-of-my-comfort-zone, dodging speeding lane-changers and trying not to crash or end up in Sacramento.

Somehow, I manage to snag a parking spot on the street a block from Nick's apartment. After a few calming deep breaths and a tissue-mop of my face and pits, I ring the front buzzer and the main door unlocks.

Up a flight of stairs where dust bunnies lounge in the corners, I knock on the beat-up wooden door that should be his. It's papered with torn-off bumper stickers from the last fifty years: *The Oakland A's, Make Love Not War, Four out of three people have trouble with fractions.*

A guy in a black T-shirt and plaid boxers answers the door.

"Hi!" I say, all chipper. "I'm Del, a friend of Nick's. Is he around?"

He regards me over his glasses. "Hey, Del," he says like he knows me. "He's gotta be over at the lab. You know where it is, right?"

"I forgot."

He gives me vague instructions and I thank him.

According to my phone, it's kind of far. I walk several blocks to the edge of campus, then hike through the massive Sproul Plaza, which is crowded with crisscrossing students and tourists. I'm breathing a little hard and it can't be from the walk. I slow down, count breaths, and study the university buildings around me—traditional brick, and clunky modern concrete. It would be so cool if I were smart and balanced enough to live in a dorm or an apartment at Cal. But it's huge. Intimidating. Scary.

SFSU is not that different, I remind myself. It's big, too, but feels easier somehow. A reduced schedule for the fall will be okay. Good, even.

Baby steps.

I pass through the wrought-iron Sather Gate, and coming right at me in a small group is a tall, dark-haired figure in glasses, accompanied by a dog in a harness.

Ohmigod, Nick!

He's with two other guys.

And a girl.

Long glossy dark hair, slender.

*She's holding Nick's free hand.*

I crack into a thousand ice shards.

"Hey! Del!" Nick calls. Surprise amplifies his voice. He drops the girl's hand.

I pivot to run. Only they're too close. I have to turn back.

"Hi, Nick!" I try to sound upbeat even though all my internal organs shriveled.

"Hey, guys, this is my friend Delilah." He introduces someone and someone, and then, "This is Bassima."

"Hi." I stretch my lips. "Nice to meet y'all." Noor looks at me impassively.

"Delilah's aunt and my mom are childhood friends," he says.

"Yeah, we've known each other since we were tykes," I add. Omigod, did I say *tykes*?

Bassima is studying me like I'm a formaldehyde-pickled appendix. She's beautiful.

Everyone stares at me. No one says: *What are you doing here?* Even though it's clear the question is flaming in each and every brain.

"Yeah, I happened to be in the neighborhood," I say. "Um, stopped by your place, and then was going to head this way, and—so amazing that here you are. Ha."

Nick says, "We're going to grab a quick pizza. Want to join us?" His tone is as neutral as Switzerland.

Bassima crosses her arms.

"No! That's okay, I just ate," I lie. Having a garbage truck back over my legs sounds like more fun. "I was just going to say hello and all. So, hello! And now I better get back. To the city. Nice to meet y'all."

I missile out of there.

# 37

I jog my leaden self as far as the edge of campus, where a DON'T WALK crosswalk sign to Telegraph Avenue stops me. *Get back to the car. Then you can melt down in peace.*

"Del, wait!" Nick calls from behind me. I turn. He's breathing hard, Noor jogging at his side. I must've run faster than I thought.

"Is there something you want to tell me?" I blurt out when he's a few feet away from me, gripping Noor's leash. Maybe he can explain everything. Maybe it's not what it seemed like.

He hesitates as determined pedestrians weave around us.

"About Bassima?" I prompt. But my voice cracks.

Nick sighs. "This is a tough summer for you. I don't want to hurt you."

That sinks in for several beats.

I croak like a frog, "Seems like it's kind of unavoidable, huh?"

He talks to the ground. "We work together."

"Nick. I know we're not, like, together." *Other than in your brain.* "I'm glad you've met someone you like." I force this huge lie past my lips. "She's another intern?"

"No, she's an undergrad here."

"Premed?"

"Yeah," he says sadly.

"Damn. I see. Don't forget, though. I'm your type."

He doesn't respond.

"So is *she* a suicidal, alcoholic fuckup?"

He reaches for my arm, then stops himself. He's looking at me like he might kiss me! Isn't he? "Nothing's happened yet, Del."

"But it could."

The WALK sign across the street counts down from "5" to the stop hand.

He makes a frustrated noise in his throat that prompts Noor to glance up at him with concern. "Not how I wanted to do this."

*This* could only be telling me there's someone else and to leave him alone. I get that I like him more than he likes me. But my bones are cracking, crumbling, my rib cage caving in.

"Can I still talk to you and stuff?" I ask.

"Of course!"

With Bassima in the picture, our texts and calls will become rarer and rarer. He's only here for another week anyway. Then he'll be in school or interning at some hospital for the next ten years at least. I need to let him go—wrench him from my heart, like hacking out an entire ventricle-chamber thingy.

"Okay," I say. "If she does anything you don't like, I'll come kick her ass."

He doesn't laugh but says, "Good to know." He's standing so close. I imagine I hear his heartbeat. His warm hand rests on my upper arm as a slight breeze ruffles his hair. The limey scent of his soap and his trace-of-peanut-butter-cracker breath fill my head. He's gazing into my eyes. "I don't—We—"

I clench my fingers until they cramp.

"How's Fran?" he asks.

"You already know she's on hospice care. They give her a couple of months. It's what I came over to talk to you about." That, and how she wants to off herself now.

"Oh! Really sorry! We could grab a quick coffee!"

"I have to get back. I'll give her your best."

"Wait. I could come over—"

"No!" I burst out. "It will just make things worse. Do not play with my—with my—affection!" I cross the street and don't look back because if I have to watch *him* walk away, my bones will disintegrate right out from under me, and my three-chambered heart will drop in the middle of that big red puddle of pain and sorrow that is me, and someone will have to mop all that shit up.

# 38

I drive in slo-mo, hugging the right-hand lane on the bridge even though it's closest to the edge. Because it's closest to the edge.

The wall between me and the bay below is much too thick and high to crash through, but probably I could get enough speed up, hit the side and flip over. I'd hurtle toward the bay below and hit the surface like a brick on concrete. Then sink gracefully to the bottom as seawater rushes in. I might be upside down. If I were conscious, I could breathe in the air pocket. Until I couldn't. Then slip down into the icy, deadly darkness.

People pass and honk. I focus on the white lines running by the car for dear life.

;

Fran's door is open. She's watching an old movie. I burst into her room instead of heading straight for the comfort box.

"Sugar? You look . . . like the cheese fell off your cracker," she says. She clicks the remote to turn off the television.

"Nick's seeing some girl." I should leave it at that, but I can't help myself. "I ran into them together. On campus."

"Oh, sweetie." Sympathetic as she sounds, her face says she's wondering how I got over there.

"I took the Prius but it was an emergency."

She doesn't say anything. I should've asked. Six months ago there would've been consequences. Now it just slides by.

"She's beautiful and intellectually way more up his alley than I am. Cal student. Premed."

Fran tries to sit up. Winces. "Don't forget . . . opposites."

She means they attract. And that I'm the opposite of calm, smart Nick. "Plus, I never told you. A man I talked to at the crisis line completed suicide a week and a half ago. I messed up."

"Oh, no." Her face collapses.

"So I've been wrestling with that." I can't help but add, "People have no idea what a psychic mess they leave behind. I completely understand how beyond caring they are by that point. But they have no idea."

Trying to convince her. And myself.

She doesn't react.

"I just—" I plop into her chair and pull at my hair. "Anyone else would've turned this summer into a beautiful love story. But I'm too messed up for a real relationship."

"Nonsense." She reaches out and pulls me into a weak hug. "I'm so sorry, darlin'. I know. How much . . . you feel him. So hard. I wish . . ." Her forehead's wrinkled in pain, or the frustration of trying to talk.

My fatigue, hurt feelings, and fear all spill over into tears. I bow my head so Fran won't see. But she does.

To my horror, she lets out a strangled sound as *her* bleary eyes fill, and she rocks forward and back. "My fault."

"Oh! God!" I cry, swiping at my face. "It's—it's okay, Aunt Fran. It's not your fault! Please, ohmigosh, it's really okay."

But it's so not okay. I'm going to implode.

# 39

I tell Aunt Fran I'm going to see a friend and don't wait around for her to ask any follow-up questions. With my backpack, I flee down the hill to a Fisherman's Wharf park bench on a triangle of grass across from the old brick Cannery. The sun has already slipped behind Fort Mason. It's twilight, normally my favorite time.

Not day. Not night.

Balanced. On the edge.

This evening's fading light is weighted with premonitions of the gaping, dark, boundary-less void. Not to mention an icy wind. I don't answer Esmerelda's call—we were going to work on my ninth step after tonight's meeting, which has come and gone. She's texted me twice. So now I text back: **Something came up. Sorry!**

It's only a matter of time before Esmerelda checks with Aunt Fran, or vice versa, and then my game is up.

It doesn't matter.

⁏

Everyone gets a glimpse of the void at some time in their life, but otherwise it's "out of sight, out of mind." Its presence often hovers ahead of me, an immense and icy fog bank. I've floated, frozen, within it like castoff space junk endlessly rotating around Earth. It's *not* just in my head. The void is really there. It's the infinity of space, or time, or what's beyond the material world, or *inside* the world at the subatomic or quantum levels. All of which are 99.9-out-thirteen-decimal-points-percent *empty space*.

Most people's realities are shielded from the void's gaping maw. Those of us with brains whose protective mechanisms are rattle-y or missing are constantly reminded of the way reality really is, in all its crushing immensity.

It's freezing, and the fog is rushing in over the whole city and the bay. Foghorns bellow.

One of the pseudo-British, bright red double-decker tourist buses roars by, blasting me with diesel exhaust.

"Fran's dying and cannot get better," I say to no one. I lean my head back against the bench edge.

*I* could get better.

And was.

Until now.

A completely silver-clad robot performance artist walks by, balancing a boom box like Fran's on his shoulder, headed home from Fisherman's Wharf. He stares a little too long at me before he moves on.

His silver hat reminds me of Osgood's black one.

*So. Del. Why did you call this meeting?*

I'm afraid. I can't take it anymore. Fran's so sick. Wants to speed things up for Chrissakes.

The cold, damp breeze whips my hair.

*At least you're past denying it.*

I've already practically lost her. She's too sick to be there for me anymore.

I'm scared about where she's . . . going. Nowhere. Big black nothing.

I might have to go live with Dad. I hated being in London whenever I visited. All the clouds and rain and giant buses on the wrong side of the road. All the evidence that Dad sees me as a burden.

And, yeah, Nick can't be there for me either. Have I ever been there for *him*? No. It's been all about me.

*Because you're too unstable and self-centered for an intimate relationship.*

I wring my hands. I know I should fight it with all my might, but I'm slipping into that place.

*The true, dark nature of the world reveals itself when you stop pedaling so hard.*

The drugs in the comfort kit. Would be so comforting.

*So would vodka.*

I hug my shoulders and rest my chin on my chest. The void. Where nothing matters. Everything is gray and pointless.

A big crowd of zitty adolescents file by with their chaperones. They look like they're from somewhere in the Midwest, all wearing matching navy sweatshirts with Christian fish on the back. A couple of them stare at me.

I remember the homeless guy on the bus.

And Osgood.

Osgood flying off that building.

All the black nothingness of space. I hold out my thumb and forefinger like an olive's pinched between them. Our tiny marble of blue and green, only half in the light. Up beyond the clouds and the atmosphere, dark outweighs light a million to one. Nothingness outweighs something—same kind of ratio. Give or take.

*Darkness will always prevail. The sooner you accept that, the sooner you'll find peace.*

Peace. Ceasing the struggle.

I stand up. My hands and legs tremble. I can't take it anymore.

# 40

I get on the next bus, which goes through North Beach, then crowded red-and-gold Chinatown, past vegetable markets, ginseng and herb stores full of products probably offloaded from those huge tankers coming into Oakland. International banks, dim sum parlors and bakeries, and on toward Union Square and all the department stores and label boutiques.

On Market Street, I switch to a pumpkin-orange streetcar originally from Milan that's heading for the Castro and lean against the window. My finger traces the semicolon on my wrist. I picture my head exploding.

First things first. At the next stop, I jump off and walk into the grungy convenience store that sells liquor.

A middle-aged woman sits behind the counter cluttered with candy, gum, breath mints, and five-hour energy-shot display boxes. In a mature voice with a reasonably good French accent, I say, "A bottle of vodka, please."

"ID," she says, putting her palm out. Her dragon-red fingernails with tiny black beads across them accuse me.

I pull out my official-looking fake European Union student ID that I got when I was sixteen.

"Hmmm, never seen one of these before," she says. "Madeleine L'Oreal?" She holds it up to check the hologram in the light.

"Oui."

"From France." She squints at the card, then studies me with one eye closed.

"Yes, but here for a year. How you say? Working." The sweat glands in my armpits are what's working.

"Pretty good English."

"Thank you."

She hands me a dusty bottle of vanilla vodka.

"Um, do you have mandarin orange? Or blackberry?"

She gives me a look.

"This is trés bien." I pay and stick my cash in my jeans pocket.

Back behind the store, I park myself on a curb by the trash bin, despite the odor. One weak alley light glows urine-yellow back here. A beat-up old VW van painted with psychedelic mural art leans in the far corner. The smell of rotten food settles around me like my mood.

A big swallow from the bottle is lighter fluid going down and tastes absolutely terrible and awesome at once. No time has elapsed since my last shot of peach schnapps in the dark Ridgefield broom closet. Such a relief to cease the struggle, to give in to the warmth and ease and rightness.

Another couple of glugs hit my empty stomach like napalm. Easy there, Captain.

I'm not supposed to mix alcohol with my meds.

Too bad.

A few minutes later a young, smooth-skinned security guy shows up. Where the hell did he come from? A couple of inches of the vodka is already gone and hitting me like a velvet-covered hammer.

That would make a dope drink name. Oh, it already is.

Used to have a high tolerance. Probably don't now. Might should keep that in mind. I screw the top on and stash it behind me. It tips over, clunking. *Omigod don't break!*

"Ma'am, everything all right back here?"

"Yep. I'm, uh, needed to do some . . . thinking," I reply.

Rhymes with drinking. Don't say that out loud.

"Outdoor consumption of hard alcohol is illegal. I need to see your ID."

He's not a real cop.

"What alcohol?" I hand him my ID.

He rolls his eyes. "We check back here regularly. This is not a good place to hang out. France, huh?"

"Alll righty. I'm practically a cop myself, by the way," I say. "I deal with desperate people."

"Excuse me?" He's frowning.

"Bay Area Crisis. Ever heard of it? I talk people into not completing suicide. Among other things." I pull out my phone to illustrate.

The guy takes a step back. "Bay Area Crisis. You're calling them?"

"No, dude, I *work* there."

"You work on the crisis line," he states. Not sure if he believes me.

"Yep." I prove it. "Hi, Bay Area Crisis, this is Del. Are you feeling suicidal?"

His walkie-talkie crackles. He pulls it out with one hand and gives me back my ID with the other. "What's your address in the city?" he asks me.

I give it to him.

"Okay. This isn't a good place."

"So I gathered from the needles and shit back here."

"You might want to head home."

"Fine. Fine. I'll go home. No problemo."

He's shaking his head as he jogs back around to the front, presumably toward something more important than a French girl trying to get hammered. Oops, forgot to use my French accent.

I shuffle out. My legs are all rubbery and the parking lot is tilting. I haven't been drunk in so long. I aim for the bus stop.

On a streetcar, the crowd swallows me and I barely flinch. *'Cause you're brave.* Someone gets up and I fall into their seat. People's faces sharpen and recede. The warmth and looseness coursing through me from the inside out makes me glow like a spotlight.

The Castro! I get off at a stop. Looks like a good bar street. Whoops, stumbling down the steps. Only a little. *You're okay.* The rest of that vodka is waiting in my backpack.

Where the hell is my backpack? Shit. Left it on the bus.

No, ha! It's on my back. But not worth the struggle, practically gymnastics to get it off.

A rainbow bar ahead is a good idea. With lots of people.

It's kinda dark, but that's some shiny zinc. My ID again, act sober. Cute bartender and a fireball shot.

Sooooo good. Wham! Burns going down. Say that out loud. "Burns so good going down!" Ha! Pretty funny.

Here's some friends.

"My name's Del. I mean Madeleine. Some people call me Del for Delilah. I, um, both."

Ha! We're all funny! Shana and Ashley from Twin Peaks. Which one?

"Nice to meetcha, Christian. Are you? Ha!"

"Thanks! I like your tat *too*. That's why they call 'em that!"

"Another round! How old? Just turned twenty-one. Celebrating."

"Here's a twenty, plus one quarter."

"No, I said, Not going to think about *Fran!*"

"Fran and Dad have an ancestor from flipping Jamestown. And Mom's Czech grandpa died in a mental hospital."

"I wouldn't be in this mess. If Mom hadn't crashed. Yep, a wall."

"I'm here 'cause Nick dumped me! But I'm okay."

"Right?"

"No dude I suuuuck at pool."

"I jus love him SO much we're soul mates but not anymore. Yeah, text him! Good idea."

"Gotta cigarette? Getta pack."

Gotta pee. Whole 'nother stinky bathroom. Not that drunk.

Gotta sit down a minute. Didn't answer.

Concert in the park? For sure. Woo-hoo! Up for anything.

;

Crowded in here nobody should wear seatbelts. Where'd you get this car? Mongolia?

Anyone want wanilla wodka?

Twenty-one questions! Pass that blunt.

Shit for lungs.

Fuck I'm high.

No, the answer is . . . canola oil.

Jus following you. Look out for . . .

Can you hear the music what is that shit?

Just a puff.

Bourbon's brilliant. Dancing's easy. Did ya think I was easy? Ha! UN-easy! Not likely gimme that bottle.

Know what? I won't survive with no Fran. Poof. I'll be gone. Like that. No, I need a grown-up to live with my whole life.

Better band for sure. Gotta pee. Whose mom? No, Fran's my mom.


;


Portapotty smells like shit can't see get up iss okay whoa spinning . . .

As a skunk

How did that get there?

How did I get here

Wait that's not them was on this side right? Where are youuu? Chriiiiiiiistian? Can you hear me


;


Dancing jus a little.

Forgettin' jus a little.

Whoa spinning.


;

One foot afront of the other
    Sorry, 'scuze me. NOT sorry.
    Fuck you. No, fuck YOU. Watch your Hey! ass out you don
wanna mess wanna piece of me?
    Fuckin asshole! Don touch me! That pushing me!
    Running super girl shit Soorrrrry
    Whew
    Oh god
    gonna be sick—

# 41

## Thursday, August 20

I wake up in gray early-morning light. Under a ratty blanket. In a bush. My mouth tastes like used kitty litter.

Where the hell am I?

Golden Gate Park?

A raggedy older lady in a worn purple T-shirt and beat-to-hell hiking boots is a few feet away. She was pulling me by the arm at some point? Pushed me into the bushes! Oh, yeah. Two guys. Grabbing at me. I remember running, like through Jell-O. An adrenaline rush. She must've saved my butt. Oh, god, my head hurts.

What a flaming brick I am.

My phone and some cash are still nestled in my jeans pocket. Miraculous.

The woman stirs and bolts upright. "Motherfucker!" she exclaims to no one in particular.

"Thank you," I say.

Not what she was expecting. "You one dumbass lucky bitch," she says, shaking her matted hair. "Got an angel watching out for you."

I stand, and a huge wave of nausea crashes over me. Deep

breaths in between gags.

I hand two twenties to her, along with the blanket. Keep the ten to get home.

"Thank you," I repeat.

She grimaces. Or maybe it's a smile.

My backpack is nowhere to be found.

Shit.

Had it in the bar but don't remember it in the car. Nausea hits again. My credit card, MUNI pass, and un-cashed Lone Star paycheck.

Oh, no, no, no.

My locket.

From Fran. Her grandmother's. Why did I take it off?

*So you wouldn't lose it.*

My eyes and throat burn and I blink hard.

I don't know where in the park I am, don't know the park that well to begin with, and heading east toward the sunrise won't work because, fog. I hike to the nearest road, JFK Drive, and follow it out to the avenues. My head throbs with each step. Another wave of nausea forces me to stop to puke, and there's nothing to puke. A sniff of my T-shirt suggests I emptied my stomach pretty well last night.

I pick at the pottery-shard memories of the last eleven or so hours. The couple who listened to me wail about Fran and Nick. Faces, sympathetic and amused in the darkness of that bar. I got in a car with them. Yeah. We were smoking and vaping some powerful shit. Drinking, of course.

Tromping through the park with them, oblivious to a crowd of people. Flashlights. Some concert.

Oh, yeah. Like weird folk music. Dancing! Was I dancing to *folk music*? Hope I kept my clothes on.

I'm lucky to be alive.

Sudden fear guts me and I check my phone. The screen has a crack the shape of a pitchfork.

Two texts from Esmerelda. One text and one missed call from BAC.

Oh, crap! I missed the fill-in shift I said I'd take last night.

Two Aunt Fran where-are-you texts, then a bunch of missed calls from her, the first one at 11:05 p.m. and again at 11:52 and 2:05 a.m. A last text at 5:24 a.m.

I text Fran so fast I make a mess of it and have to delete and start over.

**I'm all right. Home within the hour. Are you okay?**

Thank god she texts back. She doesn't answer my question.

Then I see the text I sent Nick. Double crap.

**Pleasant don leave mean**

I might as well step into traffic now. Nick'll never talk to me again.

It's 7:58 a.m. and when a bus headed east comes, I get on and stagger to a seat. Crude oil boils in my stomach. At the next stop, someone sits down beside me, then gets up and moves to a forward seat.

I rub my face but it jiggles the pain in my head. "Ow."

I need crackers.

The next stop is Divisadero Street and I get off. In a small convenience store, I grab a package of Cheez-Its and a bottle of water.

From the drink case, I gingerly take a cheap beer. Rows of pint bottles of hard stuff beckon from behind the register.

Just one beer for relief. The lady doesn't card me when I pay, probably because I've aged ten years. My fake ID is gone with my backpack.

Outside, I chug the whole can.

After a good burp, my stomach does feel better.

The next bus isn't due for eight minutes, so I perch on the seats at the bus stop shelter. Nurses in scrubs, moms and kids, and surly adolescent boys with their pants below their asses parade by as I pine for a couple of those bottles of crystal-clear vodka inside.

Facing Aunt Fran will suck sewer pipes.

*What do you want to do, Delilah? Go drink some more? Go to one of the bridges and jump?*

Behind closed eyes I picture both of those eventualities. A shot sounds better for now.

My cracked phone rings. It's Esmerelda.

I'm about to send her to voicemail. Instead, I tap to answer, even though it'll be a shit tornado.

"Hi, Ez."

"Hi! Del!" She didn't expect to get me. "Are you okay?"

"Yeah," I say.

"Where are you?"

"At a bus stop."

"We had a date yesterday. You stood me up, lady."

"I know. My bad." I massage my forehead before realizing how filthy my hands are.

"Besides that, I was worried about you. So were others." She pauses so I get her drift. Fran must've called her. "I know what's going on with you right now is tough. But I also know it's not anything you can't stay sober through. You want to tell me the latest?" she asks.

"I went out. Got blotto last night."

I wait for her to say something. She doesn't.

I continue, "Spent the night in the park. Oh, and . . . just chugged a beer."

"I'm glad you're okay. Anything precipitate this?"

"Besides everything you already know about? Nick's seeing someone else. And Fran—well, she's not doing well. At all."

"Christ on a crutch. Sorry. What are you going to do now?"

"I don't know."

"Do you want to get sober?"

That beer helped. Even my eyeballs hurt. "Maybe tomorrow. I was actually thinking about getting more vodka."

She doesn't say anything.

"Just for one day," I assure her. "I already ruined my sobriety. It's not like I'm talking morphine or oxy. If I drink just enough to get through this epic hangover—you know, to smooth things out a little—then I'll be in better shape to meet you at the noon meeting *tomorrow*."

"Yeah, that's pretty normal," she says.

"It is?"

"You want to know why?"

"Yeah."

"Because you're a fucking alcoholic. In fact, you're what the Big Book refers to as a 'real alcoholic.' And your plan is a flaming busload of bullshit."

"Whatever." Heat blooms across my face as I focus on my dirty knees.

"You're at a turning point, Del." The traffic light over the intersection turns yellow, then red.

"I guess. I don't know. I don't know what to do."

"Besides going out last night, that beer was drink número uno today. You know once you take that first one, every cell in your body will scream for you to drink more."

The rising sun momentarily breaks through clouds over the top of the medical building across the street and slices my retinas like death lasers. Disappears again. "Ohmigod. I hate this."

"Mmmm-hmmm," She says, "Maybe you do need to drink more."

"What?"

"Sounds like you still think it will work some fairy-ass magic for you."

"What? No, no, I—I know it won't work any *magic*. Christ, it's hard to think. My fucking head is about to fall off."

The bus pulls up.

"If you want to get sober today, I'll meet you at the noon meeting. That's three and a half hours from now. Can you make it that long without vodka? Hm, I could meet you in the Mission at ten—"

"Hang on." I hobble onto the bus and pay with my change. "Okay, I'm on the bus." I sigh. "Gotta get home, shower. Take care of Fran. I'll meet you at noon."

"Magnificent," she says.

# 42

Fran's BFF, Charlotte, is sitting at the kitchen island when I walk in. Her oversized highlighted blond hair is smushed, and I barely recognize her with no makeup. Saggy, bloodshot eyes-of-Sauron narrow at me.

"Where. Have. You. Been? Your aunt was in such pain last night she dialed me and could only groan."

"Oh, god." I hang my head, which makes it pound. "I got drunk."

One of the living room couches is heaped with folded sheets, a comforter, and a pillow. She must've driven over in the middle of the night.

"I knew you were out partying somewhere so loud you couldn't hear your phone. But *all* night?"

I'm not going to explain myself to Charlotte, who's been suspicious of me ever since Fran took me in. I march to Fran's room.

"Don't wake her up! She's resting. Finally," Charlotte hisses in her Antarctic Expeditions sweatshirt and rhinestone flip-flops.

Aunt Fran is asleep, her mouth open. I tiptoe to her and gently kiss her on the forehead. Murmur, "I'm so sorry."

Her eyes open.

"You're alive," she croaks. "Charlotte didn't . . . kill you?" She's gray and disheveled but forcing her lips to turn up.

"She restrained herself. Are you okay?"

"Okay. Now."

"You took your morning meds?" I ask.

"Yes. You have no idea," she says. "How scared." Her voice is barely audible.

There's nothing to do but give her a hug, though even *I* can smell the cloud of alcohol, sweat, and vomit around me. "I'm so sorry." I repeat. "I was wrong and regret what I did." This last bit is official AA Ninth Step making-amends wording, because friends and families have heard "I'm sorry" till they're numb.

It's the first time I've said it to Aunt Fran, though.

Officially, I'm now back at Step One.

The last part of making amends goes, 'What can I do to make it up to you?' It catches between my teeth because I know her answer.

She says, "You look . . . even worse than me."

"I slept under a bush."

"Ah. Would explain it." She points to her forehead. "Dirt there."

I wipe my face. Sucks if I've been walking around with dirt streaks.

"Nick texted me . . . that you might be . . . upset. Maybe drinking."

"What a snitch."

"He was worried." Her expression says, *Nowhere near as much as me.* She doesn't trust me now.

"It's his fault anyway." I heave a sigh at my own childishness. "No, it's not."

I picture Fran texting me after hearing from Nick. Calling

Esmerelda when I didn't respond. Then having a bad, stress-induced pain spike. Oh, god.

"I'm going to shower and make you some breakfast and change your bed. I just need to go to the noon meeting. Then I'll be back and won't leave again. Except for groceries or something. I take full responsibility for my slip."

Charlotte comes in. "Sweetie," she says to Fran, "I'll head home. If you don't need me." She sniffs and squinches her face like she smells something awful.

Aunt Fran lifts her head and says with emotion, "Thank you, dearest."

Charlotte gives Fran a kiss. I step back, muster all my maturity, and grit my teeth. "Thank you, Charlotte."

She stares me down. "I informed the pharmacy to deliver only two days' supply of Fran's pain meds at a time. Since there's an irresponsible addict in the house."

My face heats.

She marches out. We hear the front door clunk.

Aunt Fran asks, "Do you want to . . . talk about it?"

"There's nothing to talk about. I turned to alcohol to help me through difficult emotions and of course it didn't help. I know what I have to do." Besides call the credit card company.

"I'm sorry, sugar." Her mouth is turned down.

"I appreciate you not lecturing me," I mumble.

"Good. Because it's taking every . . . strength. May I rest? Not worry?" Her tone is sharp.

"Yes, of course. If you weren't sick, you'd be a *lot* madder," I point out helpfully.

"Silver linings," she says.

"I'm so sorry, Aunt Fran."

"I know you are, sugar. Me too. Life's too short."

I want to say, *That's why I refuse to make it any shorter!* But I don't.

I pull all her midmorning pills out of her pillbox. Fran's oxycodone or ohmigod the liquid morphine would be so soothing to my pounding head and aching body and heart about now.

The only thing to do is get to the meeting.

I shower all the grit and vomit from my skin and hair, feeling sick as a salted slug. I just chucked nineteen months of sobriety out the window and have to start over today.

One fucking day at a time.

Aunt Fran's fear for and disappointment in me stings worst of all.

She'd be better off without me as her nurse. All I've done is fail her. But I won't do the one thing that could make it up to her. I won't help her die.

;

On the way to the meeting, I get a text from Nick.

**You OK?**

**Yeah. I fucked up. Headed for a meeting after checking on Fran. Sorry about the juvenile texts (embarrassed emoji)**

**Want to talk?**

**Not really**

**It's cool. Just glad you're ok**

# 43

## Friday, August 21

The next day, Fran takes a shower while I hover outside the bathroom in case anything happens or she needs something. I guess I'm being extra attentive. But a half-cooked, sticky, lasagna-noodle curtain called Death with Dignity still hangs between us.

Now, Harold's here and she's in clean lavender velour loungewear and her pink fleece bathrobe, sitting in the wing-backed chair in the living room like a giant Easter egg. I sit on the couch.

Harold straddles the ottoman and pulls out his stethoscope and blood pressure cuff. He holds her hand. "How are you feeling, Fran?"

She took her meds about twenty minutes ago so is likely at the peak of her pain relief and "goofiness," as she calls it.

"Was born tired," she says, smiling, "and have since suffered a relapse."

"She's had a couple of bad pain spikes." I reach for my locket before remembering it's gone.

"Yes, I know. Her friend called me during the last one." He turns to me. "How are *you* doing, Delilah?"

"Fine," I say. Still nervous that Fran is going to find a way to off herself.

"You're doing a great job of taking care of your aunt." He doesn't know about my slip. "It can be tough. Not for the faint of heart," he adds.

Faint of heart. Good title for my next collage.

I excuse myself to get us some tea and to eavesdrop.

Harold asks about her sleep, memory, bowel movements, and pain.

She's slow to answer but informs him that she slept restlessly last night and is foggier today. Having trouble with words. Tired. Always. But she cracks, "Last bowel movement? May of 2014."

Harold smiles as I bring in a tray. Thin wisps of steam curl off the mugs. Fran lights up when she sees the plate of pastel-colored macarons that her friend Lacey dropped off. Dr. Smith wouldn't approve, but one small departure from the Cancer Cure Diet probably won't matter.

"Must be from . . ." Fran trails off, scrunching her face to help remember. "That place." She makes a little bursting motion with her fingers near her head to show that the name has gone up in a puff of smoke.

She doesn't take any, though, and gives the plate to Harold. He chooses a pale pistachio one that looks the size of a nickel in his catcher's-mitt hand.

Fran says, "I hate . . . being groggy."

Harold gets serious. "Fran, as we expected, the cancer is progressing. It's very important to stay on top of pain management. To not let it get ahead of you."

"Porch light's on, but nobody's home," she says. "Tried taking less, but . . . big mistake. I'm home now. Not all the way."

"It's a trade-off," says Harold. "Being groggy, or fogginess, is a necessary side effect of pain control. You're going to have to put up with one or the other."

"Don't want to . . . miss things." Her gaze is unfocused. "There's such a collage in my mind right now. Salvador Dalí."

"Melted clocks?" I ask. Sometimes we can really read each other's minds.

Harold's deep voice interrupts. "Fran, as we've discussed, we're dealing here with a fast-growing small-cell carcinoma. Pain may be a bigger issue for you. We may eventually want to put you on something stronger, a hydromorphone, which is more like morphine."

"I'd be thrilled to be high on morphine," I joke. Fran and Harold both stiffen. Should've let that thought mosey on by.

Fran hasn't looked at me the whole time. She does now. Harold wrestles a frown like there's a goldfish in his mouth.

"Jeez. Just kidding, y'all!" I say. "Harold, can you give us any idea of a timeline here? Like, an average? Dr. D'Silva said six months, but Fran's . . . changing so fast."

"Do you want to discuss this, Fran?" he asks.

"A timeline? Yes. A lifeline." She shifts in her chair. "A life jacket."

Harold clicks the steel and plastic ear-parts of his stethoscope together. "There's really no way to know for sure. People can die much sooner or hold on for much longer than you would think."

"How about a range?" I ask.

Fran's gazing out the window, tracking a jet and its contrail over the bay. She mumbles, "The Sierras. Home on the. Avocado."

Harold says, "Somewhere between a few weeks and four months."

WTF? "Seriously?" And I just wasted two days of it. "But you said there are patients that get better, right? Sometimes?"

Harold sighs. "Del, it's rare. Fran, you could live for another three, maybe even four months, but at the rate that your cancer is spreading, it's unlikely."

My face stings like I've been slapped.

"I should get busy, then," Fran says.

;

That afternoon, I'm at the Fell Street DMV to get a replacement driver's license for the one that was in my backpack. I've been sitting in this red plastic chair, waiting to be called up to the block-long counter, for the last hour and forty-five minutes. Such a waste of precious time.

I push back the sleeves of my lightweight sweater, revealing a Nevada-shaped purple discoloration on one forearm. My hangover was so epic that I didn't even realize how many ugly bruises splotched my legs, arms, and hip. From drunkenly plowing into things. From falling. From fighting off predators. From sleeping on rocks. Let's hope that's all.

I reach for my locket chain around my neck. And remember again that it's lost in the void with my backpack. Along with my stability.

I press my wrist tat, count breaths, and concentrate on the automated voice calling out wait numbers.

The big crowd here is making me sweat, but the stress is under a thick foggy layer of numbness. I'm not even fidgeting. Everyone in here looks like they're in some terrible dystopian future waiting to have their organs harvested. Well, as my old pal Matt always said, *Life is hard and then you die.*

On my phone again, I check my schedule for the fall semester.

Classes start this Monday.

If I stick with a full course load, I would have to be away from Fran for most of the day during the week.

Two of the prerequisites for an education major won't be available again until *next* fall, so I have to take them now. As someone calls, "A-114 for window eighteen," I hit the confirm button to drop the other three.

# 44

## Saturday, August 22

The next evening, I let myself into the apartment. I went to a meeting, then skated for almost two hours, trying to work off some anxiety.

I tiptoe to Fran's room and open the partially closed door. She's lying on her side, facing me. Her bare legs stick out from her nightgown that's bunched almost up to her butt. Her eyes are wide open but not focused. Her lips and face are all the same ash-gray, and some of her sheets and the comforter are in a pile on the floor.

"Aunt Fran! Are you okay?"

"Okay."

I tug her nightgown down and arrange her sheets and comforter over her. "What's your pain level?"

"A four. Five. Had . . . a little flare-up." The morphine drops are on her bedside table.

I left her here with another friend, Mari, who came to see her at lunch. She's only been alone a little over an hour.

"You could've called me, you know!" Our new health aide, Libby, starts tomorrow, and not a moment too soon.

"To do what?" She closes her eyes.

"To come home sooner." She doesn't even trust me anymore.

I get the drops and make her take one more dose. She's not due for more pills for an hour and a half, and Dr. Berg's going to have to up the dosage again.

"Can I bring you some cottage cheese gloop? Or, shoot, scrambled eggs? Or toast?" I plead.

"Maybe some water." We keep a big plastic container of ice water by her all the time. The meds dry her out.

;

I whine about wanting to be a grown-up. That means being able to consider the feelings of someone other than your own damn self.

So why am I insisting she eat cancer sludge at every meal?

I'll make her some homemade chicken noodle soup. I find a recipe and order the ingredients online with Fran's credit card—tossing in the pricey, lotion-soft tissues that she won't buy herself. I forgo Pop-Tarts.

Next, I upload all the music she loves on her phone. Some New Age flute and tinkling bell stuff for when she wants to meditate or relax. Plus all her old-school favorites, from Bach to the Bee-Gees, and lots of Earth, Wind, and Fire.

I quietly prop it on her bedside table with the options of both my speaker and her earbuds, and a sticky note that reads, "Play me."

;

I'm at my desk cutting out pictures of rain clouds and granite countertops, and pieces of upholstery samples. Even though I know it's a bad idea, that he might be with Bassima, I text Nick. I need his counsel.

**Do you think there's life after death?**

His mom is Catholic and his dad is agnostic; he doesn't attend anything regularly.

I pull out an old *Macy's Home Sale* catalog of Fran's and cut out an electric mixer. Fran is asleep. I keep checking.

**Yes.**

**Why?**

**When I was in Children's Hospital after my bike accident, I was between worlds for a long time. For a short time. There was no time. I know there's another one besides this one. Maybe lots more.**

**WOW**

That was way more than I bargained for.

No response, so I send, **You're not afraid of death then?**

**No**

**No you're not or no I'm wrong?**

**Not really afraid. But I want to live. And work.**

**I hate work.** I'm kind of kidding.

**Not if you're doing what you're meant to be doing**

Am I doing what I'm meant to be doing? How are we supposed to know what that is?

I'm meant to stay sober. So far, so good, today.

Meant to take care of Fran: check.

Meant to talk people off the edges of tall bridges and commuter rail platforms. Uh, check, mostly.

Meant to be getting educated. Yep. In so many ways.

What else should I be doing?

# 45

## Sunday, August 23

I tap on Fran's partially open door with a mug of tea. She doesn't respond, but her bed is raised and she's upright. The lamp brightens the dim room, and the newspaper is folded beside her. On the bedside table now sits the framed black-and-white yearbook photo of her and her high school boyfriend, Jerry, studying side by side.

I have a soft flash of last night's dream. Mom, with a red rose. Usually, Fran would love to have a go at interpreting something like that, but she looks a little sad. Maybe later?

"Hey, I made a mushroom and Emmental cheese omelet. Want a piece?" Ordinarily she would praise me for thinking of it and preparing something like this.

She's gazing into space. The air's a little stale, and smells of cocoa-butter hand cream with an undernote of the garbage bin behind that Market Street liquor store.

"Aunt Fran?" I brace myself. She has that same serious expression as when she asked me to help her die. "Are you okay?"

"Yes," she says with a sigh. "A funny thing." She picks up the newspaper beside her. "I know this . . . picture." She points at the front-page photo of a woman in a headscarf cradling a small child, surrounded by rubble. "I can't understand this."

"It's so sad, isn't it?" I sit in the bedside chair. There must be some relief for her in thinking of leaving such a sad world.

"What does it say?" she asks. "I can't read it."

"Oh. Your glasses. There they are." I hand them to her.

She sets them down. "No." She closes her eyes and presses two fingers against the space between her brows. "It's just . . . funny marks."

"What, the print?" I study the article.

"I know . . . it's supposed to . . . make sense." She gestures at the front of the newspaper. "It doesn't."

"Wait. You can't read it?"

A terrible question tortures her face. "Is it the cancer?"

I put the paper aside and cover my throat with my hand. Is it? Because this is bad. I thought all her brain problems were due to the chemo and the drugs.

I intertwine my fingers and squeeze. "Oh. Hmm, well, it could have something to do with your retinas, or . . ."

"Don't. It's not. It's . . . the brain."

Even though I love denying it, I know she's probably right. Nodules and tumors are in her lungs, liver, and pancreas—it's in her system. Harold did say it could spread to her brain.

"I'd love to read to you, Aunt Fran."

"Not the news," she says. "Too sad."

"Anything you like."

"Could we . . . *Little Women*? End of the chapter," she instructs.

"From *Hold your tongue, you disrespectful old bird!*?" We're already well into it.

She nods.

Using funny voices, I recite the page. She practically knows this book by heart. She's lived a life that's sort of like Jo's, or maybe more like Louisa May Alcott's.

Fran's eyes are shut but she's smiling, so I continue into the next chapter.

I close the book when she emits a soft snore.

⁏

I've been waiting at the bus stop for what feels like hours. As soon as Libby showed up for her shift, I headed out to visit Savannah, but I really need to talk to someone who understands what's going on with Fran. After a cigarette, I lean against the wall of the nearest storefront and tap my phone. A deep voice answers.

The bricks are warm and rough against my back through my sweatshirt. "Sorry to bother you, Harold. I just need to ask you something. Well, tell you something." I rock from sneaker to sneaker.

"Go right ahead."

A steady stream of happy tourist families files by. "Fran can't read anymore. She says the newspaper print looks like squiggles to her. What does this mean?"

"How is her vision for other things?" he asks sensibly.

"Fine, I guess. But it's like she forgot how to read."

"That's probably a tumor affecting the brain. But, Delilah," he says gently, "it's all part of this final stage of her life. Things will be breaking down from here on out."

Oh my god. I'm already losing huge chunks of her.

"Isn't there anything we can do?" I ask, hugging my middle with one arm. The bus pulls up.

"You could read to her."

"I am. Anything else?" The bus doors open.

"This is the time for letting go," he says. "Remember when we were discussing timelines?"

"Yeah."

"You may want to think in terms of weeks, rather than months."

"Oh." Weeks. For real now. The dirty sidewalk rushes up to meet me. Then drops back down. Cars honk; a siren sounds from a few blocks over. People walk past with strollers and backpacks and groceries. All so alive and oblivious.

I stare at the driver as he waits, closes the doors, and pulls away.

# 46

## Monday, August 24

I arrive at BAC for my shift a little early. I pleaded an "emergency" for my missed shift when I got drunk, but if Quentin finds out what really happened, he'll can me.

I have to beat him to the punch.

"Hey, Del!" he calls. "What's going on? How's your aunt?"

"Oh, uh, fine." I hug my new backpack in front of me. "I mean, not *fine*. At all. But we're hanging in there."

"I noticed you've missed your last two shifts." He says this not accusingly.

I zip and unzip my backpack's outside pouch. "Yeah. Really sorry about that. And, um, I'm sorry but I do need to take a . . . leave of absence. I don't know for how long."

He steeples his fingers and studies me. "We'll miss you, but completely understand."

"Uh, thanks." Whew. He's letting me off the hook and we're both saving face.

"You're on today, though, right?" he asks.

"Uh, yep."

;

Isabel is on a line when I sign in on a computer. My phone rings. "Bay Area Crisis. This is Del."

"Del? I talked to you before," says a gruff male voice. I don't recognize him as one of the regulars, but lots of people call more than once. Policy is that callers have to take who they get and can't ask for a particular volunteer. This is to discourage dependent relationships.

"What's your name?" I ask, silencing my cell and lining up a notepad and pen.

"Arthur."

"Arthur, are you feeling suicidal?"

"Sure as hell am."

"Do you have a plan?"

"I've been saving meds for a while now. Might have enough."

I sit up and glance at Isabel. "Are you thinking of carrying out your plan today?"

"Probably not until the end of the week."

I recognize his voice now—not quite as raspy as I remember it. Arthur with all the life-threatening illnesses, the deceased wife, and the seemingly negligent son. And the death wish.

"Tell me what's going on, Arthur."

"I'm in constant pain and feel like a piece of shit. I'm just a big burden sitting here. Doc only gives me a couple of months. Why won't they let me go sooner?"

Like Fran. "I'm sorry to hear that. What can I do to help?"

"I want to know how many pills I'll need to shut me down for good."

"Uh. That depends on what the pills are," I hedge. This is what happened last time. He does seem to have us confused with suicide *assistance*. "Hang on a second. I might have some information for you."

216

I google *assisted suicide* and click through to a group that promises to provide information on 'advancing the time of one's death.' Bingo. "Here we go. Final Dignity." I give him the number. "They can help you and answer your questions better than we can."

"Thank you," he says gruffly.

"Sure thing. Good luck."

Ha.

I write up call notes, with a nagging feeling I've done something illegal or at least unethical. Except that it did help Arthur.

When Isabel ends her call, I swivel around in my chair. "Hey! How's it going?"

"Good." She smiles in that impervious way. "How's Nick?"

"He's leaving Wednesday. To go back to Austin."

"Is that good or bad?"

"Both, I guess. It was planned and, um, he's seeing someone else," I say evenly. "So, good."

"Oh *hell* no."

"Okay, it's terrible because I kind of blew my chance with him."

Her face muscles morph with concern. "What happened?"

"He was busy, and Aunt Fran and everything, and it was complicated. I'd like a do-over for the whole thing. Maybe the whole summer." I gather my loose call notes and stack them.

"That sucks." She passes me a bowl of peanut-butter pretzels. "How's your aunt?"

"So-so." I pop a couple of pretzel pods. "The call I just had?"

"Yeah?" We often compare notes.

"An old guy in a nursing home. Really sick. Alone. In pain. I, um, gave him a referral for Death with Dignity." I walk my notes over to the shredder.

"You mean assisted suicide?" Her eyebrows pull together. The shredder eats the paper with a hum. "Yeah."

She crosses her arms. "I don't believe anyone has a right to take their life."

Jackson has disconnected from his last call. "What are you talking about?"

"Assisted suicide," says Isabel.

"Advancing the time of your death," I say. "But he would only be speeding things up a little, like a couple of weeks. Trying to make things easier for himself and his family. If it's what he wants, and he's been thinking about it for months, can it be so bad?"

"Sometimes depressed people contemplate suicide for months. Years. That doesn't mean their lives can't or won't feel worth living ever again."

"I know." I sit back down. It's not like I disagree.

Jackson says, "If someone is hella suffering, like from radical tumors and shit, and of course *wants* to, I would totally vote for a lethal dose of . . . whatever." He smooths his ponytail.

Isabel pauses. "Like putting an animal down."

"Do you think *that's* wrong too?" I ask.

She grimaces, either annoyed or embarrassed by the question. "No."

"You still think it's wrong for people?"

"Okay, maybe there could be a situation, like you outlined, where I would agree. An exception." She leans back in her rolling chair. "But don't dying patients have access to all kinds of drugs that make the pain bearable?"

I say, "Even when you're taking mega oxycodone, or morphine and steroids and all that, there are some forms of cancer that you have to race to stay ahead of. The pain keeps getting worse, at the same time that you're getting used to the dosage, so it doesn't work anymore. A patient can end up in unbearable pain more than you might think."

"A form of mercy then." She tilts her head.

"Yeah. Exactly."

"But still kind of a shortcut."

"My aunt isn't looking for a shortcut! She's in pain that gets torturous and she sees no point in drawing this out!" My volume and conviction surprise me. And when did I stand up?

"Then of course it makes sense," says Isabel, wide-eyed.

"Totally, dude," says Jackson.

# 47

Back on the bus heading home, I formally withdraw online from SFSU's fall semester. It takes me longer than I thought, and when I look up, I've completely missed my stop.

It will be *next* fall, over a year away, before I can take two of my prerequisite classes.

Fran will be gone then, one way or another.

I'll be . . .

Hanging out in a crack house? A psychiatric ward? Probably back in the void.

*You cannot possibly go there again.*

I get off at a far stop in the marina and sit down to wait for a bus back the other direction. It's dark. My elbows on my knees, I hold my bad-hair-day-hatted head and let the cold, black night air wash over me.

I might just be gone too.

God, I could use a shot. Or three.

I fill my lungs with the deepest breath I can and whisper, "Gotta stay sober. Just the rest of today."

An old, pumpkin-colored Chevy convertible low-rider rolls by, blaring Latin music and jumping on its rear wheels. People seated at the heated outside tables for the vegan restaurant on the corner only briefly glance up from their quinoa.

No buses anywhere I can see. I call a Lyft. But not to go home.

;

The driver lets me out at the Golden Gate Bridge parking lot. The bridge looks otherworldly, glowing against the backdrop of the earth's largest, deepest, dark ocean, which is blanketed by fog.

Trucks and cars speed over the steel grids and thunder that unearthly thrum.

Baker Beach, site of my cringe-fest with Nick, stretches around the point to the west.

I stride along the bridge-access pedestrian way only to arrive at a locked gate that blocks the way onto the bridge itself. It's way after 9 p.m. and closed for the night. I breathe out in relief.

But no.

Everyone slows down for the tollbooth not far behind us. After a moment's hesitation, I vault over the railing onto the highway edge and sprint the twenty feet to get past the gate, chain-link fence, and razor wire.

A red BMW in the closest lane swerves, honking long and loud. Beads of cold sweat bloom on my skin.

I scramble up the shoulder-high steel-and-cable rail. Throw myself over it and back onto the wide concrete walkway.

I brush off my hands and stride with purpose, like I'm supposed to be here. If I'm lucky, the bridge police won't be by for a while.

The night air is sharp, and the stiff wind is frosted with car exhaust. The high chain-link fence separates us from the long drop to the old Fort Point beneath us.

I walk slowly and try to catch my breath.

I could help Fran die. But if I do that, I might as well go too.

*That's silly. You've got so much to live for. What about studying to become a teacher?*

It's going to take forever. I don't even know if I want to teach. Or can. It's such a tough job.

*How about your work at the crisis line?*

I suck at it. I've started helping people kill themselves.

At the first giant concrete stanchion, a sign reads, "Emergency phone and crisis counseling" above a yellow call box.

"Ha!" I laugh.

Another sign informs me of the illegality of throwing anything over the bridge and warns of surveillance cameras.

*So, what about Dad?*

Dad doesn't need taking care of. He would be sad, but hardly surprised.

"Whoops!" My hat blows off and I watch it tumble down, down, down, through the patchy fog below.

"Ohmigod." A bowling ball is stuck in my chest.

The wind whips cruelly out here. It's come all the way from Japan with nothing to slow it down.

*Isabel, Quentin, Soo Jin, Jackson, and many others who spend so much time and heartfelt energy fighting this would be crushed. Not just because they like you, but because they would take it personally. And Savannah and Ez would never get over it.*

A truck downshifts and I flinch. Traffic booms, clatters, and drums over the steel grid sections.

*And what about Nick?*

If Nick heard I jumped, he'd be upset for sure. He'd probably feel like he did something wrong.

I let out my breath. I want him to be happy and healthy.

Even if it's with someone else. Even though he's due to go back to Texas in two days and our lives may never intersect again.

I'm all the way out over the deep black water. Layers of incoming fog partially obscure how far, far below the bay is. The red railing is thick and rough with a bit of rust and chipped paint, hard and cold in my grip. I'm clammy with sweat.

I hate heights.

A wide steel beam with nothing between it and the plunge is a few feet below the sidewalk on the other side of the railing. Pennies are strewn on it as if this were some gigantic wishing fountain. Or people can't resist letting *something* drop over the railing.

It would be easy to climb over and perch there.

The water churning underneath the wispy fog has an inky, cosmic pull that radiates through the steel and concrete, up through the soles of my tennis shoes.

*Even though you're only toying with the idea, what you're doing is . . .*

Risky.

Good thing I'm not drunk.

*Free will.*

Fran can't take care of herself now, but she's not a child. She should be able to make her own choices.

The wind moans.

I freeze, gazing out toward the city. I've always wondered how active a choice Mom's was. Did she plan? Or did she just, with a flick of her wrist, make the decision to put herself out of her misery in a split second?

Does it matter?

Yes. Premeditation versus a crime of passion.

But I believe that, underneath the pain of her illness, Mom wanted to live.

*Do you want to live?*

I do. But sometimes I really don't.

Still, I'm *supposed* to be alive. I have . . . potential. Like a flipping pumpkin seed.

The city blinks in the distance through tendrils of fog. One of those lights glowing is Fran's, for a while longer anyway. I love her. I want to do right by her.

I hold up the inside of my left wrist. "This is ridiculous!" I say out loud. "I'm a sworn Suicide Prevention Girl. Woman. I won't even help my poor aunt end her suffering and she wants to die to escape torturous pain. What the *fuck* am I doing here?"

On the bridge.

On Earth.

I pull out my phone. It's 10:11. Shoot—I was supposed to be home by now. There's a text from Fran, from four minutes ago.

**Pains increasing I need you.**

**COMING!** I text back and pull up my ride app. I sprint back the way I came, suddenly desperate to get to the parking lot. The walkway door is unlocked from this side, thank heavens.

# 48

I hear Fran's moans as soon as I'm in the front door. I run to her room. "Fran! I'm here!"

She's writhing in her bed, sheets and blanket tangled around her.

"Did you take your last meds?"

A groan that may mean "yes."

I'm sure Libby would've given them to her. And she should've only left twenty or thirty minutes ago!

I run to the kitchen to get the breakthrough drops. From her bathroom, I snatch Fran's thirty-five-compartment tackle box of pills. Her early-evening meds aren't in here.

I fill up the dropper, then push it between her lips and squeeze, hoping it goes down okay. I take her hand. She pulls it away and keens softly.

Libby left with no one here. But I had assured her I'd be back in time, and she had to pick up her kid. There's a note from her on Fran's bedside table.

*Refill never arrived! There's enough for tonight, but she'll need more by tomorrow morning. Thanks for understanding about picking up my son.*

Gripping Fran's almost-empty prescription bottle, I tap my phone.

"Harold? This is Delilah, at Fran's. We've only got two more oxycodone left! Another order was placed the day before yesterday, but nothing's been delivered and when Libby called the pharmacy today, they didn't have anything for us."

I let things slip! This is *my* job. And we're only getting two days' worth at a time because I can't be trusted.

I add, "She's having a pain spike right now! I just gave her drops."

"Good."

"We've been doing a lot of those lately."

Harold says, "I'll get Dr. Berg to call in the prescription refill again and have the pharmacy deliver it to you pronto." His deep voice is even and reassuring. "That shouldn't take more than an hour or two. She'll probably increase Fran's daily dose again. For now, Delilah, keep giving Fran the drops as needed, every fifteen minutes until it's under control. You're doing a great job."

"Okay." Thank goodness he didn't accuse me of stealing them.

I sit beside her. Replaying her text reaching me on the bridge, Nick holding hands with Bassima, Dad minimizing everything and not listening to me as usual. Everything is beyond fucked up. I give Fran more drops ten minutes later. She finally drifts off. Her breathing falls into a steady rhythm. Mine does too. Her hand is soft and limp. Her mouth is open, and her hair all thin and flat. The bridge of her nose and the bone hollows cradling her eyes jut sharply from her discolored, gray and puffy skin.

I'd give anything for her to be healthy and her old self again. I know that's impossible.

I'd give anything for her to not suffer anymore.

*Anything, Delilah? How about some death with dignity?*

I text Dad. It's early morning his time, **WHEN ARE YOU COMING?**

**How's Fran?** is his response.

**She's dying. Don't ask me that again. Stop stalling.**

**I'm working on it. Everything's been delayed here. The main office had a fire. We suspect arson. Aiming for early September.**

I roll my eyes, sorry about the headquarters but sick of his excuses, and not worried about his safety. He might put himself in harm's way just so he'd have a good excuse not to come. I send him three red, angry, cursing emojis.

An hour later, Joel buzzes. "Pharmacy delivery," he announces.

I run down all the stairs, too antsy to wait for the elevator.

I clutch the white paper bag in the elevator coming back up, as my blood somehow floods to an impossible volume, and the thin walls of my arteries and veins stretch and strain to the bursting point. My heart's gone into overdrive and I'm panting. The cables holding me sway and fray and the whole thing is about to smash on the concrete at the bottom of the shaft.

Just what I need. And Dr. Vernon already upped my anxiety meds.

The door opens on the fifth floor, and cranky Mr. Todd gets in. "Good Lord. What happened to *you*?" he asks.

Instead of answering, I breathe into and out of the paper bag until the doors open on our floor and I stumble out, unlock our door, and finally sink into the cushy couch in the dark living room. I breathe slow and deep, counting breaths for a long time.

Unclench.

I unscrew the new plastic bottle of oxycodone, full of tan-colored pills.

I pull one out.

Everyone expects me to. So why not?

Just one *half*. That would actually be a lot. Fran's dosage and tolerance are high now.

I cradle it in my palm.

Sniff it. This tablet of compressed magic dust brushes the tip of my nose.

I'd give anything for some relief. From fear for Fran, from dealing with anxiety and suicidality, from anger at Dad, from disappointment in Nick, and most of all, from disappointment in myself.

I already ruined my sobriety. Now's the time.

Just this once. Just one.

*Look at what you're doing!*

I imagine the pill traveling down my throat, without water. Sticking to first one patch, then another of the mucous membrane that lines my esophagus. The inevitable warm numbness that makes everything A-OK and flows like light-infused honey through my body—

*Think it through. What will happen?*

I'll feel good! High! Happy. Numb.

Obliterated.

Out the dark window, the Alcatraz light blinks at me sternly, rotates, and insistently flashes me again.

Once high, I'll want more and more of Fran's pills. Or I'll go find more vodka to drink. Or both.

Then what?

I tap Esmerelda's number on my phone.

"Ez? It's Del a new big bottle of Fran's oxycodone is in my lap I almost swallowed one I still really, really want to."

She takes a deep breath and says, "Okay, baby. You

remember when you asked me to sponsor you, I asked you if you were willing to go to any length to stay sober?"

"Yeah."

"That's still true. The fact that you're calling me instead of popping Fran's oxy proves it. So, high five!"

"Yeah, I guess you're right." I put up my palm for the long-distance slap.

"Where are they now?" she asks.

"There's one in my hand."

"What are you going to do with it?"

I drop it into the bottle, close it with one hand, and stuff it in the bag. "It's back in the bottle. I'll put it in Fran's bathroom. That's the usual and safest place."

"Where are you now?"

"In the living room. Hang on."

I sneak into Fran's dark room, listen for her even breathing, and quietly set the pill container on her bathroom counter.

A few moments later, I tell Esmerelda, "I did it. I'm in my room." I turn on the light.

"What are you going to do now?"

"Exercise and dance around to *Intoxicated* with my headphones on."

She laughs. "Sounds spectacular. What's your emotional temperature? Can you make it until tomorrow knowing all those kickers are waiting in the next room?"

"Uh."

"Babe, you know I'm not judging, just gathering info."

"I know. Yeah, I think so." I sit on the edge of my bed. "If I start feeling weird about it, I promise I'll call you. Is it okay if it's the middle of the night?"

"Of course. My phone will lie right next to me."

"Thanks, Ez." I swallow. "Can I ask you something?" The question is about to burn a hole through my sternum.

"Shoot."

"When we—I know they're an escape, but are drinking and drugs—I mean abusing them—a kind of suicide?"

"What do you think, baby?" she asks gently.

"Yeah. An immediate way to obliteration, for a little bit anyway. And I guess, often a quicker way to death." I lie back on my bed. Breathe in. Breathe out. "See you at the noon meeting tomorrow."

# 49

## Tuesday, August 25

Fran sleeps most of the next day. In between doing laundry, I do some research online. The California legislature is debating its own Death with Dignity bill right now. But even if it passes, it would take time to go into effect. Time Fran doesn't have. We have to focus on the existing options.

I successfully ignore the meds. Except the ones I give to Fran.

In the evening, after Libby goes home, I bring Fran squash soup that I made from an easy online recipe. First, I have to help her to her bedside toilet. It's not that big a deal, mostly just pulling her up out of bed and holding her arm in case she loses her balance—she does everything else. I'm useful.

She eats a bit of soup and I sit in the big chair, strangely nervous, like I'm here for an interview.

"I've done some research. On Oregon. Death with dignity."

Fran puts her spoon down and waits.

"You fit the requirements—adult, sound mind, terminal illness as stated by two doctors."

She ought to perk up at this news, but she grips and ungrips her hands.

"Dr. D'Silva's office is sending us a statement about your diagnosis and prognosis. To show to a doctor in Oregon. The only thing we don't have is Oregon residency, but we should be able to establish it."

Her eyes widen in amazement. "Can we?"

"Yes. There's a group there who help people like us take care of the legal requirements. Then we have to make two oral requests to whichever doctor we find, about two weeks apart. Then a written one, signed by two witnesses. Then you have to give yourself the lethal dose of pills. That means swallow them, or dissolve them in water and drink that. They don't give you an injection."

"Right," Fran says like she already knows.

"Want me to go ahead? Call the organization, get help finding a doctor in Oregon and becoming residents?"

"Amen, sister." She clasps her hands at her breasts. Her face is lit with relief. Maybe joy.

"Ha. Okay." I kiss her forehead and whisper, "Sorry it took me so long."

I'll help her do anything she wants. Even take her own life and speed up the time of her departure from me.

She grasps for my hand. Squeezes it. Hers feels both bony and puffy. "I'm not giving up?"

Worry and pain crease her face and I'm not sure how she means it. By dying? Not fighting the cancer more? Can she not remember what she asked me?

I shake my head, an all-purpose reassuring "no," and squeeze back.

She visibly relaxes. Her body softens, her breaths lengthen, and her grip loosens. I move her tray and settle her back into her pillows. I sit beside her until she drifts off.

Living can be so hard. Dying looks to be harder still.

We all have some suicide in us. Even if it's only a little bit. We smoke, bungee jump, drive too fast, get liposuction, sunbathe, don't get enough sleep, do tequila shots or illegal drugs.

We're all moving toward death, and we all push it sometimes.

I know Mom loved me more than anything. And I know she tried to be healthy for me for a long time. I've always understood that her mental illness, especially when she was so depressed she could barely move, became more than she could bear. Of course, at the time, I wished with all my heart that she'd get better and be a regular mom. But I rarely felt anger toward her. I was furious at the universe, not at Mom.

Now I wonder, did Mom have the best medical and social help she needed? Survey says probably not, based on the way Dad, her mom, and most of her friends behaved at the time—acting like all she had to do was buck up.

Osgood, too, was weary of being mentally and physically ill, and alone. He'd been off and on the streets so long. Off and on meds. Everyone who loved him enough to help him was gone. I'm not excusing myself—I still failed him—and I don't agree with his choice. But I don't live in his shoes, and it was *his* choice.

Osgood wasn't near natural death as far as I know. BAC teaches us that preventing a suicide can be a simple matter of connection and care and getting someone through the next twenty-four hours. Osgood's suicide proves we were not watching out for him enough. If we have support from others when the going gets tough, maybe we won't want to bail. Thank god people were there to save me from my bad choice and help me afterward.

But maybe when the going is so much tougher than anyone can imagine and is leading you inexorably toward the end—when there's no second chance waiting around the corner, and you've got confirmation of that from professionals—you need nonjudgmental support to make a carefully thought-out decision for yourself.

Aunt Fran has always been there for me without question. With minimal judgment about my poor choices. And no judgment about my mental health, or lack thereof.

Taking your own life is still a terrible idea, but her situation is so different from mine, different from 99 percent of the cases I've dealt with at BAC. She doesn't want to do this because she's tired of life. She wants to do it because she loves life too much to endure an ever-diminishing version of it.

She dozes quietly beside me, her face sunken and her eyes shadowed.

The air in here is heavy with humidity. Creaky and stiff, I finally take the tray back into the kitchen.

Through the living room windows, the Alcatraz lighthouse blinks at me every few seconds. Steady. Dependable. Floating above thick, gray fog that flows like a river from the Golden Gate. A deep bassoon of a foghorn belches, long and low and mournful.

A huge tanker, all lit up, appears and disappears as it slowly glides through the fog toward the Golden Gate.

A jet passes far overhead. In a city at least, if you pay attention, they're flying over all the time.

Aunt Fran wanted to learn to fly. A small plane anyway. It would've been so awesome to go up in the air with her.

What is it about flying?

It's the idea of slipping gravity to choose to go anywhere.

Flying can also be *hurtling* like a fired cannonball, out of control, headed for devastating impact.

I leave a message with Final Dignity, the organization that helps the terminally ill—the same one that I referred Arthur to. Right after I hang up, my phone dings with a text. From Nick!

**Got a moment to talk?**

# 50

Before I call Nick, I sit right next to my partially open window to sneak a cigarette. I can't leave to go downstairs.

"You can handle it, whatever it is," I whisper to myself. It will be a scrawny crow compared to the fiery winged dragon of Fran's demise.

I tap his number. "Hey. What's up?"

"Going back to Austin tomorrow," he says.

"I know. Summer went fast, huh?" Maybe it will be easier having him far away again instead of across the bay.

"I'm in the city. Can I drop by?"

I almost drop my phone. "You are? Of course! Sure!"

"Okay. I'll be there in about ten minutes. Can't stay long but wanted to say goodbye."

Not sure if he means to me or Fran, but who cares? At the end of the alley, the rectangle of lights over on Telegraph Hill twinkle and glow.

Ten minutes! I click into overdrive. Now I'm sorry I smoked. I brush my teeth and hair, and swipe on some lip gloss.

The doorman announces Nick on the intercom, and I slip out to the foyer so he won't ring the loud doorbell.

The elevator doors open. Nick stands there with Noor. His thick dark hair's a little disheveled, hers sleek and smooth.

He's in a button-down blue shirt and newish jeans, holding a bouquet of coral-colored roses. He gives me a shy grin.

We embrace and cheek-kiss. I want to glue my lips to his but refrain. I lead him and Noor into the apartment.

"Is Fran awake?" He holds out the flowers.

They're for her of course. "She'll love those." I point toward the kitchen. "There're some vases in that end cabinet. Let me go check on her."

When I tap on her door, she struggles to sit up and turns on her lamp. "Bring him," she croaks. "Warn him . . . a wheel's down . . . and my axel's draggin'."

She still doesn't miss a thing.

Out of all Fran's pretty vases, Nick has put the flowers into what was once a large mayonnaise jar, which he now balances in one hand. I push him in ahead of me. Fran knows exactly who he is but might've forgotten what to call him. "It's Nick, Fran. He's come to see you."

Fran says, "Hello, Nick! Hello, dog."

"Hi, Fran," he says shyly. "These are for you." He lets go of Noor and places the jar on her bedside table.

"From your wedding?" she asks.

Nick's eyebrows pop above his glasses.

"No," I say quickly, "These are get-well flowers for you."

"Get well?" she asks. Her clock ticks loudly.

Nick says, "Feel-better flowers."

"Medicine," she says. "Good dog." Noor sits at attention by the bed.

When Fran puts out her hand, Noor licks it before Nick takes it gently with both of his. "Has Delilah been taking good care of you?" he asks.

"The best," she says.

"Whew," I say. "Yeah, ha."

"Are you going to take her?" Fran asks him.

I shoot Nick a look, trying to communicate to roll with it. She's loopy all right but using it to full advantage.

He smiles and says, "I'm going back to Austin tomorrow. Delilah wants to stay here with you."

"No, she doesn't," says Fran.

"Yes, I do," I insist, even though I know what Fran's doing—lovingly.

Nick glances at me. "I wanted to say goodbye to you both."

I don't know when I'll next see Nick, but Fran probably won't ever see him again. In this realm.

"Such a sweet boy," she says. "To come all this way."

"I'm sorry I can't stay longer. Bless you, Fran."

Fran closes her eyes. "Thank you," she murmurs.

We head for the door.

"Nick?" she calls clearly.

"Yes?"

She's looking off to the far corner of the room. "I saw . . . a waterfall." She jerkily sweeps her hand.

"Oh." Nick smiles and answers her non sequitur without missing a beat. "That's so awesome."

"Indeed. Literally," she whispers.

We slip out. I close her door and lead Nick and Noor toward the living room.

"Thank you for coming," I say. "That meant a lot to her. To me too."

He pauses by the front door, shuffles a little, breathes in.

"Do you have a few more minutes?" I ask. "I need to tell you something." He lets out his breath and nods, like he was going to ask the same thing.

I sit on the end of the couch and he sits in the chair angled next to it. Noor lies with her head on her paws.

I scratch behind her ears, grateful she's been watching out for him. And that she's being well-behaved. "She's downright mellow these days."

"She's a good dog." Her ears perk up. "We're both learning a lot."

"I think we'll be going to Portland soon—so Fran can advance the time of her death."

"Really?" His hand reaches for Noor's back. "You're going to help her?"

"Yeah." I pull back my shoulders and lift my chin.

"When did y'all decide this?"

"About twenty minutes ago."

"Wow. How do you feel about that? Like, with your background and work and all," he adds, like I wouldn't understand the question.

I blink. Last time we got into this I overshared. But I'm glad he's asking. "Yeah, my psychiatric background is particularly ill-suited to this situation," I deadpan.

He pauses. "If you go deep enough into anyone's head you'll find some weird shit. I like that you're honest. And trust me enough to talk about it."

"Really?" He was so silent and stiff after I told him all about my attempt. Or maybe that was because I threw myself at him.

"You don't think it's messed up?" I pull at my fingers.

"Of her?"

"Of me."

"No. It's her life, and you're honoring her choice." Over his shoulder, a tiny restaurant sign down on Fisherman's Wharf blinks bright blue and green.

"Yeah," I agree. "You'll be a great doctor. You just rolled with that waterfall comment."

He shakes his head. "No, I'm pretty sure I know what she meant."

"What are you talking about?"

"When I came by here at the beginning of the summer and you were getting ready. Before Beast Burger."

"Oh, right. When she told you she had cancer before she told me."

"Well. Yeah. We were talking about sickness. I told her that when I was in the hospital after my accident, I had this single memory of a dream, only it wasn't a dream, it was like a place I'd been. Where there was a waterfall of all colors." He gestures vaguely. Drops his hands. "Pretty impossible to describe."

"Wow."

"She liked it. Thought it was 'otherworldly.'"

"Ah. Now she saw one too?"

"I guess so."

"That is truly awesome."

"Yeah."

I spin the silver ring on my finger. "Nick, if there really is something beyond our material world, something that's so beautiful and peaceful, why should anyone bother with this one?"

He shrugs. "Heaven is static. *Here* is where we learn and grow." He states this like it's obvious.

"Hm. Like, improve?"

"Yeah. Or not." He stops petting Noor and rests his hands in his lap. "Speaking of which, I got the scholarship."

I sit up. "You did? That's great! Congratulations!" I lean over and punch him lightly on the shoulder. "Way to go."

"I can start at Cal in January."

"Oh my god! That's fantastic." And it is. "I bet Bassima's psyched."

"She and I are, um, finished. Have been for a while." He presses his lips together, then pushes his glasses up his nose.

"Really? *Yes!*" I throw my arms over my head and pump my fists.

He smiles. "Knew I'd get an honest response."

"Are you okay? Tell me what happened." I prop my elbows on the armrest and hold my chin.

"Fine. She needs someone more . . . sorority-compatible." His expression is all neutral like he's reading a prescription.

"Ha! Did she break it off?"

"Fizzled out. I didn't want to go to some event dinner with her. She asked someone else. Then we haven't seen much of each other." He shrugs.

I ask him, "Are you sad? Be honest."

"Nope." He grins.

"You sure? Want me to kick her ass like I said I would?" I punch my fist into my other palm.

He laughs, probably because he knows she would definitely kick mine, but says, "Why not?"

We're getting a little loud and I don't want to disturb Fran. Or have her eavesdrop. I say softly, "Oh, okay, we can drive over right now. Unless you want to skip that and go straight for your rebound."

"You're way overestimating my attachment to Bassima. It was a . . . flirtation. Made me realize some things." He confesses this last part to his lap.

"Oh, yeah? Like what?" The lamp between us throws one side of his face into soft shadow.

He studies the bones of his knuckles. "Like that the whole summer I would rather have spent what little time I had hanging out"—he looks into my eyes—"with you."

The mineral blue and silver in the upholstery brighten. "Really? Then why didn't you?" And why did he bolt every time we were together?

"It was just hard. I wanted to be . . . um, careful. Not jump into things."

I clear my throat and tug at a ragged cuticle. Maybe he was being respectful of me. Or at least trying not to take advantage of my impulsive behavior. Worried about ruining our friendship if we did hook up and it didn't work out.

He fidgets with the hem of his shirt. "The whole thing with Fran was kind of hanging over things from the start. And logistically, it was hard." He pauses. "Maybe I was, um, nervous."

He *was* afraid of me in the beginning. Wary of my instability. Thought I was too fragile, too much of a mess. Now he sees I'm not? Or that I am, but there's more to it.

"I—" He pauses. I lean forward. "My vision."

"Oh. Okay."

He adjusts his glasses. "I don't know what's going to happen with it. Some people are already . . . uncomfortable with me. I—I just don't want to—" He sighs. "I guess I'm afraid . . ." He looks at me steadily in that slightly sideways way he has. "That I could, um, really care about someone, and then they might not be able to handle what's coming. And bail out."

"Seriously? You think I would do that?" A weird relief hits me. All this time his reserve and awkwardness have been about him, not me! "I trusted you with my numerous psychiatric problems."

"True. And that was awesome. But—"

"Nick, I could not care less about how well you can see, including if you can't at all—except caring about whatever is hard for you."

He smiles and takes my hand. "I'm really sorry for acting like an asshat. Can we be, um, like, open? To the future?"

"Open to whatever might happen between us, you mean?" We could use a little more clarity here.

"Yeah. But not rush anything?"

"Sure. You're about to fly hundreds of miles away. So, no worries there. And you are my favorite asshat."

He laughs.

"Can I just hug you?" I ask.

He answers by springing to the couch and putting his arms around me. I giggle. Part nerves and part incredulous joy.

I take off his glasses, carefully, and set them on the coffee table. Noor lies with her head on her paws. Our lips meet.

We're slow and careful but there's a current running through our touching flesh, as well as through the material of our clothes, that could heat the whole room on a freezing night. Part of me feels like a little kid. *Am I doing this okay? Does he really like me? Do I smell okay? How's my breath?* My usual anxious questions dart around my brain, but they soften and evaporate in the warmth. Just go with it, Del. Smelling *him*— he smells like caramel and fresh basil. Loving being so close to him, having my arms around his body. It's all *now*.

# 51

## Wednesday, August 26

The next morning, I bound out of bed with new energy. And hey, the only big thing on my agenda today is getting Fran's suicide set up!

If I did a self-portrait collage right now, I would cut up only yellow things—marigolds, sunflowers, photos of French's mustard, tofu curry, yield signs, corn, baby chicks. Yes, it would look patchy, but definitely bright and sunshiny.

Final Dignity should call me back today. Meanwhile, I do have to go to the gallery for a shift. I leave Libby in charge. Thanks to Harold we have three days' worth of pain pills for Fran now, with an auto-refill and delivery.

Sure enough, my phone rings while I'm cleaning the Lone Star coffee machine and a woman is browsing some of the paintings. I signal to Louis that I've got to take this call upstairs.

I beeline up to Fran's bright office, mildly hyperventilating.

A friendly lady named Catherine asks, "What can I help you with, Delilah?"

"My aunt is, uh, under hospice care and I need some information. She's interested in advancing the time of her death."

"Where are you located?"

"We're in California. San Francisco." Out the second-floor window is a calming multicolored collage of buildings and roofs topped by blue sky.

"You know your state legislature is debating an act similar to Oregon's right now."

"Yeah. It won't be a law in time to help us, though, right?"

"I'm afraid not. What's her diagnosis?"

I pull over a note pad and Fran's fancy fountain pen. "High-grade neuro-endocrine cancer in the colon, liver, pancreas, and the lungs too, I think." I don't mention her brain since it's not official.

"Her doctor referred her to hospice with a terminal prognosis?"

"Yes. Dr. D'Silva said we needed to stop chemo treatment and then, yeah, she referred us to hospice." I doodle a lighthouse, easy to draw.

"How is your aunt feeling?"

"Sometimes okay, and sometimes in a *lot* of pain."

"Are you with her often?"

"I live with her. I'm helping to take care of her." Some defensiveness creeps into my voice. A silver-framed desk photo of dorky, eight-year-old snaggle-toothed me with Aunt Fran at the old Exploratorium museum stares back at me.

"Have you or she discussed your concerns with your hospice doctor and team?"

"Yeah. They're really great but they're not exactly pro death-with-dignity." I tilt back in Fran's leather desk chair and study the Richard Diebenkorn print of a lone woman in profile staring out a window.

"What your aunt would need if she were truly set on advancing the time of her death is somewhat complicated." She gives me all the details and I take notes. I already know most of them.

I ask, "What are the meds that the doctor prescribes?" Morbid curiosity.

"Usually Seconal, I believe."

"Hmmm." I managed to feature a couple of them in my overdose cocktail at Ridgefield.

She finishes describing all the steps.

I say, "They don't make it easy, do they?"

Catherine says, "It's this way for a reason. It has to be what the patient wants and can do for him- or herself, and not what anyone else is pressuring them into."

"Totally. But believe me, in our case, all the pressure is coming from my aunt."

We talk about establishing residency in Oregon.

She notes, "It means relocating someone very ill and having them die in an unfamiliar place."

"A hospital fits that bill too."

"You're right. Then she has to find a doctor who is willing to help her."

"That's my next step. Do you have names?" I've drawn a lopsided water dragon by the lighthouse.

"No, but we can suggest Kaiser Permanente, for example, which has excellent palliative and end-of-life care, and where she should be able to find a doctor. She has to be counseled on other options."

"What other options?"

"One is doing nothing and letting the disease take its course."

"Kind of obvious, I guess."

"Another is what we call VSED. Voluntary Stopping of Eating and Drinking."

"Oh." Fran now regularly pushes her bowls and plates away.

"Near the end of life, patients generally don't want to eat or drink anyway," she says brightly.

"Yeah. I made a really good chicken-spinach casserole the other night and she only ate a tablespoon. That was a lot for her, come to think of it."

"Hmmm. How do you feel about what your aunt is considering?"

"Um. Not great. Better than I was, though. I don't want her to suffer."

"I'm glad she has you with her. Is there anything else I can help you with?"

"No, you've been a big help. Thank you." I'm staring at the lighthouse I've drawn. "Um, actually, one more question. Have *you* ever been around someone who wanted to advance the time of their death?"

"Delilah, I had a brain tumor the size of a grapefruit removed from my skull almost fifteen years ago. I permanently lost the ability to see and to walk."

"Whoa." I sit up. Fran's chair squeaks beneath me.

"It was unclear what else might go wrong, except that I'd probably have more loss of bodily functions before it was all over. I, myself, was interested in the options surrounding terminal illness and end-of-life care. I knew mine might be right around the corner."

"Ohmigod. That's intense." I pause. "And now you do this."

"That's right."

Maybe having been through really hard things firsthand actually makes us the ideal ones to help others through similar things.

# 52

## Friday, August 28

Dad's back in London. I call him on my computer to bring him up to speed—and to urge him to get to California. Fran has said she wants to talk to him too.

I work on one of my collages while we talk. On a map of France and the British Isles, I arrange a baby sock, a thin heart-shaped black stone, edelweiss, a large red dragon, and mother-of-pearl chips on plywood. *Origins*, I'm calling it. It's for Fran.

Dad and I are only on audio, more comfortable talking to each other when we don't have to make eye contact.

I get right to the point. "Aunt Fran is getting worse fast, dealing with a lot more pain and way more confusion—"

Dad interrupts, "I talked to her last week. She told me the new health aide 'talks ten words a second with gusts up to fifty.'" He chuckles.

Fran didn't mention she talked to Dad. "Did you call her?" I ask, amazed.

"She called me."

Figures. "She was obviously making a big effort with you. Just following a conversation can exhaust her for days."

"Hmm."

"She's gone downhill fast in the last week or two." A photo in an old *National Geographic* catches my eye: a woman, a farmer, in a field blooming with weeds and wildflowers. "She also wants to 'advance the time of her death.'"

Dad pauses. "Do you mean assisted suicide?"

"It's death with dignity, Dad." I cut out the farmer and field.

"Did you suggest this?"

"What? Are you—Jesus!" I put my scissors down for safety reasons. "How you can say something like that when you are on the other side of the world and I'm here taking care of your sister, when I would do anything to keep her here longer, but instead I have to watch her dying painfully—"

"Delilah. I'm sorry." He pauses. "This is difficult for me."

"You think it's easy for *me*?" The nerve! I would be shouting if I weren't worried about Fran overhearing. "What the hell are you smoking?"

He doesn't answer.

I close my eyes and count to five.

Finally, he says, "I'm not good with family sickness. I make it worse."

I don't ask why he's working for an international medical organization then. "Fran wants to see you. I know you don't like the S-word. It may surprise you but I don't either."

"I didn't say you did."

"Yeah, you kinda did."

A big sigh heaves up to the satellite and back down to me.

"Dad, I don't want her to do this, *at all*, but she does. I promised I'd help. It's her life and her death and she should say how it goes."

He says nothing for a few beats. I hope it's sinking in.

"I guess you're right."

"Damn straight. I'm going into her room. She wants to talk to you."

I balance my laptop at Fran's bedside.

"I've got Dad here, Aunt Fran." I click the video on so he can see Fran in her early-morning grogginess: puffy face, rheumy eyes, bones where you didn't used to be able to see them.

"Hello, Tommy?" Fran struggles to sit up. I raise her bed. To my surprise, Dad turns on his video, appearing as his dark-haired, unshaven self. His eyes are wrinklier than I remember.

"Hi, Frannie," Dad says softly. He looks like someone shoved him hard at the edge of an open elevator shaft. He blinks three times.

"I see you," says Fran. "Are you here?"

"No, I'm in London. At home."

"Please come," says Fran. "I need you."

Dad stares through the screen for a long pause, or maybe it's satellite delay. "Okay. I'll be there soon as I can."

Fran smiles.

I walk back to my room as Dad says, "I need a little more time here to get everything wrapped up so I don't have to rush back. I'll aim for early the week after next."

"The week after next? Really?" He's unbelievable.

"You're not going to do it before then, are you?"

"We'll see."

# 53

## Saturday, August 29

The next morning, I bring Fran tea and sit by her bed. I have to talk to her about anything important in the late mornings and keep my fingers crossed. Too early, she's all groggy. In the evenings when she's tired, she has way more trouble with pain, words, and thoughts—and can be cranky.

What should I do about Oregon? I haven't even called Kaiser yet. I'm not sleeping well and Dr. Vernon adjusted my meds a little because my thoughts are racing more and I'm jittery as spit on a hot skillet. With Dad, we'll probably need two rooms at the Executive Inn. I don't know what to do next.

*Pretend you do.*

In Fran's room, an arrangement of giant roses, sunflowers, and those pink-throated lilies sweetly masks the smell of decay. Libby must've brought it in.

"Who sent these?" I ask Fran, moving them away from the edge of the table.

"Nancy." Nick's mom. I've been texting with Nick every couple of days since he got back to Austin. I'd love to talk to him about what's going on, but I'm scared of pushing it too fast since this new thread between us is not that strong yet.

"They're gorgeous. Aunt Fran, I talked to a woman at Final Dignity—"

"Who?" she says.

"A woman. Who gave me a lot of information about death with dignity."

"About death?"

"About going to Oregon and taking a lethal dose of medication. If you still want to pursue that. She would be happy to talk to you."

"I do," she says firmly, and I think she knows what she's talking about. But I'm not 100 percent sure.

"Then I'll make reservations. You know that Dad's coming out, right? He'll join us too."

She nods. I'm never sure what she remembers and what she doesn't.

"Do you want to talk to the lady?" I ask.

"You do it," she says.

# 54

That afternoon while I'm making her some soup, Fran totters into the kitchen, thin and unsteady. She's barefoot and in her flannel nightgown the color of sliced honeydew melon. It's foggy and cold today.

"Uh, Aunt Fran? Do you need something?"

"Yes." Her bloodshot eyes pop from her pale face.

"Pain okay?"

"Fine." Her expression is set, almost stern. Something's off.

"Where's your robe? Are you warm enough?" I sound like her parent, but she gets cold easily and never comes out without her warm robe. "How about some tea?"

She pushes aside the cutting board with my carrots and onions on it, then takes the Granny Smith apples out of a ceramic bowl from the counter. She goes to the refrigerator and pulls out a rectangle of Vermont cheddar cheese.

"I'm making some vegetable soup for us," I announce, sliding the cutting board over to where I can chop and watch her.

She roots around in the top of a cabinet that only she's tall enough to reach, and in a couple of drawers.

"Want me to help you find something?"

Her hands flutter in front of her chest. Her breasts and nipples show through the thin flannel. I'm more familiar with

Aunt Fran's body now than most of her doctors and nurses. "I . . . *flour,*" she says with conviction.

"Right over here." I pull down a package from the right cabinet. The first time I made blueberry pancakes was with Mom when I was about seven. From a mix that came with a petite tin can of blueberries.

"Don't . . . move it," she says, steadying herself on the counter edge and shooting me a look.

"I didn't," I whisper.

She rips opens the top of the flour bag and dumps a bunch in the bowl. A cloud of it settles like dust on her skin, the flannel, and the counter. She unwraps the whole block of cheese and studies it. Breaks it in two with her hands and puts both chunks in the bowl.

My stomach flips. She's trying to make cheese straws. For which she should use the food processor, although I'm not going to say a word about that. Having her lose a finger in those moving blades on top of everything else is all I need.

"Can I help?" I ask evenly.

Ignoring me, she opens the drawer with the aluminum and plastic wrap, then the drawer with potholders and tea towels. When she opens the knife drawer, my pulse really picks up. The next one holds the silverware, and she takes out a tablespoon and leaves both drawers half open.

Back at her bowl, swaying a little, she tries to stir the flour and cheese blocks.

I chop onions, my brain racing. She grips the bowl.

"I can't . . ." she says. Her eyebrows are pulled together in fierce concentration.

Helping her when she's confused is one thing. But this is like dealing with a possibly dangerous stranger. I'm not sure whether to laugh or run from the room in tears.

Instead I ask, "Do you need butter?"

Fran just sticks the bowl under the faucet and adds about a cup of water. She opens all the cupboards in growing agitation until she finds the blue carton of iodized salt, fumbles to open the little metal spout, then pours too much into the bowl. Her movements are jerky and her hand trembles. She tries to split one of the cheese chunks with the spoon and the bowl tips, spilling out the wet and the dry and the solid.

When I'm really depressed, my brain doesn't work at all. When I'm anxious, my mind stamps and back-steps and then gallops erratically on a wild ride. Fran's yanking at the reins and kicking that horse, and it won't go where she wants. She's the last person I ever expected to see struggling like this.

With Mom, my expectations were different. For a long time I thought all mothers sat in dark rooms by themselves during certain months, or once in a while drove home impulse-purchase farm equipment. Our usual "normal" behavior is just a network of thin, shaky paths we've hacked out by repetition from infinite possibilities.

"Dammit to hell!" She bangs the counter. She's shaking now from exertion, in danger of collapsing.

I pull my shoulders back and stand up straight to project authority. "It's okay, Aunt Fran. You can do it later." This lie falls out of my mouth weighing about fifty pounds.

She grips the counter and leans against it, deflated. "I've done it all wrong," she whispers.

I gently take her arm. "It doesn't matter. Here. Let's go to your room and you can rest a little. I'll bring you some tea."

Her face softens in relief. "What about . . . ?" she gestures weakly at the bowl and the mess all over the granite.

"I'll finish up the cheese straws and stick them in the oven,"
I say cheerfully.

After I settle Fran in bed, I straighten up her bathroom. In
the drawer under the bathroom counter I find a piece of note-
book paper scribbled in Fran's handwriting.

*At the edge of night,*
*where darkness advances*
*in an arc that swallows the universe,*
*to my surprise,*
*almost everything is growing.*
*Like ivy shoots,*
*tenderness curls and attaches*
*over my walls and fences*
*intertwining with forgiveness*
*into a hemp safety net.*
*Grief floods and loosens the soil of me.*
*Fear*
*pokes like brambles.*
*Fantastic liquid dreams*
*crash and foam into the three-dimensional.*
*Cancer chokes the pink and spring green of me*
*to slick, putrid brown.*
*Pain devours with blunt bovine teeth.*
*Yet, wonder blooms—*
*a field of dandelions,*
*seeds helicoptering into the dusk.*

；

Back in my room I watch an online video of the life of a dandelion. Recorded over two days and reduced to two minutes, one blooms electric yellow. It soaks up the sun, then slowly folds up like a parasol. Or like hands clasping in prayer. Finally, in one split second, it bursts into the globe of white fuzz we love to pluck and blow apart. Each one of the seeds' long, thin stems is topped by tiny filaments that, once airborne, spin and carry the seed to a new life.

# 55

## Monday, August 31

Libby, our health aide, comes every afternoon now, and can stay until late to help out with bathing or treating Fran's sores from lying in bed so much. Meanwhile I grocery shop, pay bills, or go for a walk/skate/smoke. Fran isn't in diapers yet, although that may not be far off. It's getting grittier.

I book three refundable tickets to Portland for September 18, plus a reservation at an Executive Inn. Dad is supposedly making arrangements to come right now, but I won't believe it until he walks through the door.

Cards and letters continue to pour in, and Fran seems barely interested. Friends want to visit and she mostly doesn't want to see them. One woman I don't even know gets mad and insists. I reluctantly go ask Fran again. She shakes her head; she definitely does not want to see her. I apologize to the lady but want to say, "If she's so important to you, why haven't you seen her in the last two years?" Most people make it about themselves. *I'm* the only one who's allowed to do that.

Yesterday, a man named Mike Cruz who worked with her almost thirty years ago asked to come by and she said firmly, "Absolutely."

This afternoon, he arrives in dark brown cowboy boots with a big box of cherry Danish. I walk Fran to the living room, reminding her who's here and that she's looking forward to seeing him. I've combed her hair, and she wears her plum silk robe. Her movements are calm and deliberate. I remind myself that my job is simply to support her. Not to figure out who this guy is to her.

His jaw tightens as we walk in. He probably hasn't seen her in a long time. "Mike," she says, smiling bigger than I've seen in weeks.

"Oh, Fran." He can't keep the dismay out of his voice. His salt-and-pepper hair and beard suggest he's her age.

I try to see her as he does. She's still so tall but stooped, which she never was before. Moves stiffly like she's breakable. Her red-rimmed hazel eyes are puffy and her skin has a thin, gray, translucent quality to it.

"Taking its toll. I'm fine," she says, as if answering a question. "Thank you." Her one eye bulges slightly and is cloudy and unfocused. I still haven't gotten used to that.

They don't embrace. I seat her and park alongside, hoping this man won't faint.

"You . . . uh." He tries again. "Do you . . . er?" He's censoring the question, *How long have you got?*

I say, "You used to work together?"

"Back in the nineties," he says gratefully. "We worked together on an investment and pension project for the state, in Sacramento, for almost two years. We had some fun up there, didn't we?" he asks her.

"I think so," she says. "I wanted to take . . . that one . . ." she looks at me, shakes her head. "A . . . maple fog. Which one was it?"

The ornate gold clock ticks like a bomb.

"You wanted to take something, Aunt Fran?" I try.

"Never mind. A tight spot," she says. "Mike?"

"Yes, it's me. I came to see you, old pal." Some people can fall into a rhythm with her. A few panic, especially lately as she's gotten harder to understand and follow. He's going with it pretty well, but his forehead has small beads of perspiration on it.

She furrows her forehead. "Do you take me to . . . work?"

"Er, I don't think so." He looks at me.

"Nope," I say. "You're on vacation, Fran." I add, "You haven't worked at MacDougal for a long time." It kind of amazes me that this comes as second nature now, to steer the conversation for Fran.

"Me neither," pipes in Mike.

"Right. That's not what I'm thinking," she says in a silly-me voice. "Were we going to do something?" She's more scattered even than usual, probably nervous. We all are.

"Yes, water's boiling for tea," I say, glad for the excuse to go to the kitchen. "I know you would like some Earl Grey. Mike, how about you?"

"That sounds fine," he says. But his face says, *Please don't leave me here alone.*

"I'll be right back," I assure him. If I'm honest, it's kind of refreshing to let somebody else sink or swim with Fran for a few minutes and endure what I deal with every day.

When I come back with a tray, Mike has moved over next to Fran on the couch, like Nick did with me, and is holding one of her hands with both of his. He's saying, "Then the *governor* called Noriega and chewed him out. Remember?"

She nods a little, like a bobblehead. "Jensen," she repeats. "A . . . glug."

"Oh yeah! Jensen was sort of a glug," Mike says, laughing. "He made us pay for that."

Now Fran is grinning. "He called the boss," she says clearly.

"He did! To complain about insubordination!" His face is lit with relief and mirth.

I pop a piece of cherry Danish in my mouth. It's delicious. "Would you like some, Aunt Fran?" I cut her a small piece. Place it in front of her on a napkin. Once she would've made me go get a plate. She doesn't care now.

Silver linings.

"We used to live on that stuff." He points at the pastries. "Didn't we, Fran?"

"Did we live together?" she asks.

He hesitates. "Uh, no." Grins. "I certainly would have."

"Ah," I say.

She's concentrating on something.

"How long did you work together?" I ask, still chewing. I don't ask, *How long were you a couple? Or were you?*

"We were in the same division for three years, but at Mac-Dougal together for seven or eight. Fran was an excellent financial analyst and executive."

Fran says, "Your family?" She might be trying to change the subject. Or not.

"They're all well, thank you. My oldest daughter is at law school." He adjusts his shoulders.

"Wow," I say, impressed. "That's great." I'm jealous of how proud he is. *When did you get married? Before or after you knew Fran?* For an old guy, he's not bad-looking.

Fran grimaces and lets out a puff of air. This has taken a lot of energy and she's fading quickly.

After a moment, Mike leans toward Fran. "I'd better get

going. Fran, it was a privilege knowing you and I am so sorry you're ill. I see that you're being well taken care of. I wish you all the best, old pal." He stands and awkwardly reaches down to give her a hug. "Thank you for the tea." He backs toward the front door.

I follow him. "It means a lot to her," I say needlessly. "But she tires out fast."

We step out into the carpeted foyer.

"It's hard," he says. "Hard to see. She was so sharp. Such a wit. Such an intelligent and principled woman."

"Thanks for coming," I say. She's never mentioned Mike before, that I remember. Were they lovers? I can ask her in a clear moment, but something tells me she's not going to answer.

His eyes are a little shiny, and he jabs the elevator button twice.

# 56

## Wednesday, September 2

In the back of the bus on the way to my AA meeting, I take a deep breath and call Final Dignity again.

"Catherine, this is Delilah Wilson."

"Ah, yes, how are you doing? How is your aunt?"

"I'm okay, but I am worried about Aunt Fran." People are staring. Maybe I'm being too loud. "We're planning to go to Oregon in two weeks, after my dad gets here," I say softly, "and I contacted Final Dignity there. I forgot to mention—she's— I'm not sure about her brain."

"How so?"

"Sometimes she's good, but sometimes she's really confused." I take a breath. "She can't read anymore. It all looks like squiggles to her. I think her brain has been . . . affected."

She pauses. "Have you talked to the hospice doctor?"

"They think the same thing."

"I'm sorry to hear that. Advancing the time of death can only be done if a patient is fully mentally competent. It's highly unlikely that you'll find a doctor willing to do it now."

"Oh." My skin prickles and my breath comes in small bursts. The news is so double-edged.

I'll have Fran a little longer!

But. The cancer *is* in her brain, no denying it. Plus, she'll be all defeated at this news. She may suffer more as a result.

I'll think about that later.

"That's what I was afraid of," I say. "I'm so worried about her being in pain and distress. What do I do?" The bus stops, and the back door opens. I get off and head for the church basement entrance.

"What you've already been doing very well. Stay with her. Make sure she's comfortable. Her body will take over. It knows what to do. I wish you fortitude and good luck, Delilah."

How am I going to tell Aunt Fran?

# 57

## Saturday, September 5

I open Fran's bedroom window and let in the chill summer fog —although it's finally warming up now. A revolving fan also helps ventilate the sickroom smells.

I help Fran out to the kitchen. Unless she's had a bad night and is sleeping, she still often joins me at the small table for breakfast, as a matter of pride and discipline. It's her best time of day. These routines are good for both of us.

I offer Fran a half of a toasted English muffin with olive oil and salt. She insisted two days ago, and again yesterday, that's what she wanted. Today, she pokes it and frowns.

"This is not right," she announces.

I put my hands on my hips. "It's. What. You. Asked for." It's hard not to get exasperated with her sometimes. It's like dealing with a five-year-old lately. Maybe I'm not cut out for teaching real five-year-olds.

"No, I don't think so."

"What do you want then?" I demand.

She wiggles her fingers and closes her eyes in thought. "Strawberries? Do you have them?"

"No." I sigh. "But I can get some."

"Now?"

"Later today."

"What about . . . passion fruit?"

I count to five. "How about I cut you up a nectarine?" She only nibbles at meals. Pounds keep dropping off her. I'm afraid she's going to disappear.

She smiles. "How about . . . a dirty martini?"

I try not to encourage her. "Nope."

A minister from the church Fran used to attend is coming today. Even though Fran's been hanging out at a Buddhist spiritual center the last couple of years, apparently there are no hard feelings. I'll use the time to get some desperately needed exercise. "Are you looking forward to the rev's visit?" I ask as I slice a nectarine.

"Rev?"

"You know, the reverend. From your old church."

"Oh. He's here?" She glances over her shoulder toward the front door.

"*She's* coming. After lunch."

"Senior Tuesdays?" she asks, fingering the soft fleece collar of her pink robe.

I'm not sure what she means. "At the church?" The new muffin pops out of the toaster.

"Yes. Where else?" Now she's annoyed. Not with me, with the disease. She's too young to have gone to senior Tuesdays. Maybe she volunteered at them or something.

I give her a new muffin with butter.

She takes two bites and closes her eyes. She's been known to doze, and I worry about her falling off the kitchen chair.

"Everything okay?" I ask, sitting down at the table next to her.

She blinks. Instead of glassy or vacant, her eyes are alert. "I really thought . . ." She trails off.

"What did you think?" I prompt, reaching for her hand. Her nails are a little ragged. I should give her a manicure.

"I'd have more time." She touches her plate and the muffin. "Every day's a gift."

"For sure." The sudden clarity in her voice and gaze come from the old Fran, but like on *Family Feud*, I think we've only got ten seconds. "Are you afraid?" I blurt out.

"No," she says, shaking her head. " . . . No."

I breathe out in relief. "You're happy with your life?" *Do you miss Mike?*

*Will you miss me?*

And as if she heard my last thought, she says, "I'd like more time with . . . you. The woman . . . you're becoming." She puts her hand on top of mine.

"Me too, Aunt Fran. But I'm so glad we have the time we did. And do." She's as with-it as I've seen her in the last two weeks at least. It's weird stepping into our old roles, and I fight to tamp down a jolt of familiar panic. "Don't get mad"—I pull out my phone for distraction—"but I want to take a quick selfie with you. I know you don't like them, but this is something I need."

"Okay."

I lean over by her and click one. I try to smile for the camera but I know it looks forced. She's trying too.

"I never learned to fly," she says, scrunching her face as if in pain.

I'm not sure if this is literal or figurative.

She's gently stroking the quilted blue-and-silver placemat. There's no time to waste here. I guess my biggest question is, is she still counting on ending things on her own schedule?

I was going to wait until she asked before explaining about Oregon, but she never has. I won't cancel our reservations until the last moment in case anything changes. But I need to tell her.

"Aunt Fran, about Oregon," I start.

She looks at me blankly.

"We're afraid we won't be able to get any doctors to sign off on . . . advancing the time of your death."

She flicks her hand dismissively. "Friends and family. The . . . what? . . . we have?"

"Uh, relationships?"

"No. Between . . ." She puts out her palms and raises one and lowers the other. "Oh, I hate not being able . . . to find!" She bangs the table.

"Do you mean 'balance'?" I ask gently.

"Yes, with them."

"We have to balance what we want versus what they want?" I guess.

She nods, deciding it's close enough. Or else she's already in another cloud. "He didn't like him. Or my friends."

She doesn't care about Oregon, or she's forgotten? I'm following her in a dance, but there are no choreographed steps, no stage, no music. She's Texas-two-stepped to the far side of the Golden Gate. She's waving at me. The bridge is clear but is going to disappear back into the fog any minute.

"Who never liked who?" An old boyfriend? Mike? Dad? Her dad? There's so much about her I don't know. Things close to her heart.

She wipes her hand absently on her napkin. "He liked Tommy's."

"Grandpa? Liked Dad's friends?"

"He was . . . so sad he didn't come." Her eyes are glistening. "Heartbreak."

"When Grandpa was sick."

She nods.

My throat thickens again. Their dad gave Fran a hard time about her friends? And who she was. He loved his son better? But it was Fran who took care of him.

"And Dad never even showed up."

He'd damn well better this time.

She squeezes my hand, a little hard. "I'm so sorry . . . I didn't know. How depressed you were. Thanksgiving." She means before my attempt.

"It doesn't matter, Aunt Fran! You've done so much for me."

"Should have." Fran rubs her eye. "Your mom. Told me. Not long before she . . . left us. That her depression was back."

"And then she died," I say, taking a deep breath.

Aunt Fran nods.

"On purpose." I blow that breath out. First time I've said it out loud.

"Should've seen it. In you."

"It's not your fault," I say. "And you save my life every day."

# 58

## Monday, September 7

Harold checks on Fran, then snags me to sit down in the living room. The beginning of the fall semester has come and gone. I'm only working a couple of shifts a week at the gallery for Louis. For now, anyway.

"Want some seven-layer bean dip?" I ask him. "A friend of Fran's brought it by."

"Thank you, no. Tell me, how are you doing?" he asks.

"Good, I guess." I feel for my necklace and find only the naked cleft between my collar bones. Even though I know dozens of therapists and psychiatrists, Harold suggested I talk to one of the hospice grief counselors. I have yet to call the number. I'd rather talk to him.

"Yeah?"

"I try not to think about it," I admit.

"Think about what?" he asks pointedly.

I look him in the eyes. "That Fran is dying. But . . . this is what tripped me up in the past. Not thinking about feelings that are there even if you pretend they're not. The longer you won't admit they're there, the larger and harder they get." My whole life is figuring out what to deny and what to admit.

He nods slowly. "You got that right."

"Remember we were talking about how kids handle death? My mom's was harder because everyone danced around her mental illness. She had bipolar disorder."

"I see."

"So she took her own life."

He makes a noise of surprise and sympathy.

"By driving into a wall. I think she wanted to protect us from the stigma of suicide." I hook my fingers in quotes. "It was 'a car accident.'"

He bows his head. "Hmm-hmm-hmm."

I add, "Fran said that Mom knew another depressive episode was coming on."

"I'm so sorry about your mama," he says as softly as a bass tuba can. "You are carrying a big load here, Delilah. Losing Fran would be hard any way we look at it. But it will be especially hard for you."

His kind voice washes over me like a warm bubble bath. Acknowledging the difficulty. Validating my feelings.

"I've been afraid that my, um, mental health, or lack thereof, would make me want to take my own life. If Fran died. Um, when Fran dies."

"Do you think that now?" He sits up, his eyebrows slightly raised. "Are you feeling suicidal?"

"No. Not at all. But thanks for asking."

He hands me a tissue from a packet he must always carry in his pants pocket. "Remind me, Delilah, is your father coming?"

"He's supposed to be here a week from today. Finally."

"Good. And Fran knows he's coming?" One elbow rests on the blue-and-cream upholstered arm rest.

"Yes, sir."

"Then she'll likely hang on until he arrives."

"She'll wait to die?"

He sits back. "Yes, within reason. She's got other things to do too. Often in these last weeks and days, there's a lot of work going on. Even if a person is unconscious."

"Work? What do you mean?"

"Reflecting on the life you've led—regrets, triumphs. Getting ready to say goodbye to and let go of all you love. And cross over."

"How do you know all this?" There's nowhere to put my used tissue except in my jeans pocket. *Don't forget to take it out before doing laundry.*

"Occasionally someone will go right to the threshold of death, and then come back to consciousness. It's rare, but when people do, we learn more about the process." He gestures with his large hands. "That's how we know, for example, that the death rattle isn't really uncomfortable for the patient. They may not even notice it, but it bothers their loved ones to hear it."

"You mean people have come back from having a death rattle—when you're like an hour or two from the end, right?—to tell about it?"

"Yes. But it's very rare."

A small thread sticks out from a pleat on the chair armrest. I tuck it under. "I know Fran's probably not going to be one of those . . . rarities."

"Probably not," he says gently.

"So, what do I do to help her?" I ask.

He picks up his medical bag from the floor and balances it on his lap. "What you're already doing. Support her. Reassure her," he says. "Let her know that it's okay to go. That you love her, but that you'll be okay without her."

"What if I won't?" I mutter.

He dips his chin as if to acknowledge the weight of that. "Then she may fight going."

# 59

## Sunday, September 13

Fran is extra tired and has a pain spike. I get it under control with drops but it takes longer than usual. I blame Charlotte's visit earlier this evening. Charlotte exhausts everyone. She's leaving tomorrow morning for New York because her daughter is about to have a baby. Thank god.

Fran sleeps a lot more. We wake her up for her meds during the day, though, because if we don't, the pain will, and then we can't get her comfortable again for hours.

;

"Daddy!" Fran calls from her room. It's 11:32 p.m. now, and I've been asleep for about fifteen minutes, at most.

I run through the dark apartment to her room. "What is it?" I'm so tired, that I slur the words. Please, not an emergency.

She tries to sit up. Focuses on me and glares. "You've got thirty seconds to explain!" she cries.

"Explain what?" I turn on her bedside lamp, my heart thumping.

"You know you shouldn't be here!"

"Aunt Fran. It's me," I say. "You called out."

She exhales, frowns, and leans back. "Who are you again?" she asks softly.

"Your niece. Delilah."

"Delilah?" Her eyes dart around in confusion.

So I add, "We're in your bedroom. In San Francisco."

Her expression is amazed. Like it's a place she's always wanted to go and now here she is. My heart is ripping inside-out. "It's okay, Aunt Fran. I'll get you some tea." I start for the door.

"But the map," she says. "Where is it?"

"Map? Do you want your phone?"

"My map. They have . . ."

"You mean one of the ones you gave me to use for my art?"

She shakes her head. "To get to . . ." She's gripping her comforter.

"For traveling somewhere?"

Guilt grabs me around the throat. Our reserved flight on September 18 is only a few days away.

There's a long pause. "Yes," she says.

"Oregon?" I ask softly.

"No."

Oh.

"Do you need drops?"

She shakes her head.

"Tea?"

No.

I sit in the chair by her bed. "It's okay. I'll stay with you until you go back to sleep. Don't worry. You'll . . . you'll find the way." As if I know. The cold night air prickles every inch of my skin.

"Tommy is coming?"

"Yes. Dad gets here Wednesday."

She closes her eyes and seems to be resting. I let out my breath in a puff. Now that we've gotten this far without him, part of me wishes he'd stay away. His presence will definitely add to *my* strain. A few minutes go by and she's asleep.

But as soon as I stand, Fran blinks. "Ohhh," she breathes out. She gestures to the far dark corner of the room. Her eyes are shining, and her mouth is open in wonder.

"What?" I ask.

"There." She reaches out as if she wants to touch something far away.

Now the hairs on the back of my neck and arms stand straight up. "I—I don't see anything."

"Lipstick?" she asks. She pulls her heavy hand up to her mouth.

"You want to put lipstick *on* you?"

She nods almost imperceptibly and holds her fingers to her lips. "Shhh."

With shaking hands, I get her favorite color, Hothouse Tomato, from her bathroom drawer.

A folded envelope sits beneath the compartmentalized makeup box. Looks like a poem so I slip it into my pocket.

I dab a little lipstick on her lips, keeping my focus on her because I'm afraid of what I might see if I look again at the spot she's watching.

"S'all right," she assures me. Just before she drifts off again she mumbles, "Doll Boy."

;

In my room, I read her poem:

*I pull,*
*over and over*
*to stay*
*centered.*
*To see*
*what is now.*
*Hold gently*
*to what is me*
*as it switches and whips and pirouettes and fades.*
*I'm everywhere.*
*I'm nowhere.*
*An unfathomable greatness*
*with no edges and*
*no center*
*patiently*
*waits.*
*Happy helpers*
*whisper*
*candied nothings*
*without air,*
*without sound.*
*How quirky and quark-like*
*are words:*
*crux,*
*edge,*
*ledge,*
*time,*
*soon,*
*place,*
*leave,*
*arrive.*

# 60

## Wednesday, September 16

Joel buzzes the intercom and announces, "Thomas Wilson, Ms. Wilson's brother, is here."

"Oh, crap," I say instead of "Thanks." I never offered to pick him up at the airport, and he never asked.

The doorbell chimes, long and loud.

Deep breath. I open the door. Dad stands on the threshold in a blazer and scuffed brown leather shoes. For having come some five thousand miles, he's clean-shaven and his eyes, the same light hazel color as Fran's, are bright. The gray hair in his sideburns and at his temples is the only change in him since the last time we occupied the same space. He holds a bakery box, and on his arm hangs a shopping bag with a bottle of wine. Hmm. He must've already checked into his hotel and left any luggage.

We hug around the big pink box. He hangs on to me longer than usual, crunching the cardboard. He's wearing his usual spicy and grassy aftershave. The smell is an ache and a frustration for me, but it also means competence is here.

I pull away. "I—I'm glad you're here, Dad," I stammer, probably for the first time since I was a toddler. "Better late than never," I add.

"You've been smoking," he says with a light sniff.

"My, what a good nose you have. But not drinking." Not since last month. I'm twenty-seven days sober.

"Del, with a grandfather who died of lung cancer and an aunt dying the same way, I wish you would consider stopping."

My whole head vibrates in disbelief. "Don't start, Dad. You are in no position to give advice of any kind."

"I'm sorry," he says to my surprise. "You're right."

He hands me the box. "Go ahead, open it." I do, while he heads to the kitchen and puts the wine on the kitchen counter.

Coconut pecan frosting. A German chocolate cake! I stop my third-grade self from dragging a finger across the top.

"Frannie's favorite. She used to make them when we were kids."

"I didn't know that." If he thinks a cake is going to make up for being completely missing in action for the whole war, though, he's going to have to dodge some grenades.

I close the box and join him in the kitchen. He stares at my wrist. "Is that a tattoo?"

"It is." Einstein.

He sighs but refrains from asking me more about it. Instead he opens the white wood cabinet that holds flour, sugar, spices, and condiments. Fran's attempt to make cheese straws pops into my head and I cringe.

"What are you looking for?" I demand. He should not be making himself at home.

"A plate? Something I can put this on."

I point.

After Dad deftly transfers the cake, I expect him to go to Fran's room, but he walks toward the living room windows. He gazes out at the lit-up Golden Gate Bridge. The amethyst sky, veined with ruby and gold, peeks through the clouds.

Dusk again.

"I forgot what a beautiful view this apartment has." He pivots. "How is she?"

"You might want to go in and see for yourself," I say so evenly I should get an Oscar.

He makes no move. Toes the carpet with his eyes all tight and wrinkled. "I just need a couple of minutes . . . to prepare."

"Give me a break, Dad. You've had months to prepare." So much for competence. It's exhausting just to keep an even tone and not throw the cake at him.

He swallows. "Can they estimate how much time she has?"

"Not really. No more than a week or so at the most. She's been asking for you"—I rub it in—"like every day. I gave her pain meds twenty minutes ago, so we should have a window of opportunity. Now."

I start toward Fran's room but Dad will not move. "Is there a nurse here?"

"Not yet, but we have a night nurse now who's been coming the last few days. She'll be here soon." After Fran's last pain spike, Harold recommended adding Eileen to the roster.

"I'm so glad she's on hospice care," Dad says.

"She *is* happy to be at home," I allow. "It's probably for the best that we're not in some hotel in Oregon."

"So that's definitely off?"

"Yes." I've messaged him about all this, without much reaction from him.

He puts his hand on my upper arm. Breathes in deeply. "Delilah, you've been doing a really difficult job here, an adult's job."

No shit. I guess he's trying to give me a compliment.
"Okay, Dad, Let's go."

Dad grips the cake platter with white knuckles.

We walk into Fran's curtained, dim bedroom.

"Is it time?" Fran looks confused as I raise the hospital bed so she's sitting up.

"A special cake for you, Frannie," Dad says. Unlike when he saw her via video, he shows no shock at her appearance.

"A birthday?" asks Fran.

I take it from Dad and put it on the bedside table.

"Daddy?" Fran asks as Dad gently hugs her.

"It's Tommy."

"Oh, that's nice!" Fran is smiling bigger than I've seen in weeks.

"And Del," I add.

"Oh, Del," she says, like I'm also a delightful thought.

I unclench my fists and take charge. "Charlotte left us a casserole. Do you feel like coming to the table? Or would you rather we have some dinner in here on trays?"

"I've got company," Fran says.

"Right. The table it is."

Dad says, "I'll take you out." He helps Fran into her plum robe and slippers with non-skid soles.

I set the table with Fran's favorite woven mats and the good silverware. If we don't use it now, then when?

They hobble out of Fran's room, Fran leaning heavily on Dad who's the same height. His face is contorted in concentration.

Fran winces and cries out.

"You're going too fast, Dad!" I blurt out. "You're hurting her!"

He's freaking clueless and thinks he can waltz in here and take over.

"I'm sorry!" Dad stops and lets Fran reposition herself against him. They proceed at a snail's pace.

I shove the casserole into the microwave to reheat, reminding myself that dealing with this situation would be hard for any nonprofessional just entering into Fran's complicated and fragile world.

Dad gets Fran situated in the big padded chair, propped with extra cushions. We need to make this quick. For Fran to hold herself erect and stay comfortable takes a lot of strength.

The crab-artichoke casserole is cheesy and hot, and I serve it with salad from a cellophane bag with an easy Dijon vinaigrette Fran taught me to make.

Dad asks me, "Do you object if Frannie and I have a glass of wine?"

"Nope." I would like one too.

Fran watches my face as Dad pours himself and her small glasses of the French Chablis. He places the bottle next to his mat.

Esmerelda met me at an early morning meeting, and we talked by phone this afternoon about Dad's arrival. I also got a pep text from Nick. All I can control is my reaction to him. My (big) job is to remember that this is Fran's time.

Dad and I sit down and are about to start when Fran puts up her hand. "Please," she commands, a little loudly.

We wait, forks in hand.

"To give thanks." She puts out both of her puffy hands. We gently clasp them, and Dad reaches across the table for my other hand.

She recites painfully slowly but perfectly,

*Thank you for the world so sweet,*
*Thank you for the food we eat,*
*Thank you for the birds that sing,*
*Thank you, God, for everything.*

"Amen," we say.

"That's the blessing we used to say when we were little," Dad says quietly, running his finger around the edge of his glass. "Dad always asked for the 'bird blessing.'"

"Shh." Fran grips my hand harder. She's not done. "Dear Lord," she says, "we thank you . . . for this. For everything. This life. The kids . . . inside . . . important people. Together. We're thankful . . . Just thankful. *Now.*"

"Amen," Dad and I say again.

"That was so nice," adds Dad, glancing at me for approval, which has never happened in my life. I affirm his humble progress with a nod.

Fran wears a big smile and gazes at each of us with her good eye. She takes a sip of wine and smacks her lips.

"I like being called a kid," jokes Dad.

"I don't," I say.

"Ain't No Mountain High Enough," Fran says.

Now Dad looks like he's about to bolt. I try to communicate back wordlessly that this is normal and that he should go with the flow.

"Tommy's here," Fran adds, grinning.

We dig in and slowly relax. Fran listens or goes off in her own world, only eating a few bites, but that's more than she can manage at most mealtimes lately. The faintest pink colors her cheeks. Dad's arrival has given her a second wind.

It's only mildly annoying.

"We didn't forget," Fran pipes up at one point when Dad and I are discussing the complications of healthcare and education for isolated, impoverished women and children under strong-arm dictatorships.

"Nope. We didn't," I confirm, even though I don't know what.

We all have slices of the German chocolate cake. Fran gets a forkful into her mouth, closes her eyes, and lifts her chin with a smile. "Like Momma's," she murmurs.

Dad agrees, "Like Mom's." He pushes his empty dessert plate away and says, "What a delicious dinner. With lovely company. Truly one of the best I've ever had." He takes Fran's hand.

This might be our last supper. The weight of that is supported by what's between us. Pushed up against the edge of Fran's life like this, old hurts and awkwardness with Dad have mostly evaporated, at least for the time being.

I don't dare think about anything beyond this moment.

It's not that hard.

# 61

We help Fran to her bed and she collapses into her pillows. I administer all her meds and sit beside her in my usual chair. Dad carries a dining room chair to the other side of the bed. She grips my hand and reaches for Dad's hand too. She's been working so hard to enjoy this time, and tired as she is, she's not ready for us to leave her yet.

She says with effort, "Every day's a . . ."

We wait.

"A blessing?" asks Dad.

"A gift," I state, having heard this before.

"No." Fran smiles, pulling her fingers together near her face as if to catch her thought. "A bad hair day."

We laugh, lightly at first, then harder maybe than we should. It's true, her hair looks kinda awful. It's amazing and lightening to be able to laugh freely.

It is a gift. My throat thickens and aches with gratitude.

"Tommy is so handsome," Fran says.

"You're beautiful, Frannie," says Dad sincerely. He sits on the other side of the bed. "And you're much braver than I am. You always have been."

"The crosswalk," says Fran. "The big bike."

Dad looks at me and I shrug.

Fran's elbows rest on her lap and she points upward with both hands. She says clearly, "Momma let me ride . . . my big bike. Through the alley. Tommy led me."

Dad's face softens. He knows what Fran's talking about.

Fran speaks slowly and with fierce concentration. "To the crosswalk . . ."

"At Preston," says Dad quietly. "And then on to school."

"Held traffic . . . I walked my bike." Fran smiles. "A big truck. With lawnmowers. Sweaty . . . sunburned men. They waited . . . patiently. You waved them on."

"Ha. What grade were you in?" I ask Fran.

"Third."

"And I was in fourth." Dad's eyes are shining. Their parents were in the middle of their messy divorce. "Remember Madame Faivre?" he asks Fran. "Our music teacher," he informs me.

"Oui," Fran responds, not missing a beat.

"She liked you best," he says.

"Hand span."

Dad says, "She did always say you had an exceptional hand span." He laughs, then catches himself.

So this is how it was between them. Dad the spoiled, handsome, charming boy, receiving and shrugging off compliments. And Fran hanging on to any she could get. I'm ecstatic Madame Faivre liked Fran best.

Dad says softly, "I love you, Frannie."

"I know."

;

Dad and I clean up. More than half a bottle of the wine is left, but as I bring dishes in from the table, Dad stands at the kitchen sink, holding it higher than necessary, pouring it down the drain. When he turns around, I force a smile to show I understand. At least he doesn't know about my slip. I hope.

After Dad's gone, I put Fran's mega pill box back in her bathroom, then lean down to kiss her, certain she's out cold. But she reaches for my hand. Holds it.

I sit down beside her. This is way more than she's done in weeks. She's got to be exhausted. Her one eye is swollen and cloudy, but her left eye is focused on me. She's wide awake.

Harold said to reassure her about leaving me.

"Del," she says like she's trying it out as a name. "Sweet girl."

"Well, thanks." I grin.

"Thank *you*," she says, gazing at me with tenderness. She means for dinner, for helping to take care of her, for being here. But forgiveness is in those words too —for Oregon, for my slip, for dragging her to *Beach Blanket Babylon*, for bashing her Prius, even for the time I spilled all her white truffle oil. I love her so much in this moment, I might blow apart like a dandelion on a summer breeze.

"It isn't too hard?" she asks, reaching for my hand.

I tell her the truth. "It's been hard. But I wouldn't miss it for the world."

She smiles gratefully. Closing her eyes, she lets out her breath, which becomes a deep, guttural moan.

I flinch. That sound electrocutes every cell in me. She fooled me tonight. Made me think she's better. "It's okay, Aunt Fran, I'm right here. Rest now."

She's breathing a little unevenly. But I'm pretty sure she's already asleep. I hold her hand for a while as the night presses in around me.

It's not okay for her to go.

# 62

## Thursday, September 17

The next morning, after Libby arrives to watch Fran, I walk down to Fisherman's Wharf to meet Dad for coffee, at his insistence. Even after our happy dinner last night, I'm tired and a little anxious about Dad being here, but it's nice to be outside. It's cool and foggy again today and I pass a gazillion tourists. Actually, I'm struck by the fact that I'm not a whole lot *more* anxious about Dad.

Still, I keep repeating, *For Fran, we will get along.*

Dad's already sitting in the nautical-themed restaurant, at an oak-plank table under a brass porthole. By a large cannon. With a tankard of coffee. "Morning, sweetie. How is she today?"

I sit. "Asleep. Last night wiped her out."

"It wiped me out," he says.

I maturely neither comment nor roll my eyes. "How's the hotel?"

"Great. But I'd really like to stay with you all." He tilts his head enough to suggest it might be a question.

"There's no place for you to sleep," I say quickly.

"I'd be fine on the couch. I can give them notice and check out tomorrow or Saturday."

I cannot suppress a sigh. "Okay. Whatever."

Fran will be glad to have him around more, even if I'm miserable. All that old awkwardness has re-congealed.

He asks, "What happened with the assisted-suicide business?"

"Death with Dignity." I fold one of the extra treasure-map placemats for my collage file. "She's not mentally competent enough now."

Dad wraps both hands around his coffee mug as if for warmth.

"But she was," I say. "I totally blew it."

"What do you mean?"

"It all would've worked out if I hadn't been so freaking slow and selfish. I wasted precious time fighting her."

He puts his coffee down. "Sweetie, it shouldn't have fallen on your shoulders. I should've come earlier."

"Yeah, you should have. Decaf coffee, please. Large," I say to the pirate waiter, with a weak salute.

"Aye-aye."

Dad says, "I talked to Louis about the gallery this morning. He's very capable and is doing a great job."

"I know," I say.

"Anyway, I'll handle all of that. With your input, of course. You've been doing an excellent job, whatever you may think." He sips his coffee. "I'll stay with her this afternoon and evening. You go do something with friends. Or whatever you want. I've got things to talk to her about too."

Our waiter plops down my tankard of coffee. "Thanks." I pour in sweetener and cream.

My phone dings with a text.

"Everything okay with Fran?" Dad asks, frowning.

I check it. "Uh, yeah. It's Nick. I'll text him back later."

I slide my phone into my backpack. Nothing will piss Dad off faster than texting at the table while we're supposed to be conversing. He and Fran have that much in common.

Dad says, "He was out here this summer, right? How is he? How are his folks?"

"Fine. He already went back to UT." We are not going to discuss Nick. "Dad, did you ever have a dream about your dad, after he died?"

"Not that I recall." He frowns, either at the subject change or at the mention of his dad.

"Aunt Fran said once you both dreamed about him at the same time, right after he died. About going fishing."

He pauses. Exhales. "Yes, I forgot about that. We did. He was healthy and looking forward to fishing." He smiles sadly. "She told you about that?"

"Yeah. I get the feeling he's back."

;

That evening I bring Fran her dinner on a tray. The bedroom curtains are open partially and Coit Tower on Telegraph Hill's all lit up. Downtown San Francisco glows, twinkles, and flashes beyond.

"Hmm?" she says, fighting to sit up.

"Hang on. I got it." I push the button to raise her bed. She falls back against the pillow, eyes closed.

Her hair is stuck to her scalp. She's so pale she's almost see-through. I turn on her lamp and the warm yellow light transforms her to the color of custard.

"I've got some soup for you," I say cheerfully. "Homemade vegetable broth with organic leeks. You love leeks."

She wrinkles her nose and shakes her head. Maybe it's parsnips she likes.

"Come on, please try it," I beg. Harold said she doesn't need food now and her body is turning away from it. But I can't bear starving her.

She lets me place it in front of her but pushes the bowl to the other end of the tray. The soup sloshes. "Yuck," she says.

"All right. Fine. It's there if you change your mind." I sit beside her bed. "Want your oxygen?"

She nods. I hook her up. The skin beneath her nose is a little chapped where the tube plugs into her nostrils. I smooth on a dab of Vaseline.

"Sip of water?" I ask.

I hold her plastic water cup with the straw in front of her. Her mouth gets really dry. I use one of the moisture swabs to clean off her scuzzy teeth a little.

"Pain okay?"

She fumbles for my hand and I clasp hers. Her eyes are closed but she nods. We just upped her dosage for the umpteenth time. "Crepe myrtles love the heat," she mumbles.

"Aunt Fran, I know you're a little worried about me," I start. This is my chance, served to me on a lacquered tray. "About my mental health, and my stability. You don't need to be. I have tools I didn't have before I came to live here. And I have people who'll support me—"

Nobody like her, though.

No other words will come.

Fran opens her eyes and smiles reassuringly at me. Doesn't let go of my hand.

# 63

## Friday, September 18

It's the day we were supposed to fly to Oregon. For Fran to have to travel somewhere at this point would've been torture. Thank god she doesn't have to.

Only it's late now and I'm in my room obsessively thumbing through a stack of Fran's old cooking, traveling, and fashion magazines for new collage content. I started *Faint of Heart* with a vodka ad.

My phone rings. It's Nick.

"How's she doing?" he asks. "My mom says she hasn't heard much lately."

"She's going downhill pretty fast. But Dad's here now, and it's going as it should. I guess."

"How're *you* doing?"

"Okay." I give myself away with a sigh.

"You guys being so tight, losing her is going to be hard."

"Yeah." My voice cracks a little. "I'm really glad you called. How are you? How are your eyes?" He mentioned scheduling a checkup with his doctor in Austin.

"Good. No new problems anyway. But it's hot as hell here and I miss the fog. School's fine and I'm getting the transfer worked out." He pauses. "I've been thinking of you and Fran a lot."

"You have?"

"Weird thing is, when you're familiar—like, intimate even—with death, it can call you, pull you, make you feel . . . almost homesick."

"Yeah," I whisper. I can't believe he knows this.

"I was thinking about a kid who was in Children's Hospital with me. I was eight and he was nine. We shared a room for a while."

"What was he there for?" I'm lying on my bed. The brass light fixture on the ceiling is tarnished.

"He broke his neck in a four-wheeler accident."

"Oh, jeez."

"But he was a total live wire. Really fun. The nurses would open the blinds and we'd watch the big crane working on this nearby building for hours. We made up, in great detail, how to operate one, what we'd do if we were driving."

"That's sweet."

"Not really. We were planning wild crane rampages."

I laugh.

"Neither of us could move much. All we wanted was to be outside, playing and running."

"Of course. How long did you share a room?"

"Just a few days. But he somehow knew how to use each hour he had to its fullest, no matter how much pain he was in or how many limitations were put on him. Even eight-year-old me could see that." He pauses. "Then he got pneumonia and they had to move him to the pediatric ICU."

I have a feeling I know where this is going. I make a sympathetic noise but don't try to form words.

He pauses again. "They let me visit him even though he was really sick. He was so weak, and super subdued—not cheerful anymore. But he told me he wasn't scared about dying. He was letting go."

"Like Fran is," I breathe.

He goes on, "He said a *light lady* was there to lead him to what was next. He was psyched."

"Oh! Fran sees people too." I don't really get it, to be honest. What if your belief system doesn't include "light ladies," or imagines them completely differently? I say, "Fran says Buddhists don't believe in heaven the way Christians, Jews, and Muslims do—and I'm pretty sure there are contradictory teachings and opinions even within the same faith."

"Yeah," Nick says. "But all religions envision something bigger than our material world."

Maybe each person's experience is unique. I lean my head back against my headboard. "But is it . . . real?"

"Yeah."

He could ask, *What's real?* The alley behind our building is only barely lit by a streetlight at the bottom of the hill. Sometimes I see shapes in the dark outside my window. My collages make my internal worlds multidimensional. My tattoo represents a whole lifetime of struggle and triumph that fills my head whenever I look at it. The meaning of all these are very real to me but maybe not to someone else.

"I so, so hope you're right." I hug my knees.

Nick pauses. "The night he died, I dreamed that we played soccer finally, after talking about it for so long. In a big field miraculously right outside the hospital. We had a world-class game, scored lots of goals. When I woke up . . .

I knew. And I was sad, but I was also happy. Because he was no longer suffering. And I'll never, ever forget him."

"Thank you for sharing that with me." I swallow. "Wish I could kiss you."

He laughs. "Me too."

# 64

## Saturday, September 19

At 6:30 a.m., Eileen, the hospice night nurse, knocks on my door and asks me to come into Fran's room.

"She's unconscious, not responding to speech. Her blood pressure has dropped too. I gave her drops at 2:30 a.m., and again ten minutes ago. That's what we'll be using now if she regains consciousness or appears to be in pain. No more pills."

Fran's puffy right eye bulges even though it's closed. It looks worse, scary. I remember what Harold said about tumors in her brain.

She's resting comfortably. Breathing evenly.

I take her hand and squeeze it. "I'm here, Aunt Fran."

There's no response.

Eileen folds a cotton blanket. "We'll give her drops on schedule and we'll be here round the clock. To turn her and keep her comfortable."

"What should I do?" I sound like that third-grader I keep trying to grow out of.

"Just be here with her. She most likely can hear you."

Mom could probably hear me too. When she was on life

support and I had to say goodbye. I cried and begged her not to go. Feel kind of bad about that now.

Half an hour later, another hospice nurse—Constance, early thirties—arrives with an air of bossy but reassuring efficiency. These hospice nurses are the experts. She checks Fran, cleans her, including a shampoo, and changes her sheets while I make some coffee. When I come back in, Constance turns Fran on her side and supports her with pillows.

Fran moans, and I wince.

Dad's checking out of his hotel and moving in here today, but I should text him to hurry up.

Constance swabs out Fran's mouth, gives her morphine drops, makes notes on a clipboard. She puts a pillow at Fran's back, one between her knees, and one propping her in front, over which her arm can rest. She places rolled cloths in Fran's hands as her fingers are curled and gripping.

I retreat to the kitchen, plopping into a chair at the table and putting my head on my arms.

"How is she?" I ask when Constance comes out.

"She's resting comfortably." Her green scrubs have little yellow smiley faces all over them.

"What does that mean really? How long does she have?"

"Answer to the first question is that she's not in pain, and to the second, there's no way to know. Everyone's journey is different." More quietly, she adds, "I think she's pretty close."

"But in the next thirty minutes?"

"Probably not."

I wonder how much longer she can fight.

Or what happens if she stops fighting. Is that when she'll go? Isn't that what she wants now?

It's what I want. For her to die peacefully and to stop suffering.

"She's aware that we're here and can hear us." Constance fills her bottle with water from the faucet.

"Even out here?"

"Well, no, probably not." She sips from her water bottle.

"I thought maybe she's developed supernatural hearing all of a sudden."

Constance cracks a smile. "Sitting with her, keeping vigil, is a gift to her. She may be more sensitive to touch, though, so try not to hang on to her. You can also let her know that everything is going to be taken care of. That she can go when she's ready."

*Buck up, Delilah.* I head into Fran's room to sit beside her.

I text Dad: **She's taken a downturn**

He fires back: **Be right up.**

# 65

"Aunt Fran," I say.

Constance's use of the word "gift" has stuck in my mind. I don't have to think of it as saying goodbye. Think of it as giving Fran peace.

This is my last chance without Dad hovering.

"Here we are." A cough of emotion rises in my throat, so I clear it. "You and me. You already know how much I love you and how important you've been to me, like, forever. You understand how I *am* and don't get all disappointed in me. You help me get back up, and learn, get stronger, and move on—you have been really . . . far out. Thank you with all my heart."

Her face is so pale and slack that her mouth's partially open and probably already dry again. I grab one of the moisture swabs and wipe her teeth. They look like dusty, yellowish piano keys. I dab some lip balm on her lips.

"You've taught me so much. Like, how to structure my life, save and budget, pick out cute clothes, cook. About art and color and composition. How to be kind. How to trust. How to cope. How to be brave. How to love."

Her old alarm clock on the bookshelf ticks decisively.

"Don't worry about me. Of course, there'll be hard times ahead. I know way better now how to deal with that. Thanks to you." I pause. "My attempt was . . . a serious thing. That hurt you and Dad and other people. Sometimes I still think about it, and about the idea of suicide. A little. Less and less. But that's not, like, unusual, and I promise I will never act on it again."

Whew. Got that out. I pat my tat.

"Plus, I'm going to work on . . . relationships. Dad and I can be better allies. We have a lot of uncharted territory to explore. I have friends I can count on, and at some point, I'll find a significant other, like you said. Maybe eventually even have children. I will be fine. That's a hardcore . . . *vow* to you."

And it is. No more nighttime strolls on high bridges. This is what people mean when they say *I swear on my mother's grave.*

"I figure there's a right time to let go, and a wrong time. My right time won't be until I'm old and sick. I hope. Your right time, Aunt Fran . . . is here."

Wherever she'll be, maybe it's not far away. Hanging out by the waterfalls with the light ladies.

"I'm so sorry I didn't help you with Oregon sooner. If I'd done what you wanted, when you wanted, we might've gotten there in time to end things on your terms. But this is okay, isn't it? To be home?"

I wish she could answer me. I imagine her winking.

Sitting in her familiar darkened room beside her, I realize I've been watching her decline and, yes, helping her die now for eleven weeks. Seventy-seven short, long days since she told me. We're so close to the finish line.

While it was far from a beach barbeque, especially for Aunt Fran, it also wasn't as scary and awful as I feared. And full of silver linings.

I get it. It's time to go. She needs to let go too. She loves me and worries about me. So I'm working to loosen my heart's need for a physical Fran to hang onto. It's like being super hungry and having to be satisfied with just imagining a pizza. But it turns out I can still smell the oregano and the fresh tomato sauce, and it brings back such sweet memories of Giancarlo's Little Italy with me, Fran, Dad, and Mom devouring a pepperoni pie and all getting along.

"Dad and I will make sure everything is handled right, like we've talked about. I love you so much, always will, and want you to know that it's A-OK to go whenever it's time. Really."

How ridiculous to say that. As if it were up to me.

I whisper, "Follow your map."

The faintest pressure comes from her fingers and I gently squeeze back.

# 66

## Monday, September 21

One of us—the day or night nurse, Dad, or I—is in Fran's room almost all the time now. When we sleep or nap, the nurse who's on knows to wake us up if anything changes.

Fran's unconscious. Occasionally expressions flit across her face like shadows on a partly cloudy, windy day. I hope she's checking out a beautiful color-coordinated world. Probably redecorating it.

She's in the twilight of her life, neither fully alive nor dead.

All I can do is stay beside her as much as possible.

I play games on my phone, and a couple of hands of Five Card Stud with Dad and a deck of real cards. We watch *America's Got Talent* on low volume. I read poetry aloud to Fran even though she doesn't respond, and it reminds me to share Fran's incredible "ledge" poem with Dad.

Harold arrives to check on us all. Dad comes out to the kitchen and I introduce them.

"Pleasure to meet you," Harold says, shaking hands. "I've enjoyed getting to know your sister and daughter." He smiles at me. "Delilah, for someone so young, has frankly surprised me with her care skills, her fortitude, and her honesty. Her love for her aunt is obvious."

Dad flushes—whether out of pride in me or embarrassment that he wasn't here sooner, I don't know. "Thank you. Thank you for your care," says Dad. He turns back toward Fran's room. I put up my hand and Harold gives me a high five. He has to go, so I give his big self a hug.

The doorbell rings.

Louis breezes in with two boxes and gives me an air kiss on his way to the kitchen. He pulls out a key lime pie and a gourmet veggie pizza.

"Thank you!" I tell him. The smell of the tomato sauce and spices puts me back at that table in Giancarlo's so many years ago with Fran. She and Dad were temporarily on good terms again; his head's thrown back in laughter. Mom's leaning in toward them, grinning. The memory of that perfect moment when all my favorite people were getting along *and* we got to have pizza makes my limbs a little shaky.

"How is she?" Louis asks.

"Close."

"And you?" He eyes me in his usual searching way, but I realize that it's concerned, not hostile. Maybe that's all it's ever been.

"Hanging in there. Thanks." I touch his arm. "You may want to tell her . . . goodbye, just in case."

He pats my shoulder and says, like an elderly relative, "My, but you're getting so grown up!" I bat him away. He heads into Fran's room, and Dad comes out.

About ten minutes later Louis emerges with tears in his eyes and leaves silently with a stiff wave.

Dad and I drift in and out of Fran's room, to my room and

the living room couch to nap, to the kitchen table or island to eat or caffeinate. We have a ton of food that friends dropped off, including a fudge macadamia Bundt cake that Savannah's mom made. It's a relief, because we don't have the bandwidth to cook or even to orchestrate takeout.

That evening I sit at Fran's side and read Psalms to her. When I look up, Fran's right eye is unfocused as usual, but her open left eye is on me. It's a little cloudy now too, but she's tracking me.

"Are you okay?" I whisper.

Her lips move but nothing comes out. Seems affirmative though.

"Do you need pain meds?"

She blinks and almost nods.

"Hold on!" I jump up and run out to get Constance, who's back on. "She's awake!" I cry.

Constance follows me into Fran's room. Dad comes in too.

"Hello, Fran. Is the pain bothering you?"

She makes sort of an assenting noise. Constance gives her drops and we wait.

"Are you comfortable?" Constance asks.

Fran blinks. They hold hands a moment. Fran weakly swipes at the oxygen clip that's in her nose.

"You want me to remove this?"

She nods.

Constance does. Fran kicks off part of her blanket, then seems to drift off.

Constance points to the sole of Fran's exposed foot, the color of lilacs, and whispers, "That's a sign that the body is starting to shut down."

Dad closes his eyes.

Within minutes Fran's breath becomes slower and more labored, with uneven pauses in between. It also sounds phlegmy, like she has a bad chest cold.

"Death rattle," I whisper. It *is* kind of hard to listen to, as if she's struggling to get air through all the gunk.

With a suction syringe that looks like a turkey baster, Constance clears Fran's throat. She props her up slightly with a pillow. "Gravity will help," she says.

Dad and I sit on either side of Fran. Constance has reiterated not to hold on to Fran near the end, to just be close by. I can't resist touching her lightly.

Dad and I listen to her breaths and keep vigil.

;

Midnight. Now it's September 22.

The equinox. The world in balance between winter and summer, light and dark. Life and death.

Life swirls outside, in an infinitely widening circle, of which this room is the center. We sit motionless as Fran's breathing slows and slows some more.

Ten breaths a minute. Eight. The nurses have stopped checking her blood pressure, which was already ridiculously low.

At 12:45 a.m., Eileen is on and I go lie down in my room. "Call me if anything happens."

I bolt upright at 1:20 a.m. Cold air is blowing in my barely open window. It was hot today—yesterday—and the fog is rushing in. I hustle into Fran's room. Dad sits at her side, deep in thought.

"Any change?" I whisper.

"Not really," he says, rubbing his eyes. "I'll go lie down for a bit."

Eileen is hanging out in the living room, ready if we need her, but giving us this time and space with Fran.

The clock ticks on, accumulating weight.

I reclaim the big chair next to Fran, where I'm aware of each slow breath—along with the fan on low, creaks in the building, a car passing every once in a while on the street below, a distant siren, and then a sea lion's bark from the wharf. The sound carries for miles.

The silence.

A foghorn.

When Eileen comes in to check Fran, it's 2:30 a.m. I've been awake, but time kind of jumped, so maybe not.

Eileen gives her drops. She pulls the sheet and blanket back and shows me Fran's mottled, more purplish feet.

"She is close," she says softly. "You may want to get your dad."

My breathing hitches, then revs. This is it. A live current of energy electrifies my nerve endings. Being beside her is the most important thing in the world right now.

Dad staggers up from the couch, wraps a blanket around his shoulders, and follows me. We take our stations on either side of Fran's hospital bed. I let him have the overstuffed chair and I'm on the other side in a dining chair. We watch Fran's sunken face, her closed swollen eye, her sternum as it rises and falls.

Her body has thinned and discolored and is breaking down from the inside out. I know that body well now, have seen 96 percent of it. But it *is* just a sack of cells—a container for her tender heart and her marvelous brain, even though that hasn't been working up to snuff lately. The old, pure, best Fran—the essence of her—is still in there.

Her breaths drift further and further apart. Like a trapeze artist in slo-mo, I swing through the space between the end of one and the beginning of another.

She stops breathing for a really long time, but then she takes another little gasp of air. And starts again.

Dad and I look at each other and hold our own breaths.

# 67

I don't want to keep her here, but I take her hand lightly and close my eyes. Maybe I'm imagining it, but the faintest pressure from Fran's fingers seems to radiate along the lifeline in my palm.

"Daaddy," Fran breathes.

My eyes startle open. Dad's red eyes do the same.

Has Fran regained consciousness? I gently let go of her hand. Fran makes no movement.

This is the only place in the world at this moment.

"We're right here," I whisper. "We love you."

"Yes," Dad murmurs. "And it's time, Frannie. It's okay to go."

Her breathing is so delicate. Laborious, although there is the occasional small, quick gasp—a stolen sip of air.

The small, hardworking sound of the clock's ticks is amplified by the silence. They hold up the entire weight of Fran's life, mountains of seconds weighed in dandelion fluff. As I wait for Fran's next breath, my hands tremble in my lap and I pray:

*Help her way be easy. Don't let her suffer or panic. Let her slip away gently. Guide her, please.*

Fran's face is . . . expectant. Impatient? Laboring. Slack.

It's been twenty seconds since her last breath.

Paintings and engravings that Fran has shown me over the years flash through my mind. The Tree of Life. Draped, winged, and gold-leafed angels. Light-from-above annunciations. Microgravity ascensions. Bleak, empty purgatory and flaming hell. Jackal-headed figures in the Egyptian *Book of the Dead*. Elaborate colorful Wheels of Life from the Tibetan *Book of the Dead*. *The Ascent of the Blessed* by Hieronymus Bosch. The engraving of *A Meeting of a Family in Heaven* by William Blake. Brilliant artists trying to make sense of something every one of us will encounter, and that those artists have since.

Was it like they imagined?

Maybe they all fall short.

It's been over two minutes. Fran is still and empty.

Dad and I stare, clasp hands, and weep.

# 68

The apartment is dark except for one lone lamp in Fran's room, the light in the kitchen stove hood, and the Alcatraz lighthouse that flashes robotically every few seconds, trying in vain to slice through the fog. While Eileen cleans and redresses Fran's body, Dad and I sit mutely on the stools at the kitchen island. Soon Dad will make the calls to let people know she's gone.

While I expected chest-crushing grief, what's amazing is the champagne-y gladness bubbling around all the chambers and ventricles in my heart.

That she isn't suffering.

That she is somewhere really "far out."

That I had her incredible company as long as I did. I'm so lucky.

That Dad and I had the honor to witness one of the most intimate aspects of her life: leaving it.

;

Eileen has put the mustard-gold dress on Fran. My choice. I can't stop looking at her body without her in it. It still looks like her, except for something fascinating and awful about the mouth, as if it belongs to someone else. Harold said time with the corpse helps us process the passing. That helps me justify gaping at her.

My fingers are shaking a little when I pin an old gold-and-pearl brooch on her, careful not to stick her. I picked it out with Mom when I was about seven. I never saw her wear it, but she claimed to love it.

My throat thickens, though, at the thought of my lost locket.

Her skin's slightly waxy. Her cheek is cool to the touch, but soft. I carefully insert her favorite pearl-drop earrings in her pierced earlobes.

She would want to look fabulous.

She needs some Hothouse Tomato lipstick.

No, that feels too weird.

Her familiar hands rest at her sides. I touch the back of her left one. It's corny but I silently thank them for holding mine when I needed it, stroking my hair, patting my back, and cooking me fabulous food. And for serving Fran so well all her life. I take a phone photo just of her hands.

Goodbye, Fran's body.

The medical examiner will come in a couple of hours, to pronounce her dead, I guess. Then the funeral home will take her to the crematorium.

That, I cannot think about.

Even though I expected it to stop, the clock in her room ticks on.

# 69

I'm so exhausted I sleep soundly all day. When I stagger up at sunset, every object, piece of furniture, and article of clothing in the apartment shivers and hums a high frequency that only I can hear. Pining for Fran.

With Dad in the apartment, I have to stop puffing cigarettes right next to my window. He can still smell them. I am going to meetings religiously because the pull to get obliterated is still inside my chest like a meat-hook. Ez and Savannah answer every single one of my calls and texts.

Dad arranges the memorial service with help from Louis and Charlotte.

Lots of people send flowers or, per Fran's wishes, donations to Bay Area Hospice and a breast cancer foundation she was involved with. My job is to keep track and send thank-yous.

I sit at the dining room table with my laptop, updating my spreadsheet of condolence gifts, while Dad sits across from me with various folders and documents piled in front of him. He's handling all Fran's financial stuff, plus the death-certificate paperwork. Thank goodness. Who knew there was so much to do?

I pause. He's staring at me over his reading glasses. Like he's never seen me before.

"What?" I ask. There's a big conversation we haven't had yet. It's been festering for the last few days. Where I'm going to live now.

What I'm going to do.

Dad reaches across the table and puts his hand on mine. "Del. You've done an amazing job. You've been more compassionate and stronger about all this than I could ever have been. I'm so impressed and proud."

*Just accept the compliment, Delilah.*

Don't mind if I do. "Thanks." He withdraws his hand and I stare at my blinking cursor for a moment. "Dad?" A question I barely even knew was there explodes in my brain.

"Yes?"

"Dealing with all this has made me think about Mom's death more."

"Yeah," he says, like he has too.

"I've always understood about Mom's suffering. And her wanting to end that. But now I think"—my voice breaks—"that Mom wasn't in her right mind to make that choice." My eyes burn and fill.

"She wasn't, sweetie." He stares down at the pen he's holding. "But I think she made the choice long before she executed it. Contemplated killing herself, and fought it, for a very long time." He takes a breath. "For what it's worth."

Man, that must've been hard for him. "Thanks for telling me that." Now I take a deep breath. "Um, did Fran tell you that I slipped last month? Fell off the wagon?"

He frowns. "She never mentioned it."

"I did. For one day. Really, I guess it was two. I've never taken responsibility for *any* of my drinking or drug abuse with you. All the lies I told you. It won't happen again. What can I do to make it up to you?" I'm jumping the gun since this is step nine and technically, I'm only back at step four now. But *carpe diem*, I say.

He tilts his head slightly. "Keep doing what you're doing, sweetheart. Turning into an exceptional young woman." He pauses. "I'm sorry too. That you couldn't come to me with your problems, that I wasn't there to support you through everything you were dealing with. I didn't . . . really realize, before your attempt, how bad it was for you. Even though I damn well should have. And afterward, I—well, I didn't deal with it any better afterward." His voice breaks. "Fran did so much for us both. I'm truly, truly grateful."

I nod. Me too.

He goes on gripping a pen with both hands. "I'm very sorry, too—for not getting here sooner. Fran was my responsibility. Not yours. The truth is I was afraid."

Really? I wouldn't have guessed that. "It's okay, Dad."

Who knew that adults are not only clueless, but also scared so much of the time? Dad and I are really different, but maybe we have more in common than we think. A fondness for denial anyway. A tendency to let our fears overpower us, in one way or another.

I thought Fran's death would kill me. Being with her for her parting is one of the biggest, and hardest, yet most life-affirming things that's ever happened to me.

I'm still anxious. But not afraid.

⁏

The service is held at the big cathedral on the top of Nob Hill. Old friends—including Nick and his parents—have flown in from all over. It's so beautiful and peaceful in here. Crowded, yes, but the high ceilings and side naves absorb the excess energy. Louis and his boyfriend, Hassan, are sitting right behind me and I have to stare between them to see Nick. Louis makes a knowing, wink-wink face at me, which I ignore.

Despite extreme sweating and flushing, I get up and try to express what Fran means to me. It's kind of a train wreck even though I wrote it out and practiced it fifteen times.

At the reception, in a chandeliered room in the nearby Nob Hill Hotel, Nick and I finally find each other. He gives me a long hug, ignoring my blotchy face and red eyes. Dad and Nick's folks are watching us, though, so we don't lock lips.

"Fran would've loved your eulogy," Nick says. "I liked what you said about the time you all spent together having so much weight."

"Thanks. She had a crush on you. I'm so glad you got to see her before she died."

"Yeah, so am I."

Ez, and Savannah with her new blue hair, break in to hug me.

I introduce them to Nick, who shakes their hands and flashes them his dazzling smile.

"A pleasure to meet you," says Ez, studying everything from his glasses and his fingernails to his shoes. Nick's neck pinks.

Savannah gives me a "he's hot" look even though I know he's a little square for her taste.

Nick's parents approach. Nancy, also blotchy and swollen-eyed, bear-hugs me. His dad gives me an awkward shoulder-squeeze. They have to head to the airport.

"Thank you so much for coming," I say.

"I wish we were staying longer," says Nancy.

"Me too," says Nick. Me three. "I'll call you later, Del."

I give him a thumbs-up, but wish he wasn't always rushing off.

While Dad talks to everyone, I walk the big labyrinth in the church courtyard outside. I make good progress, then double back over the same area again and again, take a big slip, regain ground, go over the same area again and again, switch back for more reversals, and finally, after countless steps, reach the transcendent center.

I do it all over again to get out.

# 70

Dad and I are eating takeout back at the apartment.

"So, how do you feel about coming back to London and living with me?" Dad asks evenly, in between bites of a spring roll.

"Uh. You're still leaving tomorrow, right?" Nothing like putting off these major earth-shaking conversations until the last minute. But that's Dad. And honestly, I've been avoiding it too.

"Yes, tomorrow afternoon. I've got a lot of work piling up back home." He takes off his glasses and massages the bridge of his nose. "You could follow me whenever you're ready."

London is home for him, but it's totally not for me.

I say, "Louis needs my help at the gallery, and I can work there full-time until January—and part-time indefinitely. I'm all set to start at SF State after New Year's."

His frown is just like Fran's. "You staying here all by yourself? I'm not sure you're . . . well enough."

"I think I am." I put my soup spoon down. "My life is here. Dr. Vernon, my AA group, my friends. Esmerelda. I'd like to stay if there's a way." I don't say that Nick will be arriving in January too, since that's an unknown variable.

"I don't know." His eyebrows are lowered and his mouth is set in a funny way. Looks like concern. "Will you really be okay? And stay that way?"

We both know what he's asking: Will I drink? Will I step in front of a streetcar?

I pause. "Dad, I'm going to be dealing with anxiety and depression as usual. For the rest of my life, probably, to some extent or another. But I know how to cope. I know I can handle it." Since he doesn't look convinced yet, I add, "Plus, maybe you can come visit more often." It's a long way, but he's used to flying to distant locales. "It would be, um, nice to see more of you."

I've caught him by surprise. He blinks rapidly and looks at his lap. "I'd like that too."

"Next semester starts in mid-January," I say quickly. "I have to get housing, of course. Through the university, or I can find an apartment roommate situation. Savannah said I can stay with her until then."

"Actually, I've been meaning to tell you . . ." He leans back and smiles. "Fran left this place to you."

"What?" That this beautiful light-filled home could ever belong to me blows me away. "Guess I don't have to worry about rent, then." Living on my own. Be careful what you wish for.

"You'll have to worry about the property taxes." He laughs, a little meanly, crossing his arms. "Utilities, and probably huge homeowner's dues."

Yikes. "I know what the homeowner's dues are because I've been paying them for Fran. They are kind of huge."

"Okay. Don't worry," Dad says. "We'll figure it out. We'll probably need to sell it, and the market's good right now. And the money we get from the sale would be set aside for you."

The idea of selling this place I've visited all my life, and lived in successfully for the last twenty-one months, makes my throat burn.

"But that wouldn't need to happen before the end of the year," Dad adds. "In the meantime, I guess I'd feel okay about you staying here by yourself. It's safe and central, and there are folks around who can check on you."

This is amazingly like a conversation between two adults. He's mostly listening to me. And not just passing the buck—me—to someone else either. Although we're pretty much out of people to pass me to.

"Are you mad?" I blurt out. "That she left it to me?"

He jerks his head back like a turtle. "No! Not at all. She adored you and it's a generous gift. I'm grateful."

"Maybe I could come to London around Thanksgiving," I say, "then come back here after New Year's." It means going to England at the darkest, coldest, wettest time of year. Ten-plus hours, twice, on a metal tube hurtling through space, miles above the earth over a deep, icy ocean, with hundreds of people packed all around me. But I'll live, probably.

"That would be great." He's relieved too. "Just for my own comfort, though, I'd like to communicate a lot more." He presses his lips together as if bracing himself. "Daily."

"Sure. No problem."

It's a start.

# 71

## Friday, October 2

I dream that Fran and I are flying in a jet plane. It's hers—really "snazzy," as she would joke, silver with bright orange trim and accents. White leather interior. And fast.

She wants us to jump out of it. I have a parachute on my back, but I'm still petrified. She's all, "Come on, it'll be fun!" A little yellow flower is tucked behind her ear.

I force myself to the gaping door of the plane (no idea who's piloting it since Fran is standing beside me). We both step through the open door just as I notice she has no parachute. She laughs and takes my hand and—we don't fall, we're flying!

The Grand Canyon gapes beneath us. Forests and fields and glowing, latticed cities slide by.

She lets go of me and says, "You can do it yourself, sugar."

Sure enough, I aim and go. Totally in control.

I wake up.

Happy and sad at the same time. Wishing more than anything she were here in the flesh. It's not the usual aching, gaping fear and need, though. Just a gentle missing.

For a little bit anyway.

;

At the airport's sleek, soaring international terminal, Dad and I say goodbye at the curb.

Dad gestures skyward. "As Fran would say, what a 'blue sunshiny day.'"

It's *blue-sky, bright sunshiny day*, but I don't correct him.

We hug. He smells like himself, plus dry-cleaning fluid from his wool jacket. I close my eyes and, just for a second, allow myself to time-warp into eight-year-old Del hugging my dad good night.

"See you for the holidays?" Dad asks.

"Yeah. Definitely." Two whole months away. "Maybe we can talk some about Mom then," I say bravely. "There's so much about her that I don't know. And want to." I'd like to know more about Dad's parents too, and what Fran was like as a kid. As a teenager!

He reaches out and pushes a strand of my hair out of my eyes. "Deal."

He starts to roll his suitcase down the sidewalk into the terminal. I've closed the trunk and opened the driver's-side door when he turns and says, "I dreamed of Fran last night."

"I did too!" I grip the top of the open car door. "We were flying."

"In a silver plane?"

"Ohmigod. Me too!"

Dad uncharacteristically blows me a kiss. "See you soon, sweetie." It's so weird, I don't know what to do in response, so I just wave.

He disappears through the automatic glass doors.

Back in Fran's Prius, it smells like Dad's aftershave, but also like Fran. Gardenias, fresh bread, orange rind. A wave of grief hits me like a tsunami. I cry all the way home.

Home.

Whatever.

I take the elevator up from the garage and step into the eighth-floor foyer.

Unlock the front door.

The apartment yawns, quiet and empty and weightless. *Here I am, a big girl, living on my own.*

My grief is so dense and compacted that if it escaped from my rib cage, it would expand like foam flame retardant flowing through every street in the whole city and peninsula and running into the Pacific. But it has a molecular solidness that's nothing like the weightless, hollow, infinite sadness of the void.

;

That evening, I get a surprising text from Nick.

**Thinking about flying to SF the weekend of Oct 23rd to arrange housing for when I transfer to Cal**

I clutch my phone. What do I respond?

If I had succeeded in spending every waking moment with Nick this summer, I would've failed Fran. And myself. How obsessive would that have been anyway? I'm honestly happy to be the friends we are. And to take everything one step at a time. But why tell me he's coming if he doesn't want things to . . . proceed?

I need Fran's advice. Even though her absence is a gaping shrapnel wound, I know she's probably watching and jumping up and down, telling me to go for it now.

I text back:

**You're welcome to stay here**

;

I wake up at 6:09 a.m. in my just-beginning-to-lighten dark room and wonder if Fran would eat pancakes if I made them.

The knowledge that Fran is gone backhands me.

I mourn her for a little bit under my duvet, a deep violet sadness.

After getting dressed, I sit in the living room, close my eyes, squirm, and concentrate on my breathing, trying to meditate.

It's cool because when I get all quiet like that, I feel Fran near me. No joke.

But I don't see her.

# 72

## Wednesday, October 7

The sky is pinking over the East Bay. Esmerelda sends me
a text.

**Quick coffee? The usual?**

We often met before she went in to work early on. I wouldn't
mind reviving that routine.

At 6:45, I order two lattes and grab a table in the old Italian
coffee-and-pastry shop she loves. I text Dad that I'm awake and
made it through another night.

Esmerelda and I like this place because it's the opposite
of a chain. Saffron-colored walls surround me, one covered
in a mural and another with dozens of framed photos of beat
poets, authors, and other celebrities from the last century. This
morning, only a couple of professional and bohemian types are
seated. The rush will be here soon.

Esmerelda makes her entrance kitted out in the bicycle
gear that she wears for her ride to work. We exchange a long
hug. She's a tad steamy.

"Are you doing okay?" she asks, holding me by the shoulders and searching my face.

"Yeah," I assure her. "I'm glad to see you." We sit at our

table. "I don't . . . I don't know what to do."

"For sure. What a loss." She scoots her chair closer to the table.

"No, I mean literally. Next. Today. Tomorrow. I keep thinking of things to ask Fran, not to mention all the stuff I need to tell her. I keep listening for her step, and the noises of her humming or banging around in the kitchen." I don't say that I play Fran's voicemails and read her texts to pretend for a little bit.

"Is it scary being alone in her place?" She shakes two brown sugar packets, readying them for her coffee.

I rotate one of my loop earrings. "No. Just kind of empty."

Someday, I'll be able to look at the selfie I took with her just a month ago when she was still hanging on to here and now by a thread. Not yet though.

I wish I'd taken more photos of her . . . before. But I'm so glad I did *Untitled, Growing Things, Dualities and Paradoxes*. I'll finish *3D Chemo, Faint of Heart*, and maybe even *Summer of Triumph*.

She picks up a spoon and runs her fingertip over it. "Did you see that the state legislature just passed the death with dignity act?"

"I heard. 'A day late and a dollar short,' as Fran would say."

"Ha. I'm going to miss her."

"Me too," I say needlessly.

She frowns and twirls a curl around her finger. "Are you jealous of her?"

It's like she punched me. "What? N-no! Of course not!"

The espresso machine hisses as the baristas hustle.

I blow out the breath I was holding. "Maybe. Just a teeny bit."

Esmerelda studies me. I feel like a pinned moth. "Dude. Are you feeling suicidal?"

"No." I shake my head. "Really. Not at all." And I'm not. But something strange, scary, and unfamiliar is wiggling underneath the wet cement of my grief. "I do miss my shifts at the crisis line."

"Are you going to start back up there?"

"Yeah." A guy sets our lattes down. "Thanks."

She stirs the sugar into her cup. "Doesn't it, Fran's passing, make you *really* wonder about dying? And what's on the other side?"

"Totally." I stir sweetener into mine, breathing in the creamy roasted-coffee smell. "That's kind of what I'm talking about. And it seems like where Fran went is . . . um, okay." I close my eyes a second, trying to figure out what I want to say. "Death is holy. To be respected and honored. The process. The end result. But honest to god, I don't *want* to die."

She takes a sip of her coffee and eyes me over the cup rim. "Grief can make people feel like they want to die—and you maybe more than most."

"Thanks for bringing it to my attention," I say dryly. "But that's the thing." I lean forward. "Fran's dying—makes me want to live more than anything."

There it is.

It's like a new live wire inside me with a positive current. I'm not even sure what to do with this bright burning urgency.

Even with the lead weight of Fran's loss pinning me down, sitting here breathing, seeing, talking, and thinking is miraculous. I know full well how unbearable life can get. But it's like I've never fully seen . . . the upside.

Esmerelda nods. "Grief can also crack you open to new thinking. You should take advantage of that. A mentally healthy and balanced person is integrated—all parts of you working in harmony for your growth and betterment, right?"

"Yeah. You're right." Esmerelda's words ding in my head like a slot-machine win. Being mentally healthy doesn't mean experiencing only uncomplicated happiness all the time. Being able to fully feel my emotions, instead of shutting down, is a gift. I'll do everything I can to take care of myself and protect that gift. Even though I've got to do kind of a lot.

She says, "The twelfth step. We need to help others, to help ourselves. So, what about that part-time gig at the trauma center?"

"Oh, yeah! Did I tell you about that?"

"You mentioned it." She smiles serenely.

The sky outside is spread with light-raspberry jelly and a smear of apricot between the clouds. It's still daylight savings time so the sun rises kind of late. The world spreads out beyond the plate-glass window that looks across trees and flower planters along the streets and roof decks on Telegraph and Russian Hill, greening and growing as flocks of parrots squawk over noise from the awakening city, up to the edge of the salty Pacific water in the cold and fast-moving tidal bay. Over the islands and Marin to the Russian River, the canoe rental places, and the redwood forests, mountains, and cities beyond. But it's not overwhelming. All the space between and around all those atoms holds . . . possibility.

I want to help prevent people from taking their own lives. But it's more than just fighting the wrongness of suicide. It's the sunsets. Jalapeño cheese grits. Caroline's and Jorge's paintings. Lighthouses keeping watch, ships coming in. Love. Even learning. Or working. And using my strengths to help others get out from under all their garbage to reach this vista point too.

That I would've caused my own departure from here almost two years ago amazes me. Although I'll never forget how it feels when it seems to be the only option.

Nursing Fran and being at her side for these last couple of months nuked my whole life, my whole understanding of what life is and what death is. I've had a glimpse of something that lies beyond the four walls of my room, my city, the solar system. How random, and yet sort of planned, things are.

How helping others to manage their unruly mental health issues, at least enough to make it through one more day, will be one way for me to keep a handle on my own. Just like the long list of people who have helped and are helping me.

I've got one more thought to run by Esmerelda. "Can I be Badass Suicide Prevention Woman, and still be for Death with Dignity?"

"You can be any whack thing you want, babe!" She looks at her phone. "I gotta hop though."

I gulp my coffee. "Thanks for meeting me. I'll tell you the latest with Nick later."

She freezes in mid-rise from her chair. "Uh, quick recap?"

"It's all good," I say, grinning. "But sorry, I've got to go too." To check out the psychology department at school. Maybe instead of a teacher, I could be a youth counselor or therapist. Work one-on-one with the most troubled and distraught. Could I do that?

*You can do anything you set your mind to, sugar.*

;

My latest collage features neon butterflies, feathers, a snowy white owl, skulls, doors, bones, bells, fabric with brown leaves, green budding ones, human hands, an empty silver locket, ocean waves, lead weights, and pieces of the newspaper travel section page that Fran couldn't read. I'm calling it *Intimate with Death*.

A text dings on my phone. From Quentin, as if he heard Esmerelda's and my conversation this morning:

**Checking in to see how your aunt is doing. We miss you. The suicidal miss you.**

Bless his heart, as Fran would say.

**Aunt Fran died Sept 22. Just getting things settled. I'll get on the schedule next week. I miss the suicidal!**

# 73

The airport bustles. The security line for departures snakes for miles on the other side of the glass where I stand outside the no-entry zone. The hard, shiny floor glares with the reflection of the over-bright ceiling lights.

Nick's flight is on time but I'm fifteen minutes early just in case. I pop a piece of searing mint gum and breathe through my teeth to aerate my mouth. My most flattering jeans are a little snug after all the cake I've eaten in recent weeks, but this soft blue, thin, oversized cashmere cardigan that belongs to Fran is really huggable.

*Belonged* to Fran.

I breathe in the familiar gardenia-y scent of her perfume, feeling her right here, watching this reunion.

"If you are," I whisper, "help me not dork out."

If this visit can go smoothly, maybe Nick and I can decide what we are to each other.

We're friends for sure. How often he's in my head; how being near him sharpens my senses and lights up colors; how everything he says reveals a person I admire and respect; how Aunt Fran loved him; how much I want to feel warm swaths of his skin against mine—all suggest there could be more between us. It's kind of up to him.

Nick was right. We'll figure it out.

A stream of people flows by. There he is! Way down the concourse. His tall, unmistakable figure ambles confidently toward me, Noor at his side. He's wearing one of his soft plaid flannel shirts, green and blue, and a backpack.

The security guy gives me a warning look as I edge as close as possible to the point of no return. Ironically, my grin and twitchy movements seem to reassure him. A manic humming-bird crashes around inside my rib cage.

"Nick!" I wave and bounce up and down.

From half a football field away, I see his matching grin bloom. Even if he can't see my face clearly at this distance, he can apparently hear me.

We grab each other in a hug, practically on top of the TSA dude. Noor stands patiently.

Nick holds me by the shoulders, brown eyes magnified through his glasses gazing deeply into mine. "How are you doing? Without Fran."

The undeniable fact of Fran being gone knocks me sideways once again. I grip his arm and manage, "I'm so glad you came." I mean now, the memorial, the summer, and all the Fourth of Julys.

He kisses me. It's a warm sparkler of *now* as travelers and their roller bags push around us.

Noor nudges her nose in the butt of my jeans. I give her the back of my hand to sniff instead. She licks it. "Welcome to you too. Come on," I say, "I'm driving you both to the Sausalito Chili Cook-Off and Bluegrass Festival. We've only got fifty-four hours and ten minutes before you have to go."

"I'll be back in January." He reaches for Noor. Something hesitant about his movement, about the way he's watching me, tells me he's nervous too.

I can dial it back just a tad. I say, "You may want to wait and see how the weekend goes."

He laughs. "Good thinking."

As we drive over the Golden Gate Bridge, the iconic rust-red tower soars above us and a brilliant collage composes around me. A handsome boy in green plaid. A black dog in a travel service vest. A geometric cityscape sparkling in the mauve twilight to the east. A garnet-and-gold sky to the west over the indigo ocean.

We hear a flyover by a jet that I know is silver and orange.

# AUTHOR'S NOTE

When we were in our early thirties, my best friend from high school died of pancreatic cancer, leaving behind a bereft husband and one- and four-year-old boys. I had the sacred privilege of being with Eli and her family at their home for the last week of her life, as well as for her passing. It impacted me profoundly, in fact spurring me to become a writer. I've since been with other loved ones for their final phase of life, including my mother, who declined and died from a cancer very similar to Fran's. This story is to honor them all. In every case, the services hospice offered to our families over the course of a day, a week, or months were extraordinary.

Bearing witness to someone leaving this world is a powerful experience, and juxtaposed against my commitment to suicide prevention, it posed an interesting question. It made for a story I wanted to try to tell, and doing so expanded my views. I've come to regret that modern society has gotten so removed from the dying process. Nothing teaches us better and more quickly that our days are numbered and that our best way forward is to strive to be kind. My experiences with mortality have also helped me with moral and emotional clarity, not to mention with finding purpose.

It never ceases to amaze me how crisis line volunteers and staff of all ages and backgrounds put in long hours to give compassionate and nonjudgmental support to those who are on the edge, struggling with despair. These acts of caring and connection can make a big difference. This story is also a tribute to all those on the mental health front lines.

# ACKNOWLEDGMENTS

This novel would not exist without the help of scores of people whom I will undoubtedly fail to name in full, but am indebted to regardless: my charming agent, Erzsi Deàk of Hen & Ink Literary; my gifted and committed editor at Carolrhoda Lab, Amy Fitzgerald; designer Danielle Carnito; production designer Erica Johnson, and the rest of the Lerner team.

My writing group, Beyond the Margins, takes every manuscript to the next level: Annemarie O'Brien, Christine Dowd, Dean Gloster, Helen Pyne, Linden McNeilly, Merriam Saunders, and Sharry Wright, and the late Frances Lee Hall, who cheered on early drafts of this story. Other excellent writers who offered invaluable critiques include Nancy Bo Flood, Stephanie Greene, Stephanie Parsley Ledyard, Dianne White, Candy Dahl, Deb Gonzales, Miriam Glassman, Mina Witteman, and Kris Atkins. Special thanks to YA authors Kelly Loy Gilbert, Anna-Marie McLemore, and Sarah Tomp, along with the incomparable editors Deborah Halverson and Alexandra Shelley for their expert guidance.

For accuracy (any inaccuracies are my own), I am deeply grateful to Sophie Brown and her mom, Anne Greenwood Brown; Daisy Soto; Lighthouse for the Blind of San Francisco; Kay Hendricks Mansfield, RN, and surgical oncologist Paul

Mansfield, MD, of MD Anderson Cancer Center of Houston, Texas, for their patient and detailed medical expertise, as well as Melissa Thornton, RN; Elizabeth Eisenhauer of Eisenhauer Gallery of Edgartown, Massachusetts, for all things art; Katharine Rose Kirner of Compassion and Choices; and addiction counselor Ginger Whatley, MS, LPC, LAC.

I lean heavily on my family for free expertise and they always come through. For this story, Lacey Jacobus, who knows many things; Christian Jacobus, MD, for his palliative and hospice expertise; psychologist Ashley Jacobus, LPC; and the late Catherine Jacobus for her wise and encouraging feedback. Most of all, thanks to my husband, Jim, and offspring, Jake, John, Caroline, and George, for their love, support, and delightful, warped senses of humor.

# QUESTIONS FOR DISCUSSION

1. Why do you think Del is so close to Aunt Fran? How does their relationship shift over the course of the story?

2. What healthy coping strategies does Del use to deal with her depression and anxiety throughout the book? How do these differ from her unhealthy coping mechanisms of abusing alcohol and drugs?

3. What are some of the positive impacts of Del's work at the crisis line? What are some of its limitations?

4. For much of the story, Del experiences negative self-talk in the form of a contemptuous inner voice. This voice puts the worst possible spin on everything Del does. What are some examples of this voice lying to Del about herself?

5. How are the challenges that Nick faces with his deteriorating eyesight similar to and different from Del's mental health struggles?

6. What distinction does Del eventually make between her suicide attempt and the choice Fran wants to make to end her life? What about Osgood's suicide? How are the circumstances fundamentally different for each of these cases?

7. While Del isn't religious, she does come to feel that "death is holy." What convinces her of this? How is death's sacredness connected to her determination to cherish life?

8. What sources of support does Del have even after Aunt Fran dies? What sources of support do you have when life is especially hard? In what ways might you be able to offer support to others who are struggling?

# ABOUT THE AUTHOR

Ann Jacobus earned an MFA in Writing for Children and Young Adults from Vermont College of Fine Arts and is the author of the YA thriller *Romancing the Dark in the City of Light*. She lives in San Francisco with her family, where she teaches writing for Stanford Continuing Studies and is a suicide-prevention and mental health advocate.